THE STALKER

Susan K. Droney

This is a work of fiction. Names, characters, places, and incidents are products of the author's imagination or are used fictitiously and are not to be construed as real. Any resemblance to actual events, locations, organizations, or persons, living or dead, is entirely coincidental.

World Castle Publishing, LLC
Pensacola, Florida
Copyright © Susan K. Droney 2016
Paperback ISBN: 9781629894355
eBook ISBN: 9781629894362
First Edition World Castle Publishing, LLC, March 14, 2016
http://www.worldcastlepublishing.com

Licensing Notes

Cover: Karen Fuller
Editor: Lisa Petrocelli

CHAPTER ONE

He watched from the window, the same streaked window he stood in front of every morning. He'd been watching her for ten long years. He licked his lips in anticipation, and his heart thudded irregularly in his chest just like it did every time he knew he would be seeing her. He moved the curtain slightly to get a better view. She was coming, and his heart raced. She bounded out of her door, hands tightly gripping those of her ruddy-cheeked, carrot-topped twin boys. He wished he could hear what she was saying, just as he wished it were he whom she was smiling at and talking to. The children continued looking at her, laughter in their bright eyes as their cherub faces smiled while she talked.

How he longed to hear her voice speaking to him again, but it was only etched in his memory forever. He watched as her boys scurried onto their school bus. She smiled and waved even long after the bus was out of view. How he ached for her all these seemingly endless, lonely years. Being apart from her angered him and brought the demons closer to the surface, forcing him to lurk even further in the shadows. The shadows were his only solace, where he could watch her with no one telling him it was wrong or that he was a freak. Time was passing quickly, much too quickly. He had to make a move. It was time to come out of the shadows and finally claim her for his own.

****

Ten Years Earlier

Jeremy Talbot shifted uneasily in his seat, praying that the professor wouldn't call on him. He couldn't bear the humiliation of standing in front of the class with everyone's eyes focused just on him, smirking as they silently and verbally poked fun at him. His hands grew clammy, and beads of perspiration popped out on his forehead. His eyes moved nervously as he looked at Professor Burgess, briefly making eye contact. "Dammit," he muttered under his breath, hoping the man had enough compassion to know what calling on him would do to him. He looked down at his paper, then up again just in time to see the professor catch his eye again. Burgess looked away, and Jeremy breathed a sigh of relief, wondering who would be the chosen one.

"Mr. Talbot, let's hear your short story."

Jeremy looked up in surprise. His face reddened as the familiar terror engulfed him.

Burgess leaned back in his chair with an elbow propped on his cluttered desk as he nodded his head in Jeremy's direction.

Jeremy stumbled to his feet, hoping no one noticed his wobbly legs. His hands trembled as he tightly gripped the paper. His glasses slid partially down the bridge of his long, narrow nose, and he hastily pushed them back up, leaving a smudgy fingerprint on the lens. His throat dried out and his tongue felt stuck to the roof of his mouth. He closed his eyes for a moment, wishing he would be stricken dead this very moment. Death would certainly be better than enduring the mocking glares of his fellow classmates. Why should he read his story to this bunch of morons? It wasn't like anyone in this room, including Burgess, would understand what his story was about anyway. It embellished his deepest, most personal thoughts, thoughts no one else apparently had, but his thoughts haunted him in the darkest hours of the night. He'd turned his paper in with the expectation that Professor Burgess would be the only one to read his pained and tortured words, but now he was supposed to share those words with everyone in this room. They'd know his story was about his own life, even though he'd disguised it as fiction.

"Mr. Talbot, we're waiting." Burgess impatiently tapped a pencil on the edge of his desk, a look of contempt on his face.

Jeremy heard muffled laughter. His anxiety increased as the scorching tears threatened. He fought for composure. His classmates' contemptuous eyes burned into his flesh as his back smoldered under the intense heat of their scrutiny. Perspiration beaded up on his forehead, then made a slow descent down his face, and his eyelids grew damp with the sour sweat coming from his pores. He wouldn't cry; that would be the ultimate humiliation. He wouldn't let anyone disgrace him this way, so with blurry eyes he squinted down at the paper in his trembling hands. "I..." he stammered then swallowed hard. "I...I can't," he whispered in an unsteady voice. His eyes caught Burgess's and pleaded with him for understanding. Surely, the man could see his obvious discomfort and would cut him some slack, he thought.

Professor Burgess tugged thoughtfully at his perfectly trimmed grayish brown beard. "Then sit down, Talbot."

With a judgmental look at Jeremy, he flicked a piece of lint from his tailor-made shirt.

Jeremy scrambled into his seat, staring down at the marred desk. All eyes were still directed on him, and he heard the laughter even though it was silent. He heard it every day even if no audible sounds were present. He saw it in the way they looked at him and the way they shunned him as though taking a moment to acknowledge him was too much of an effort. His face flamed as he waited for the inevitable condescending speech. *The bastard never will get off my back, but someday I'll show him. I'll show them all*, he thought.

"Talbot, why are you taking this course?" Burgess asked in a bored tone of voice, slowly shaking his head as he stood in front of his students.

Jeremy raised his eyes. "I...I want to be a writer," he mumbled. His head pounded, and he placed his hands on either side gently massaging his temples as the demons whispered, mocking him too. *Don't let him treat you like an idiot! For God's sake, for once in your life, act like a man!* Their taunting echoed throughout his mind.

"What makes you think you have what it takes to become a writer?"

Jeremy folded his perspiring hands and placed them on his desk. "I have a natural talent," he replied in a weak, wavering voice. "Writing is all I ever think about," he added.

Burgess laughed a low, husky laugh that gave evidence to his many years of heavy cigarette smoking. "There are thousands of people with a natural talent, but only a tiny amount will ever succeed, Talbot. I'm afraid it takes more than just talent. You need to convince everyone of your capabilities as a writer and why your work deserves to be read. What sets it apart from the next person's? It takes a strong, forceful voice to do that."

"I'm not a quitter, Professor Burgess. It's my dream, and I'll see it realized someday."

Burgess studied him for a few seconds. "Have you taken a public speaking class?"

He shook his head. "Next semester," he mumbled, dreading that day with every fiber of his being, but if he wanted to graduate, it was a requirement he had to fulfill.

"You realize that in my classes a big part of your grade comes from your oral presentations, don't you, Talbot? You're taking an advanced course next semester."

Jeremy heard the snickers and whispers. He cleared his throat. "I'm aware of that, sir."

Don't let him talk to you like that! He's making an ass of you.

"Shut up," he hissed to the voices. "Please just leave me alone."

"Excuse me?" Professor Burgess raised an eyebrow. "Do you have something else to add? Maybe you'd like to come up here and share it with the class."

"I...I didn't say anything," Jeremy quickly answered, hating the way the man mocked him.

"God, Talbot's such a wacko," the student sitting behind him snickered to the girl in the next seat.

Burgess frowned insolently at him. "Leave your paper on my desk on your way out, Talbot."

"Yes, sir." He knew that Burgess was thinking him a pathetic, squabbling mama's boy who'd never see a career as a writer, but he'd prove him wrong. They'd all be wrong. The sad thing was, though, he knew deep in his heart that no one would ever know his success but himself.

Later that afternoon he sat alone, as was his usual

custom, watching others conversing and strolling hand-in-hand with their lovers. He longed for a girl to look at him with love in her eyes, knowing that he was her whole reason for living. He needed a woman to hold, touch, kiss, and make love to. He'd never kissed a girl or even gotten close enough to one in that respect to get to that stage, but he'd fantasized about it night after night. Every day he listened to his fellow classmates chattering, laughing about their new conquests and parties they attended or were planning to attend, and he ached to be included in the college social scene. He was so lonely. Couldn't anyone see that? He blinked back hot tears of frustration. He wanted to be like everyone else, but the harder he tried the odder people thought he was. He often wondered when his difference had manifested itself, or had he always been different? He was trapped inside his own mind and couldn't always control the voices any longer, instinctively knowing that he had to live in isolation and forget about fitting in or someone would find out the truth. But if he found the right girl, one who truly was concerned about him, she wouldn't care when he eventually told her about the voices. She would love him and help him to cope with his demons.

When he was younger, he had many friends and acted like any other normal, healthy boy, but by the time he entered junior high school, things had rapidly begun to change for him. That was when the voices started coming to him night after night in the death-like hours of darkness, seeping into his brain until they controlled him. Maybe they'd always been there, hiding in the recesses of his mind ever since he'd been born, waiting for the proper time to show themselves to him. He'd never relinquish any power to them during the daylight hours, even though they fought him continually for total control twenty-four hours a day. He didn't know how long he could fight them off, but he had to at least until he could get out on his own and away from his parents' watchful eyes.

He'd never been one for physical sports, but to please his father and gain his acceptance, he tried out for the junior high basketball team. When he was ridiculed and pummeled in the boys' locker room, then stuffed into the laundry cart under a pile of damp jockstraps, he knew he wasn't wanted nor accepted into their elite little group. His father never again pressured him into partaking of any athletic pursuits and in fact essentially excluded him from his own life and heart. His father made it clear to him that he was ashamed of him and ashamed that his only child was an unpopular weakling.

Jeremy filled his mind with books. Books were his escape to a better place and time, a place and time that accepted him with all of his human frailties and where he never felt the pangs of seclusion. His true peace came from within the pages of the multitude of books he devoured. Then when he'd turn out the light at night, the voices came slithering out of the dark recesses of his mind, soothing his non-existent self-esteem and filling him with false hope for a brighter future, a future never destined to be his. They tried to convince him that they were his only friends, and in the beginning he believed them and their continual warnings to avoid those who would hurt him. But as time wore on, he began to distrust them too.

He sighed, pulling a paperback from his backpack. In minutes, his mind became oblivious to the noise around him as he quickly dove into the chapter he had left off at last night. His real friends were waiting for him within the words some author had penned.

"I'm sorry about what happened in class," a soft and very feminine voice said close to his ear.

He looked up, startled. "Are...are you talking to me?" He raised his eyes and found himself looking into the eyes of the most beautiful woman on campus. Rebecca Walker was not only beautiful, but popular as well. *Why would she take the time to talk to me?* he wondered, and then quickly tossed the question aside.

It didn't matter why; what was important was that she had. He refused to let his mind dwell on negativity right now, lest the demons come to the surface and destroy this moment for him.

She smiled. "I don't see anyone else around."

He closed his book.

She leaned close to him. "Professor Burgess was too hard on you, Jeremy."

He shook his head, hating the sympathy in her voice. "No, it's just that I have a difficult time speaking in front of the class." He hoped she didn't notice the weakness in his voice. "Maybe I need to take more than one public speaking course," he heard himself say, knowing that in reality he was lucky if he got through the required one.

"Don't let Burgess obliterate your dreams. Many writers aren't comfortable with public speaking. Sometimes I believe that's what makes them such wonderful, poetic writers—all those things they can't express verbally flow out on paper. I suspect that's the type of person you are, Jeremy." She gazed into his eyes.

He shrugged, trying to relax, but his stomach muscles twisted into a ball. She was so beautiful, and he wished he could think of something witty and clever to say, but nothing came to his lips so he remained silent.

"You're a beautiful writer, Jeremy. Many people speak

poetically but don't have the talent to express themselves on paper the way you do. Your words touch others deeply — at least they do me."

His eyes widened. It was as though she could see inside of him to his tortured soul. He was the type of person she spoke of — expressing himself on paper — but in person he was a blubbering idiot, and he learned a long time ago that he was better off keeping his mouth closed.

"Remember our assignment about relationships? You wrote such a tragic but gripping love story. I've never forgotten it," she said softly.

Too bad I haven't had the experiences like the guys I write about, he thought. "I've always wanted to be a writer," he awkwardly replied.

"Me too, but I don't seem to have the discipline that you do. I can't force myself to write every day in my journal. It comes out flat and forced if I press it." She smiled.

"It just comes easily to me." He wanted her to go on talking forever. He could sit for hours listening to her melodious, lilting speech. He memorized every word she spoke and every gesture she made, catching the light scent of her perfume, sparking foreign emotions within him. The only woman he'd ever been this physically close to before was his mother, and he doubted that counted for much.

"No, I think you're a born writer, just like you said today in class," she continued enthusiastically. "Someday you're going to be a rich and famous author, and none of this will matter anymore. You'll have the last laugh on everyone, Jeremy."

Oh, it will matter, he thought. *I'll never forget this moment for as long as I live. Why would I want to? Why would I ever want to forget you, Rebecca Walker?* His face flushed as he shyly smiled at her.

She touched his shoulder.

Her touch filled him with a tender warmth with which he was unfamiliar. It frightened him and thrilled him at the same time. He wasn't used to anyone touching him, especially someone like Rebecca. He couldn't even remember the last time his mother had hugged him, let alone gave him a friendly pat on the arm or shoulder.

"You've got to have self-confidence, Jeremy. You need to get out and have some fun after being locked inside stuffy classrooms all day long." Her eyes narrowed. "I never see you around campus except for class. Why don't you come to some campus parties and let people get to know you?"

He frowned. "I usually go home after classes. I don't have much time for socializing." He was lying, but he couldn't tell her what a loser he really was and that the truth was no one ever invited him to do anything or go anywhere. He suspected she already knew that, though. He saw hundreds of people every day, but he was still forced into his solitary confinement. He had no friends. No one knew he even existed, or if they did, they couldn't care less about him. He tried to see a bright, normal future, but more often than not he saw only the bleak, dark emptiness that was his life. His only friends, for better or worse, were the demons. He was never allowed human friends for long, the demons saw to that, even though at times he yearned for friends like he had so many years ago when he was a young boy — before he understood who the demons really were.

"You should join some clubs, get active and involved." Her eyes danced with enthusiasm.

"I don't know. Maybe." He yearned for the words that would show her what a charming conversationalist he was, but what he longed to say stayed trapped in his throat, not allowing him the pleasure of seeing her eyes light up with amazement at his eloquent speech.

She looked at her wristwatch. "Well, I've got to get to class. I'll see you on Thursday." She winked. "Hang in there, Jeremy."

He nodded, mumbling a quick good-bye, then watched her walk away, her curvy hips slightly swaying and her long, reddish-blonde hair falling gently over her shoulders. He couldn't believe what had just transpired. He pulled out a handkerchief and mopped his forehead. Rebecca Walker had actually paid attention to him. She'd noticed him, and she'd taken the time to soothe him after his humiliation in class. Why would she do that? She had even touched him. He could still feel her hand on his shoulder burning through to his flesh. What did this all mean? Could it be possible? Could a woman like Rebecca Walker actually be attracted to him? Was she making a play for him? Had he missed the signals most guys were aware of? He had no friends to discuss this with, so he wasn't sure. Could he talk to his father about this wonderful event? His father was at work more than he was at home, and even if he were at home, Jeremy knew that dear old Dad would offer him no hope, instead brushing it aside as wishful thinking on Jeremy's part. Nevertheless, hope was all he had to cling to.

He could barely wait to get home. He needed to look up Rebecca in the student directory. Maybe he would get the courage to call her tonight and ask her out. Yes, that was what he would do. He smiled at his newfound self-confidence, but as quickly as it had come, it disappeared as the demons of doubt entered his thoughts. *Why would Rebecca Walker want to go out with a loser like you?* the demons shouted through the corridors of his mind, laughing and taunting him. He squeezed his eyes shut, trying to get them out of his thoughts. No, he'd prove them wrong. She did want him.

CHAPTER TWO

Rebecca sat in the bleachers watching her boyfriend Nicholas Adams as he strode to the pitcher's mound. He turned his head, briefly scanning the crowd, and his face lit up when he caught sight of her. He gave her a wide grin. She shielded her eyes from the blazing late afternoon sun as he struck out the batter. The game was over. She leapt to her feet, cheering along with the rest of the fans. They won the game, and as usual it was because of Nicholas that they had. Nicholas would want to celebrate the victory with his teammates, but he'd never admit it to her, instead insisting that he preferred to celebrate the win only with her. One of the things she loved so much about him was the way he always put her first and was willing to sacrifice his own desires for her.

She met Nicholas at the end of her freshman year after her dorm mate Cassi Arnold had begged her to double date with her and her boyfriend Luke Reynolds. Luke was one of those all-around nice guys, not terribly good-looking but with a personality that drew others to him. Nicholas had recently transferred to Pittsburgh from Delaware and was recruited for the baseball team, and Luke had taken it upon himself to introduce him around and get him socially involved. Rebecca later realized that Nicholas wouldn't have had any trouble being welcomed into the campus without help from anyone. Reluctantly she'd agreed to go out with him, but by the end of the night she and Nicholas had hit it off. Before the semester had ended, they were dating each other exclusively. She brokenheartedly went home to Massachusetts for the summer and Nicholas to Illinois, and their phone calls and letters only made them miss one another even more. But when classes resumed in the fall, they picked up where they'd left off, vowing never to be apart again.

The following summer they stayed in Pittsburgh, securing part-time jobs at Burger King and on-campus tutoring duties, which allowed them to live on campus for the summer. They did the same thing the next summer, and now, in their final year of college, they agreed that as soon as they graduated they would visit their families and plan for their wedding. Nicholas had secured a position as a computer programmer in Boston, and in September Rebecca would start her position as a legal secretary in a suburb of Boston. They would spend the summer setting up their new home together, and Nicholas would live there alone until their marriage, when Rebecca would join him. Their families and friends were both ecstatic over their upcoming nuptials, having suspected that they were a couple destined to be together.

She watched Nicholas effortlessly climb the bleachers and reach for her hand. He plopped down next to her. "Good game, huh?" he said and grinned.

She tousled his shower-damp hair and then leaned closer, planting a kiss on his cheek. "You did it again."

He leaned back against the bleachers, gripping her small hand in his large one. "What do you want to do tonight?"

"I want you to celebrate with your teammates."

He faced her. "You say that every time we win, and you know I'd much rather celebrate with you."

She laughed. "I know, honey, but your teammates are counting on you."

He scratched his head. "Luke says Cassi says the same thing to him. We're two of the luckiest guys on campus to have such understanding girlfriends."

"Don't you ever forget it." She studied his handsome face, looking deeply into his sparkling blue eyes.

"What?"

She became pensive. "Can I ask you to do me a favor, Nick?"

He squeezed her hand. "You know I'll do anything I can for you, Becky."

She gave his hand a gentle squeeze back. "Do you know Jeremy Talbot? He's in my creative writing class."

His eyes narrowed. "Yeah, I know who he is. Why?" he uneasily asked.

She sighed. "I feel sorry for him because Professor Burgess is so hard on him. He looks so lonely, and I can't stand how everyone makes fun of him all the time." She saw a worried look cloud his eyes. "What's wrong?"

He shook his head. "I don't know. Jeremy is strange...I've heard rumors."

"What rumors?"

He shrugged. "He's not right in the head. He's got definite issues."

"Nicholas, how can you say that? He's a talented writer."

"Just because he's talented doesn't mean he can't be a little whacked. He never talks to anyone. I heard he became obsessed with some girl in high school just because she befriended him. He wouldn't leave her alone and started stalking her through letters and stuff."

"It doesn't make him crazy. Some people have a hard time getting over a breakup and learning to let go."

"The girl wasn't dating him," he emphasized. "I don't know. He gives me the creeps. He never smiles, and it looks like he's hiding behind that long scraggly hair. Someday I'd like to cut it off and see what he really looks like."

She laughed. "Come on. He's really a nice guy...just a little shy."

"He talks to himself."

"So, I've heard you muttering to yourself many times." She gently nudged him. "Everyone talks out loud."

"It's not the same, Becky. He has conversations with people who aren't there. That's a big difference."

"I think we should invite him to a party."

He cocked an eyebrow. "Please tell me you're joking. He'd never fit in, and everyone would avoid him. It would actually be setting him up to be hurt. Trust me on this, inviting him would be cruel."

She slowly shook her head. "No, I'm serious. He is a senior, and we should make him feel like he's part of the class. In a few weeks we'll probably never see him again."

He grimaced. "The guys will never go for it. They'll think I'm nuts!"

"Convince them," she said snuggling against his shoulder. "For me?"

He slowly let his breath out. "I'll see what I can do, but if not, he can at least come to the pre-graduation party — everyone will be invited to that one. Then we'll only have to see him at graduation and never again."

"Nicholas, it's not like you to be so unkind."

"The guy just bothers me, that's all."

She saw the discomfort in his eyes. "Okay, we'll wait till the pre-graduation party then. Will that make you feel better?"

"Yes, he replied.

****

In the solitude of his bedroom Jeremy hurriedly thumbed through the student directory. His heart skipped a beat when he saw her picture. There she was, looking back at him with a smile that was meant just for him. He stared at her bright eyes noticing that they were looking right through him. She'd been waiting for him all this time, waiting for him to make a move. If only he'd known sooner. He grinned, thinking about how they'd make up for lost time. She offered herself up to him. Yes, the time was now. Destiny had brought them together, and he would make damned certain they would never be parted. It was no accident that she had sought him out this afternoon. They were meant to be together, and he couldn't change their destiny even if he wanted to. She was his, and he was hers. His heart swelled as he fantasized what their lives would be like. He closed the book and hurried downstairs to dinner.

"Jeremy, how were your classes today?" his mother asked, passing a plate to him.

She asked him the same question every night, with the same phony smile pasted on her lips. She was hoping he'd have something positive to share that would assure her of his normalcy, but night after night his reply was always the same—a slight shrug of his shoulders—and he'd look into her eyes, sensing that she'd felt cheated by life. He often wondered if she'd ever had any dreams of her own. He recognized a long time ago that his parents were married in name only, but to the outside world behaved like a happy, well-adjusted, loving, middle-aged couple. Sometimes his father acted like it was his mother's fault for bringing such an imperfect human being into the world. Of course, neither of his parents voiced their feelings to one another, let alone to him, but he saw it in the looks that passed between them and reflected in their eyes.

Tonight was going to be different. Tonight he would finally be able to break the pattern of the past and let his new self emerge — the self that Rebecca wanted him to show off to the world. "It was the best day of my life!" He beamed.

Gilbert Talbot, a thin, balding man, quizzically looked up from his plate. "Another *A*, I take it?" He took a bite of meatloaf.

Jeremy excitedly jumped to his feet. "No, it's not about grades or classes…nothing like that." His eyes twinkled. "It's so much better!"

"What's got you so wound up then?" his mother asked, positioning her abundant frame into her chair.

"It's a girl!" he exclaimed, seeing the doubtful looks pass between his parents.

Millicent Talbot's eyes clouded. "Now, don't go getting yourself all worked up over some girl the way you did with Julie Howard," she sternly warned as she picked up a bowl of mashed potatoes and passed them to her husband. "Sit back down before everything gets cold."

Jeremy burned inside. *Why did she have to bring up that hurtful incident?*

His father laid his fork down. "Yes, I remember Julie Howard. As I recall, you drove the poor girl crazy with your ridiculous infatuation." His lips were tightly drawn as he suspiciously eyed his son.

"Infatuation?" He sniffed indignantly. "She was my girlfriend!" He slammed his fist on the table, his nostrils flaring. "Why does everyone find that so hard to believe?" Blood rushed to his head and his temples throbbed, making him dizzy. "Am I such an offensive person that it is beyond your thinking to believe that any girl would care for me? Is that how you two really see me — your son, the son you two created and brought into this pathetic world? You look at me as though I'm some kind of joke."

"Calm yourself, Jeremy." Millicent nervously glanced at Gilbert. "Maybe we should have Dr. Tate talk to you. He can prescribe some tranquilizers for you."

Jeremy's jaw dropped. "I don't believe what I'm hearing! Is that your answer to everything? Send the boy to the shrink and have him filled up with pills to do his thinking for him? He remains the obedient son, doing everything he is told but having no real feelings or thoughts of his own. Turn him into a submissive robot incapable of any human emotions."

"We should have never allowed you to quit taking your medication last month. The pressure is too much for you." Gilbert cautiously eyed him.

He glared at his father. "News flash, Dad! I haven't been taking those pretty little pills for a long time. They made a nice addition to the septic system."

Millicent's hand flew to her mouth. "But Jeremy, the medication was necessary for your emotional well-being. It calmed your nerves. Your father and I know how stressful college can be with your heavy workload. We trusted you as a responsible adult to take your medication as prescribed."

"As a responsible adult I knew those pills were only clouding my mind and forcing me to live in an oblivious fog. That's not living, Mother!"

"We need to get you back on your medication, Jeremy. I'll arrange an appointment with Dr. Tate for tomorrow. This time your mother and I will monitor you and make certain you take your pills."

He laughed bitterly. "I'm not a child. Open your eyes. You can't force me to go to a shrink or take any medication without my consent."

"You can't go on this way, Jeremy. Your father and I only want what's best for you. These outbursts and delusions of you having girlfriends are not healthy."

"Why do you find it so hard to believe a girl could care for me? How can you sit there and say that Julie and I had nothing together, when you knew that my whole world revolved around her?"

She let her breath out slowly. "Jeremy, the relationship existed only in your mind. If Julie had been your girlfriend, then she wouldn't have requested that you stop calling her and sending gifts." She peered into his eyes. "Now would she?"

"Mother, you know it wasn't like that at all. Her father didn't think I was good enough. If he would have left us alone, we would still be together today," he insisted.

"Then why has she never tried to contact you since she left for college, Jeremy?" his father reasoned. "If someone loves you, they don't call the police on you for harassment. You're lucky that I have friends in the DA's office and that Dr. Tate wrote a letter on your behalf, or charges would have been levied against you."

He glowered at his father, hatred shimmering in his smoldering eyes. Gilbert Talbot had all the answers, always getting the final word—etched in gold. *What a joke!* Jeremy laughed to himself. "Why does everyone always try to destroy my fucking happiness?"

"Jeremy, I won't tolerate that kind of language in my house!" his father said loudly.

"I'll be graduating from college soon, and I'll be moving out of your fucking house and your fucking lives for good! I swear to God that you'll never see me again." He emphasized the expletives, enjoying the shock on their stern faces, then turned and stomped up the stairs to his room and securely locked the door behind himself.

He plopped down on his bed, holding the directory with the picture of Rebecca at arm's length. He had to find out if she lived off campus or in the dorm. He grabbed the telephone and called student directory assistance, then quickly punched in the numbers they gave him as he lovingly fixed his eyes on her picture. He waited for his call to be answered. A bubbly voice soon came on the line. He swallowed hard. "Is Rebecca there?" he asked in a low, quivering voice.

"I'll get her…hang on."

His palms perspired. He was thankful the young woman hadn't asked for his name. What would he say when Rebecca came on the line? What if she truly didn't want him to call her? No, his parents couldn't be right. He'd prove them wrong. For once in his life, he'd show them how wrong they were. But what if she didn't feel the same way about him? The demons tried to convince him that he was making a fool of himself again.

"No!" he shouted, then realized that someone was talking into his ear.

He froze. Rebecca's voice was softly talking to him. He closed his eyes as she asked over and over who was on the line. The sound of her voice sent the same urges he had felt this afternoon pulsating through him. He couldn't talk to her now. All the things he'd planned to say became muddled in his thoughts until his mind went totally blank. He swept a shaky hand through his hair as he gently clicked the phone off. He took a few deep breaths to calm himself, then lay still on his bed, staring at her picture. He closed his eyes, wondering how it would feel to be inside of her, slowly thrusting in and out and watching her as she moaned beneath him, begging for the release that only he was capable of giving her. His free hand slowly crept down to the growing bulge in his pants.

****

Millicent Talbot looked at her husband. "Gil, what are we going to do?" she anxiously asked.

He removed his wire-rimmed glasses and carefully wiped the lenses with his handkerchief, then took his time putting them back on. "Do you remember when we first noticed something was wrong with him? He's regressing."

She nodded. How could she forget? She'd given birth to him, for God's sake, and had almost overnight watched him go from a popular, socially active preteen to a reclusive and moody teenager. She'd questioned him relentlessly, but he'd refused any explanation for his sudden change in behavior. When she heard him screaming out in the night to people who weren't there, she knew Jeremy was in desperate need of help. After a complete medical examination ruled out any kind of drug use, she feared a mental disorder was the cause of his antisocial behavior. "Dr. Tate was against his going off the medication and giving up his therapy sessions. Do you think Jeremy really did quit taking his meds some time ago? Should we call Dr. Tate and let him know what's going on?"

He raised his eyebrows in surprise. "I don't think we have any choice, Millicent. We can't allow another Julie

Howard incident. As far as his medication is concerned, I don't know. I'll tell Dr. Tate what Jeremy said about disposing of the medication, but he could be bluffing just to get our goats."

Millicent clasped her hands tightly together until her knuckles showed white.

Chapter Three

Jeremy sat in the student lounge sipping at a cup of coffee, books piled next to him. For the past two hours he'd pored through the volumes, trying to come up with the perfect opening for his paper, but his mind refused to stay focused on his work, which was unusual for him.

He watched other students sitting in groups, and then shifted his attention to the couples talking either animatedly or intimately. A few students sat alone as he did, but he was certain that even those who were solitary chose it only for the time being and weren't forced to live it every moment of their lives as he was. He remembered the time in his life when he'd been just like everyone else. Back then he was popular and well liked, and his many friends would spend weekends at his house and he at theirs. Things started to change when he entered junior high school, his mind seeming to shift as rapidly as the physical transformation taking place within his body. He wasn't prepared for the demons that appeared one night during the midst of his deep confusion.

The voices had always been there and kept him company when he was a child, soothing him when he was lonely and feeling the emotional abandonment from his parents. As he grew into a young man the voices became demanding, and he no longer thought of them as friends, but began referring to them as his demons. They only taunted him further.

Bad headaches had begun with a sharp blow to his temples. Then, the insistent voices began reverberating almost constantly throughout the corridors of his conscious and subconscious mind, jolting him to the awareness of their everlasting presence. They refused to give him rest, and even at such a tender age he instinctively knew that peace would never be his again. They introduced him to his dark side but refused to return him. In time, the darkness began to eat through him, slowly devouring his soul as it manifested in his mind and took complete control of all his thoughts and emotions. That was when his parents forced him to see Dr. Tate, the king of drugs. He'd taken the pills faithfully, but when he saw how they were really affecting his mind, he disposed of them.

The demons had warned him about taking the pills, and at first he'd doubted them. But in time came to realize the demons were right when he saw how the pills blocked his ability to see the truth and glazed over the ugly inconsistencies in others. Without the pills he saw right down to their black ugly souls, and the real truth — the truth everyone kept hidden from him and the world — thriving and pulsating, waiting to attack their innocent victims. His parents and Dr. Tate didn't want him to see their own ugly black souls and tried to keep him pacified, but he'd had the last laugh on them. The demons told him that the bad thoughts and deeds he saw in others were directed at him, and he had to keep his guard up at all times and trust no one. Not one person on earth was worth his trust. If he ever became weak and let someone into his world, he would be betrayed and face dire consequences.

His childhood friends could no longer be trusted, and he sensed the mind games they were playing with him, trying to trick him. They had only pretended to befriend him but deep down were using him for their own selfish gains. They waited in silence for the opportune time to expose his hidden vulnerabilities and leave him stripped to the bare bone in front of the world. But he was smarter than they would ever be. Now his parents waited in the dark, ready to pounce if he let his guard down for even a moment. But he'd outwitted Dr. Tate, and if he had to return to that drab, stuffy office, he'd play the game again, laughing on the inside as Dr. Tate took credit for helping him to regain control of his life.

When he was nestled in his bed during the long lonely hours of night, the demons came to him, infiltrating his mind and revealing what lay ahead for him. He loathed them and loved them at the same time; they were all he had. He'd tried to chase them away a few times, but they refused to leave, and in time he'd gotten used to them, sometimes even finding himself looking forward to their visits. They afforded him a welcome break from his never-ending loneliness. They watched out for him, protecting him by showing him who he needed to be wary of. When he disobeyed them, he paid a dear price. That's why things had gotten screwed up with Julie Howard. He hadn't listened to the warnings but had foolishly and recklessly rushed into the relationship. He wasn't sorry, though, because Julie had given him the hope for normalcy he so desperately craved.

He'd met Julie in the autumn of their senior year in high school. She was the prettiest and most popular girl in school, and probably the wealthiest since her father had made a killing in the stock market. She was in his history class. He'd never spoken to her, but he couldn't help noticing her and was pleasantly surprised one day when she took the desk next to his. That had to be a positive sign, so he secretly stole glances at her throughout the class lesson, longing to run his fingers through the long auburn hair that cascaded over her thin shoulders. The bulge in her sweater attested to her well-proportioned breasts, and his eyes often rested there. Her panty hose clad legs were long and curvy, and the way she crossed them showed more of her thigh than she probably intended, until he realized that was most certainly her intention. She wanted him to get a good eyeful of what could be his. She was flirting and teasing him. He felt his cock swell and awkwardly folded his hands in his lap.

She caught him staring at her chest, and as he raised his eyes she flashed him a weak smile, a smile that went straight to his heart. That cinched it for him. She wanted him as desperately as he wanted her. He smugly leaned back in his seat, blocking out what the teacher was saying, instead focusing on how things would change for him and the newfound respect he would have once everyone started seeing Julie Howard on his arm. He smiled pompously as he imagined all the invitations to parties he and Julie would receive. As everyone pleaded for them to attend the various social activities, he would promptly and self-righteously smile as Julie refused the invitations since they'd treated her boyfriend so poorly all these years.

When class ended, Julie hurried out of the room without a word to him, but Jeremy didn't feel in the least slighted that she hadn't even said good-bye. Instead he surmised that she needed time to reflect on the chemistry between them and the unspoken promises of the past forty-five minutes. He knew how a woman wanted to be treated. Years ago he'd found the stash of girlie magazines his father kept hidden in the garage and sneaked them out one at a time, reading every article until he'd memorized the techniques that worldly men professed women wanted done to their bodies. He studied the women, imagining how their soft flesh would feel as he masturbated in the darkness of his bedroom. He wondered whether his father had ever practiced some of the techniques on his mother. The thought sickened him and he quickly dismissed it. His father most likely yearned to be screwing one of those ripe young beauties, and he supposed that was the reason for his stash of magazines. His parents didn't even share the same bedroom, so he doubted they shared their bodies with one another.

In the following days, Jeremy did everything humanly possible to show Julie the intensity of his feelings, knowing that she was overwhelmed with all the attention he began to lavish on her. He sat up through the dark, cold winter nights composing torrid poems of his love. The demons lurked in the background mocking him, but he ignored them, wishing he could banish them from his mind for good. They refused to vacate and angrily hissed their warnings of doom and destruction for letting Julie into his heart.

Each morning he arrived early at school and sneaked the letters and poems to Julie's locker. With his penknife he pried it open, then strategically placed the items in different folders and books where she would find them throughout the day. He laughed giddily, picturing her expression as she read each note and poem. She'd definitely know that she was loved and desired. He took a portion of his savings and bought a heart-shaped locket and some expensive perfume like the kind his mother wore and stuffed those in her locker too. He had several bouquets of flowers anonymously delivered to her home. Any girl would be beside herself to have so much affection bestowed on her. She never acknowledged the gifts, but he was sure she knew they came from him. She had to know who her secret admirer was.

He nodded to her in the hall each time they passed, but she never acknowledged him in return and sometimes even flashed him a blank look. After a while her aloofness began to disturb him. Several weeks later, he decided that if she wasn't going to announce their love to everyone, then he would have to be the one to do it. He signed his name to the next batch of poems and letters and with anticipation waited for what he knew would be a passionate response from her.

A week passed, but she kept her silence and distance. She was ignoring him, and it couldn't be of her own free will. Someone was forcing her to avoid him. He continued putting letters into her locker each morning, but she only flashed him a vague and sometimes even frightened look when he saw her in class. She avoided sitting by him again. He longed to speak to her, but the words that so freely flowed onto the paper dissipated when they reached his lips, so he just stared at her like some lovesick idiot. After school, he followed her to her usual hangouts, hiding in the shadows as he kept an eye on her from a distance. Her vivacious laughter filled his heart with a joy he could barely contain. He wanted to sit next to her and hold her close, but he kept his distance until the proper time. He stood outside her home in the shadows for hours, watching and waiting for her to come to him. His love for her was the stuff the classics were made of, and he realized how Romeo must have felt waiting in the shadows for his Juliet. As his ardor intensified, so did the contents of the letters. He was consumed with passion. He wondered if Julie could be afraid of finding herself so passionately drawn to him. He had to find the courage to express himself in person the way he did on paper. He never got the chance.

He was shocked a few days later when he returned home from school to find his parents and a police officer waiting for him. Bit by bit he learned the fate of his love affair with Julie Howard. Her father wouldn't tolerate anyone who wasn't athletically or monetarily inclined to date his little princess, so to make sure that Jeremy stayed away from his daughter, Mr. Howard had made up false stories about him and even threatened legal proceedings. He was removed from any classes he shared with Julie, and his heart sank when he saw the personal, intimate letters he had written to her in the officer's hands. Those were meant only for Julie's eyes; no one else had a right to see them. He thought she must be destroyed for giving up those letters.

He was further incensed that his parents doubted his relationship with Julie and scoffed at the idea that he and Julie had been planning to attend the senior prom together. After all, they reasoned, if he and Julie were a couple, then why had he never taken her out on a date or called her? They had only found out what was going on when the police officer showed up with a restraining order against him. Julie had refused to defend their love to her parents and friends, and she let him suffer the humiliation alone. He was devastated. She wasn't the sweet, warm human being he'd thought, so he abruptly ended their love affair. She pretended not to care, but he saw through her act as she tucked away her pain and put on a false face to the world. He smiled smugly to himself. He knew the truth and so did

Julie.

He never understood why his parents and even that quack shrink Dr. Tate refused to accept what was real and instead seemed bent on accusing him of manufacturing the whole relationship in his mind. He satisfied himself with the knowledge of what Julie and he had shared, and it didn't matter who denied it. They'd been lovers. He wondered if Julie ever thought about him, but mostly he wondered if she regretted what she'd done to deny them the love that was rightfully theirs.

****

Julie Howard rushed into class and quickly took a seat. She opened her philosophy book. When she raised her eyes, she noticed the student sitting directly in front of her. Her heart skipped a beat as she focused on his slumped shoulders and greasy-looking, tangled black hair. *No*, she thought. *It can't be him.* She swallowed the lump in her throat, terror gripping her chest. She wondered what to do when a pencil slipped from his desk. She trembled as she watched him lean over to pick it up. "Sorry," he whispered, turning his face toward her. Relief swept through her when she saw that it wasn't Jeremy Talbot. Her hands shook and she clasped them tightly together to calm herself. It had taken her a long time to cope with the trauma Jeremy had caused, remembering it as vividly as though it had happened only yesterday. It had been nearly four years. Every time she saw someone who even remotely resembled him, she became panic-stricken and knew she'd never be able to forget it for the rest of her life.

She'd become an unwitting victim of his when she innocently took a seat next to him one day in her senior year of high school. She wanted to sit by Kerry Brewer or Samantha Stiller since they were her closest friends, but she'd been held up in her previous class, and when she entered her history class the only vacant seat was next to Jeremy Talbot.

She noticed Jeremy's gawking eyes peering at her. He was grinning like an idiot. Now she understood why everyone thought him odd. He never spoke to anyone and seemed to live in a world of his own. She flashed him a brief smile, hoping that would satisfy him, but it didn't. She felt his blazing eyes on her breasts and it sent an eerie, icy cold feeling to the pit of her stomach. She shuddered. *No wonder he has no friends*, she thought. *He's so weird.* She'd make certain in the future that she never sat by him again under any circumstances. If this was the way he acted around everyone, she could understand why he was made fun of and avoided like the plague. She sneaked a peek at his thick glasses, wondering how he could even see out of them since the lenses looked like they had never been cleaned. His too-long, oily black hair was parted in the middle, with loose strands hanging down over his glasses. His stooped shoulders and baggy clothing looked ridiculous on his five foot two frame. He looked dirty. When he turned his head, she quickly looked away. Eye contact with him gave her the creeps.

There was no excuse for his filthy appearance, and it surprised her since his parents were respected, upstanding individuals in the community. Her father always spoke highly of the Talbots, but when she'd asked about Jeremy, he told her frankly that his parents never mentioned him in social circles. He did find that odd.

Part of her felt sorry for him, imagining how terribly lonely his life must be with no one to talk to. When she began to find anonymous letters and poems stuffed into her locker and flowers and gifts delivered to her home, she questioned everyone she knew, but no one knew anything about it. She became alarmed when she had a new lock put on her locker, and the next morning found that it had been picked the same as the original one had.

She ignored the letters and gifts until one morning she picked up a letter and after reading the horrifying contents, she became physically ill. Only someone with a demented mind could have written the note. The words frightened her almost as much as the future events the author said awaited her. Every time she had passed Jeremy Talbot in the hall, he leered at her. Now she knew that he was the author of the letters. Before going to her parents or the school authorities, she decided to confront him first. If he stopped, it would be over, but if he persisted, action would have to be taken that would certainly mean dire consequences for him.

Jeremy was always in class before she was, so one day she feigned a headache and left phys-ed early to confront him and put a stop to his gifts and letters. She entered the classroom, and finding it empty sat down and waited for him. A few minutes later, he appeared, head lowered as he headed for his desk.

She stood up and walked over to his desk. "Jeremy, can I ask you something?" She kept her voice even, her gaze fixed intently on his face.

He slowly raised his eyes until they met hers. "Yes, Julie?" he stuttered nervously, his eyes glued to hers.

She wondered what was going through his mind. His eyes peering into hers gave her the chills. She took a deep breath. "Someone's been putting letters and poems in my locker and sending gifts to my home." She saw the muscle in his left jaw twitch. "Jeremy, I know it's you."

He looked down at his closed textbook, and then

slowly brought his eyes back to hers. "You're my girl," he whispered forcefully. "I thought girls liked to hear how beautiful they are."

She started to back away from his desk, but he clamped his icy fingers around her wrist. "Let go of me," she cried. He loosened his grip but wouldn't completely relinquish his hold on her. "Jeremy, I am not your girlfriend. You've conjured something up in your head that's not real."

"Excuse me?" His eyes flashed.

"Those letters were almost pornographic."

"Those letters spoke the truth."

"No," she said hoarsely. "They were sick and demented. I wouldn't do those things with anyone!"

He laughed. "No, I know what you really want. Girls always want the same thing. I was being romantic by telling you how I would fulfill every desire and fantasy you possess."

Her eyes widened. "My God, Jeremy, that's not romance."

He grinned. "I guess you've never dated a real man before. I only want you to know what to expect our first time."

She yanked her wrist free. "There's never going to be a first time! I was only friendly with you because I felt sorry for you, but I don't anymore," she said. "Stay away from me, Jeremy Talbot!"

He watched as students slowly began filing into the room. "Never, Julie, you're my girl," he whispered.

She was trembling as she took her seat, his words sticking in her mind.

Later that night she took the letters, poems, and gifts to her parents and told them about her confrontation with Jeremy. Her father quickly made a couple of phone calls, and then assured her that she wouldn't be harassed any longer. She never questioned how he'd stop it but was relieved that he would.

Jeremy was removed from her history class, and when she saw him in the hall, she made every attempt to avoid him. Every so often his eyes would meet hers, and she saw the lust in them. Those eyes would always send shivers up her spine.

After graduation she enrolled in college at the University of California, elated to be far away from him and hoping she'd never run into him on her visits home. For three years she hadn't, but just the same, she was on edge whenever she visited the old familiar haunts, expecting him to pop out of the shadows. Her life had been changed forever, and her guard would now always be up.

Chapter Four

Thaddeus Tate pored over Jeremy Talbot's file, hoping to find a clue as to when Jeremy had begun playing games with him. When Gilbert Talbot called him explaining Jeremy's digression, it angered him, and he wasn't sure which enraged him the most—being duped by a patient, or Jeremy's parents previously agreeing with their son to end his counseling and medication against Thaddeus' wishes. Now they expected Thaddeus to right their wrong.

He sighed heavily. This time he'd be cautious with Jeremy and wouldn't let him get away with anything. Jeremy was shrewd, and Thaddeus had to be even shrewder. He loosened his tie and leaned his heavy frame back in his leather chair as he waited for his secretary, Candace, to buzz him with Jeremy's arrival. He picked up the picture of his wife and sons and smiled contentedly. Minutes later the buzzer sounded. He set the picture back down.

"Jeremy Talbot is here."

"Send him in, Candace." He clicked off the intercom and watched as the door opened. Jeremy stepped inside the office, quietly closing the door behind him.

"Have a seat, Jeremy." He motioned to the leather easy chair in front of the desk, keeping his eyes focused on the young man and noting that his appearance hadn't changed much since he'd last seen him. His shoulders were still slumped, and his gait was hurried and awkward as he made his way to the chair and with jerky movements pushed his hair from his brow. "It's been awhile since I've seen you."

He nodded.

"How've you been?"

"I'm sure my father's filled you in on all of the details," he curtly answered.

"It doesn't matter what your father's told me, Jeremy. I'd like you to tell me what's been going on in your life."

"I'm fine," he mumbled.

"How's everything been going?"

"Fine."

Thaddeus tapped his pen on his chin. "What's really bothering you, Jeremy?"

He shrugged. "Nothing. Why do you keep asking the same thing over and over?"

"Your father mentioned that you were having a few problems with your temper, among other things. Is that true? I'd like you to tell me about it. I'd like to hear your side." He saw the sparks in Jeremy's eyes at the mention of his father. "Talk to me, Jeremy."

He smirked. "Why don't you just ask my father, since he seems to know exactly what I'm thinking and feeling at any given moment?"

Thaddeus studied him for a few minutes, noting his quick movements as Jeremy crossed then uncrossed his legs. He tried to make eye contact, but Jeremy hastily looked away and stared at his hands. Thaddeus observed Jeremy's body become almost totally still, barely a muscle moving, as though he were calming himself and using every ounce of strength he possessed to control his bodily movements. "What are you thinking, Jeremy?" he finally asked.

He cocked an eye. "Why my parents are doing this to me."

"What do you think your parents are doing to you?"

He jumped to his feet so quickly it startled Thaddeus. "Why don't you ask the bastard who calls himself my father? Ask him about why he and my mother constantly thwart any chance I have for happiness!" He walked to the window and stared through the barred glass to the street eleven stories below.

"Tell me about it, Jeremy. What do you believe your parents are doing to you?"

He turned from the window and looked directly at Thaddeus. "Why should I tell you anything? He's already told you his lies, so it doesn't matter what I say."

"Please sit back down and tell me your version, then."

His eyes narrowed. "I'm wasting my time. You won't believe me."

"I want to help you, Jeremy," Thaddeus said compassionately.

Jeremy frowned, then walked back over to the chair and laid his hand on the back of it for a moment, gently running his fingers across it before seating himself.

"Tell me what's been going on."

He shot the doctor a pained look. "I tried to share some happy news with my parents, and they accused me of making up things. Most parents would be thrilled when their children are happy." He sniffed indignantly. "But not mine…mine thrive only on my failures."

Thaddeus saw the sadness in his eyes but remembered the incident with Julie Howard. "Are you making things up?"

He jumped to his feet again. "I thought you were on my side."

"Please calm down, Jeremy. The issue isn't about taking sides."

"That's not the way I see it!" he shouted. "I should have known you'd listen to my father." He paced across the patterned carpet.

Thaddeus watched as Jeremy rapidly reached one end of the room, then turned swiftly on his heel and repeated the process. He kept his eyes fixed on him for ten minutes. Jeremy abruptly stopped in front of his desk and gripped the edge of it until his knuckles showed white.

"I don't know what the hell everyone wants from me," he choked, looking into Tate's eyes.

"Your parents want only your happiness."

He lowered his eyes. "Then they should leave me alone." He sighed tiredly. "That would make me extremely happy."

"Jeremy, I need to ask you a very important question."

He shrugged.

"Are you hearing voices?"

His eyes widened. "What?"

"I asked you if you're hearing voices. Do you speak with anyone when you're alone up in your bedroom?"

He laughed. "Who told you that? My nosy mother?"

"Your mother is concerned about you."

"That's absurd. Obviously if I'm alone, then no one else is there," he answered sarcastically. "It's probably my stereo she hears."

Thaddeus scribbled some notes. "I remember your first visit here, Jeremy. Do you remember?"

He nodded.

"At that time your mother mentioned she repeatedly heard you talking to someone, and she knew that no one was in your bedroom with you."

"It was the same thing then as it is now. She hears me singing along with the stereo, and sometimes I put my headphones on and lie in bed. All she ever heard was me." He squinted. "She's the one who could use your help."

"You're telling me that you aren't speaking to anyone?"

"No, I'm not!"

"Are voices speaking to you from within your mind, Jeremy?"

He snorted. "Whoa, doc, the only voice I hear is my own. Once in a while I speak aloud when I'm by myself."

"Why do you do that?"

"Get off it! You mean to tell me that you never think out loud?" he asked with a smirk.

"It's perfectly normal to think out loud, but not to carry on complete conversations with yourself."

"I don't do that," he stated. He rammed his hands into his pockets as his eyes squarely met the doctor's. Thaddeus carefully observed Jeremy's movements.

"Why did you quit taking your medication?"

"It clouded my mind and made me tired. I couldn't think straight."

"You need to be on medication, Jeremy. I'm going to prescribe something to calm you."

"Have you heard a word I've just said? I need to focus. I have finals coming up, and I need to concentrate." He removed his hands from his pockets and ran a hand through his hair.

"I promise you that these pills won't affect your ability to concentrate." He kept his eyes trained on Jeremy, hoping to read something in the young man's expression, but he only saw the blank look he'd become accustomed to ever since their sessions began. "Promise me you'll take them as prescribed."

"And if I don't?" He raised his eyebrows.

"Then I can no longer help you, and any trouble you may find yourself in, now or in the future, will be of your own making." He frowned. "You need to learn to cope with your emotions. Through our sessions and the medication, you can learn, Jeremy. I have no doubt of that. But without your total cooperation, we're just wasting one another's time."

"I don't believe you about the pills having no mind-altering effects." He shook his head slowly back and forth. "If I don't take the damned pills, though, I'm positive you and my parents will find a way to have me locked up like a wild animal." His eyes drifted back to the window.

Thaddeus watched in silence as a peaceful expression came over Jeremy's face. He cocked his head, fully concentrating on something. Finally, his gaze slowly moved away from the window and back to Thaddeus.

"Okay, whatever you say, doc," he said with a gentle smile.

Thaddeus wrote out the prescription and handed it to him. "Is there anything you'd like to talk about right now? Whatever's on your mind."

"Not really."

"How's college this semester?"

"Fine."

"Are you getting out and socializing?"

"Not too much."

"What are your plans after graduation?"

He shrugged. "I'm not sure what I'll do. I may take a position with a newspaper as a reporter."

"Do you have any long range goals of what you'd like to be doing in the future?"

"Yes, I want to write novels."

"Do you think you can make a living at it?"

"I suppose I'll never know unless I try," he sneered.

"Tell me about your girlfriend." He saw the light come into Jeremy's eyes.

"She's beautiful! She's like an angel, so soft and sweet."

"How did you two meet?"

"We're in a creative writing class together."

Thaddeus propped his chin on his hand. "I'd like to read some of your work sometime, Jeremy. Maybe that'll help me to understand you better."

"Sure." He flashed him an unaccustomed smile. "Someday my novels will be in every bookstore in the world," he confidently stated.

"What do you write about?"

"Mostly feelings…pain."

"Are you in pain, Jeremy?"

He laughed sarcastically. "Aren't we all? Isn't that one of life's human flaws?"

"Explain your pain to me."

He let his breath out slowly. "Have you ever wanted something so desperately you felt like you'd die if you didn't get it? Like a craving deep within yourself that won't go away no matter what you do until you satisfy it."

"Everyone has those desires, but as we mature we learn that we can't have everything just because we want it."

"But some things we know we're going to have and nothing can stop it from happening. Like in winter, we go through each dark, depressing day knowing that spring is just around the corner. Once in a while, in the dead of winter, we're teased with the bright rays of sunshine and feel the warmth on our faces, and the next day the cold, biting winds are blowing again. But then spring finally does come to stay. It's inevitable."

"Do the dark days of winter depress you?"

He frowned. "They depress a lot of people."

"I'm not asking about anyone else, Jeremy. I'm asking about your feelings."

His eyes narrowed. "Since when have you or anyone really cared about my feelings? My parents never gave a shit about me or the pain I was suffering. Your main concern is the big fat check they write you for every session."

Thaddeus ignored the remark, noting how Jeremy's mood was rapidly changing again. "Tell me about your pain, Jeremy."

He sat back down and stared at his feet. "I've been in pain since the day I was born, probably while I was still in my mother's womb," he replied with an acrid laugh.

"Why do you say that?"

He bit his bottom lip. "My parents didn't treat me the way my friends' parents treated them. Mine were ashamed of me." He twisted his hands. "I wasn't the son they wanted. Nothing was ever right about me as far as they were concerned. I was too short, too thin, athletically uninspired…you name it, and I'm the opposite of it."

"Jeremy, that doesn't mean your parents don't love and care about you and about your general welfare. The thoughts you're having are what you perceive, but that doesn't necessarily make it true."

"Don't try to whitewash it, doc. You weren't there

when I was a kid. Why do you think my mother's so fat?"

Thaddeus took a deep breath controlling the urge to laugh. "Your mother's weight has nothing to do with you. Why do you think her weight has anything to do with your perception that your parents don't love you?"

He pushed his glasses up. "When I was little, I used to hear them arguing late at night when they thought I was asleep. They said horrible things about me," he said in a cracked voice.

Thaddeus's eyes softened. "What did you hear them saying, Jeremy?"

"I...I heard my father yelling at my mother for the way I turned out. He told her that she'd started gaining weight the day I was born."

"That doesn't make it your fault, Jeremy. Many women have trouble losing weight after giving birth."

His jaw tightened. "They make it seem that way. They argued repeatedly about how I disrupted their lives. I've never been anything more than an unwanted freak to them. Growing up, I never received affection from either of them." He threw his hands up. "Sure, my father would take me out in the backyard and toss a ball around with me when I was a little kid just to impress the neighbors, but when we got back inside the house he'd ignore me as usual. He'd never talk to me, and instead act as though I weren't there even if I was in the same room. He'd tell me to go find something to do, and all I wanted was for him to talk to me." His eyes glistened.

"Some men have trouble outwardly showing their affection, Jeremy, even to their own children."

He emphatically shook his head. "No, he never said he loved me, not even once."

"You never told me any of this before now, Jeremy.

Why?"

He shrugged his bony shoulders. "I guess I just learned to live with it."

"Why are you telling me now?"

He shrugged again. "I suppose so you won't think I'm crazy like they do. I just want my side to be heard." His eyes pleaded with Thaddeus's for understanding.

"Why do you isolate yourself from people?"

"I don't. They isolate themselves from me."

Dr. Tate was pensive for a moment. "Tell me anything you can remember about how your mother interacted with you when you were young."

"This is just between us, right? I'm of age now, and my parents have no right to know anything I tell you."

"Everything you tell me is in the strictest of confidence, Jeremy. Your parents are aware of that." He saw tears spring into the young man's eyes and sensed that his mood was again changing.

Jeremy's eyes had a faraway look in them. "She never gave me hugs, kisses, or played with me either."

"When was the last time you remember her showing affection toward you?"

He cocked his head. "I don't ever remember her showing me anything but contempt. Sometimes I remember things from when I was two or three years old."

"Like what?" The doctor leaned back in his chair.

"How she would put me to bed, but never kiss me good night, tuck me in, or even read me a bedtime story."

"What about during the day? Your mother didn't work and was home all day long with you."

"Usually she would tell me to play with my toys or watch TV because she was too busy to bother with me. She continually reminded me that she was sorry I'd ever been born. At times she would look at me in the strangest way, and it would scare me."

"What do you mean by strange?"

He took a ragged breath. "I'd see her looking at me like she hated me. She constantly told me to get out of her way. If I didn't move fast enough, she'd take her foot and kick me, and sometimes it seemed like she couldn't stop herself. When I would see her foot coming toward me, I would try to duck and consequently be backed into a corner. She continued kicking me until she was exhausted."

"Many times, Jeremy, we misinterpret things when we don't get our own way." He held up his hand when Jeremy opened his mouth to speak. "Don't misunderstand what I'm saying. I'm definitely not implying that what you interpreted didn't happen, only that many times young children tend to exaggerate in their minds what others have done to them if their immediate demands aren't gratified. For instance, you may have, at the time, felt your mother was withholding affection for you when in reality she was busy at that particular moment with household chores."

He shook his head back and forth. "No, it didn't matter what time of the day or night. She never had time for me." He bit his bottom lip. "She didn't have to kick me."

"I'm sorry she did that to you."

"But you don't believe me."

"I didn't say that."

Jeremy lifted his shirt and walked to Thaddeus. "Look. You can still see the scars."

Thaddeus cringed, seeing the faint scars running zigzagged across the young man's back. Compassion for Jeremy tugged at his heartstrings. He could never imagine Lily or himself inflicting such terror on their own sons. He knew by the position of the scars that the injuries weren't self-inflicted or caused by playing or falling down. "Do you remember seeing a doctor or being asked by anyone about your injuries? Perhaps a teacher may have questioned you about your home life?"

"Before I ever had a chance to tell anyone what was going on, my mother would inform everyone that I was accident-prone. She even had the gall to tell them that I was a very self-centered, demanding child and would inflict these injuries on myself as a way of getting attention. She convinced them that I had a very active imagination and made up stories all the time. I couldn't defend myself against my own mother, and there was no one to help me. Everyone believed her stories. Once I tried to tell my father, but he took her side."

"Your father treated you the same way?"

He nodded. "He didn't physically abuse me, but his verbal abuse was nonstop when he was home. I had lots of friends once I started school, so it helped not to feel so lonely." He sighed. "I know my father was disappointed that I wasn't a six-foot-two jock."

"Do you think he's disappointed that you don't participate in sports now?"

"All of his friends' sons play sports, and he's always talking incessantly about them, rubbing my nose in it at every opportunity."

"Maybe you're blowing things out of proportion just a little?" he suggested, eying him carefully. "Is that possible, Jeremy?"

"No. I'm nothing more than a worthless wimp to him." He took his glasses off and wiped them on his shirt, then put them back on. "He's even asked me to stay in my room when he has friends over, because he's ashamed to let them know I'm his son."

"But your girlfriend gives you hope?"

He smiled, his eyes growing bright once again. "Yes. She would never hurt me."

"I don't believe you've told me her name."

"Her name's Rebecca Walker, and she's everything a woman should be."

"What do you think a woman should be?"

He thought for a moment. "She should be soft-spoken, feminine, and willing to do anything for the man she loves and never make him angry."

Thaddeus's eyes narrowed. "What happens if she causes the man she loves to become angry?"

Jeremy avoided his eyes.

"What does anger cause him to do?" he asked again.

"Nothing," he finally replied. "He just wouldn't be pleased, that's all."

"What type of things would she have to do to cause that anger to come out in him?"

He shrugged. "Putting him down in front of other people, making fun of his weaknesses, or not being faithful."

"If a woman did those things, then she probably never loved him in the first place." Dr. Tate kept his eyes on Jeremy. "I don't know too many people, male or female, who haven't been disillusioned about someone they've loved at some point in their lives. It happens all the time and it hurts deeply, but in time one heals and is able to get over that hurt."

"Rebecca is incapable of hurting anyone."

"Be careful about putting her on a pedestal. She's only human, and if you put her above reproach, that's putting unfair pressure on her."

"She just wouldn't hurt me, that's all."

"How long have you been dating her?"

"I don't feel like talking anymore," Jeremy abruptly said.

"Would you like to talk about Julie Howard?"

His eyes clouded. "No, that's been over for years."

"You were quite upset at that time, as I recall."

"Any guy in my position would have been upset. But I forgave her a long time ago, because it wasn't her fault."

"She denied having any type of relationship with you."

He frowned. "What could she say? She had to do everything her precious daddy said, and Daddy didn't approve of me so of course we had to end things. But I know what Julie and I shared," he stated firmly. "I remember when Julie and I were having problems, you said you believed I was suffering from disillusionment. You never believed me when I told you how much in love Julie and I were."

He contemplated Jeremy's remarks for a few seconds. "Sometimes when we want something so desperately, our mind convinces us that we've achieved it and it's ours for the taking, when in reality it is nothing more than wishful thinking on our part. We've convinced ourself beyond a shadow of a doubt that it's real, but in actuality it's nothing more than a fantasy."

Jeremy emphatically shook his head back and forth again. "No. It happened. I wouldn't have written those letters to her if she hadn't been my girlfriend. That would be ridiculous."

Thaddeus glanced at his wristwatch. "I'd like to see you next week, but please call me if you need to talk about anything. I want you to take your medication twice a day. I want your word that you will take them as directed." He paused. "Jeremy, I'm sorry about what happened to you when you were a child, and next time we'll work on helping you to deal with that pain so you can put it behind yourself."

He nodded. "Okay."

Chapter Five

Millicent Talbot wiped the sweat from her brow, holding tight to her watering can with her other hand. She gave the geraniums, chrysanthemums, and peonies a long drink before heading to her pride and joy — her roses. She lovingly gazed at each. This year they were going to be the best by far. She prided herself on the effort she put into her flower gardens and the spectacular view they gave her from her kitchen window on the gray and overcast days.

When the watering was finished, she walked over to the patio, then picked up her glass of iced tea, took a large swallow, and plopped down in a patio chair. She scanned her enormous backyard bordered by the elaborate display of flowers. Her flowers were the only things that gave her joy in her otherwise drab life. She remembered as a little girl working with her grandmother Emily in the little garden they had maintained in the yard behind their small house. Those long-ago days spent with her grandmother were the days she'd treasured the most. She'd always called her Nana Em and thought of her as her true mother, most times wishing she would have been.

Her own parents had moved from New York City back

to Pittsburgh when she was less than a year old. They hoped the move back home to family and friends would save their marriage and offer them an escape from the poverty their teenaged marriage had given them. Her mother had repeated the story to her so many times that she knew it by heart. Millicent's parents, Eloise and Tom, had fallen in love in high school, and when Eloise had found herself pregnant she and Tom knew they would be forbidden to see one another ever again. Eloise would most likely be sent away to a distant state until the baby was born and quickly given up for adoption, returning to Pittsburgh with the excuse that she'd been sent to tend to an ailing aunt. It was the same age-old story that families told over to save face when a family member became pregnant out of wedlock.

Tom and Eloise couldn't bear the thought of being separated, so one stormy night they sneaked away in Tom's beat-up truck and headed to New York City where they knew no one would find them as they blended in with the masses. The plan was for Tom to find employment, and Eloise would stay home and take care of their home and baby when it was born. They had enough money to pay the first month's rent on a small flat above a meat market. The next day Tom found a job in a box factory. As soon as they legally could, they planned to go to City Hall to get married.

Tom found ten-hour days in a hot factory more grueling than he'd anticipated, especially returning every night to a nagging wife who was lonely and homesick, and to a colicky baby daughter. The constant bickering and lack of money proved more than his nerves could take. In time they were barely civil to one another and decided that in order to save their marriage, they would take their shame back to their families in Pittsburgh, begging forgiveness. Tom's family promptly slammed the door in their faces, wanting no part of them or their bastard, as they referred to Millicent. Eloise's mother, Emily, had been widowed at the age of thirty and became the sole breadwinner for her six children, which now left her looking older than she was at the age of forty-five. Even though she had her own share of problems, she welcomed Tom, Eloise, and Millicent into her small, cramped house and soon found herself cherishing her new granddaughter.

A few months after they'd settled in, Tom didn't return home one evening after work. The next day Eloise learned that he'd quit his job at the mill and taken their meager savings from their bureau drawer. According to his friends, he headed to parts unknown, frustrated with his role as a husband and father. Eloise refused to believe that she and their baby daughter had been abandoned. She insisted Tom had set out to find a better job and would be sending for them soon. Emily never believed he'd return, and the only bright side she saw in the situation was that Tom hadn't deserted her daughter and grandchild in New York City.

Millicent never saw her father again and had been too young to remember anything about him, but her mother told and retold the story of their love and their escape to New York, and how he would send for them any day. As time wore on, Eloise became a recluse, barely leaving the house and suffering from bouts of depression so severe she couldn't even care for her toddler. Millicent soon came to think of her beloved grandmother Emily as her mother, and her birth mother as a stranger whose nerves she always seemed to get on.

She was brought up in poverty but cherished the things her grandmother taught her, and she never felt as poor as she was. Nana Em taught her how to cook and clean, assuring her that she would someday make some man very happy. Millicent didn't tell her that she wanted no part of men, marriage, or having babies. She saw what that had done to her mother, and she was determined to never let a man be her sole reason for existing. She didn't have any close friends in school, since everyone believed that her mother was crazy and pointed and whispered behind her back, but she didn't let that deter her from getting a good education and pulling straight A's. She had a dream, and that dream was to go to college to study medicine or law. She had an equal love of both, but hadn't decided which career would win out.

When she entered her junior year in high school, her precious Nana Em became ill, no longer being able to work. This left Millicent no choice but to quit school and seek full time employment to help out the family, which now consisted of only her mother, Nana Em, and herself. She found a position in the drugstore on the corner of their street and worked the counter. The job was very different from what she'd wanted out of her life, and if it hadn't been for her Nana Em needing her, she would have run away from it all. Nana Em had always freely given everything she could to her, and now she had the opportunity to give something back.

Nana Em worried about Millicent working all day and taking care of the household duties at night, when she should be dating and enjoying her life. Millicent constantly assured her that she was happy and contented the way things were, but Nana Em kept pushing her to meet the son of one of her friends, Gilbert Talbot. But she kept finding excuses to avoid meeting him. She had no room or desire for a man in her life.

She came home from work one evening to find Gilbert sitting on the living room sofa with an invitation to dinner from Nana Em. Millicent was cordial and made it perfectly clear that she was not interested, but Gilbert persisted in getting to know her better, and night after night he'd unexpectedly show up trying to win her heart. Nana Em used every opportunity to encourage Millicent to go to the movies, take walks, or sit on the front porch swing with Gilbert. In time, she became used to and even looked forward to his company. Having a friend to talk to was refreshing. She knew that Gilbert wanted more out of their friendship than she did, feeling his attraction to her and knowing she was pretty in her own right, with a good figure. When a year had gone by, Gilbert began bringing up the subject of marriage.

Tired of barely making enough money to support her family, Millicent finally succumbed to Gilbert's proposal of marriage after he promised to take care of her mother and Nana Em for the rest of their lives. Gilbert Talbot was a man of his word, and for that Millicent was grateful, but she also knew the soft spot he held in his heart for Nana Em. He came to love her almost as much as Millicent did. She wondered if he ever suspected that she didn't love him the way a wife was supposed to love her husband. His naked flesh on top of her night after night sickened her. She hated him sticking his thing into her as he grew sweaty and damp, but she'd dutifully lay there, unresponsive, waiting for him to finish when he would then roll off her and onto his side, and then promptly fall to sleep. If he was upset that she showed no interest in sex, he kept it to himself, and she had financial security so she figured the situation worked out to suit both of their needs.

Two years after her marriage to Gilbert, her beloved

Nana Em passed away, followed six months later by her mother. She was crushed by the death of her grandmother but felt nothing with her mother's passing. Her depression deepened as the months passed, her only happiness found in the flower gardens where she relived the long-ago days of gardening with her grandmother.

A year after the death of her Nana Em, she found herself pregnant. At first she didn't tell Gilbert, hoping that she'd miraculously lose the baby, but she didn't and knew she had to tell her husband. He was neither happy nor upset with her news and just accepted his responsibility. As her pregnancy wore on, Millicent's depression increased even further, and after the birth of their son, Jeremy, she was depressed so much of the time that she didn't know how it felt to not be depressed. She tried to get close to Jeremy and to nurture her helpless infant as a mother should, but he reminded her of the sexual acts that had taken place between Gilbert and herself, and it made her feel dirty. She took several showers daily, but she could still feel his throbbing penis inside of her, making her physically ill. Jeremy was the product of her sin.

At times she couldn't even bear to look at her son, then felt guilty for wishing he'd never been born. She was expected to be loving and warm, but when she looked into his innocent face, all she felt inside was contempt for this child. She was his mother and it wasn't his fault, but now she was trapped in this marriage with no hope for anything better out of life. All of the dreams she'd held so tightly in her youth withered and died. In public she put on a false front, acting like Jeremy was her pride and joy, but inside their home she gave him as little of her time as she could. She never intended to hurt him, but at times she lashed out at him, striking his fragile tiny body with her fists and kicking him until his body was black and blue. When the rage within her began, she had no control over it. It washed over her like a tidal wave, rendering her oblivious to normal actions.

After Jeremy's birth, Gilbert spent more and more time at his office, where his job as an insurance adjuster kept his mind occupied. When he was home, he read the paper or watched TV, barely acknowledging his son and leaving him to amuse himself. Millicent made excuses to Gilbert about being unable to have intercourse, but when he insisted and sometimes even took her against her will, she began to make herself as unattractive to him as she could. She wanted to repulse him as much as he repulsed her. As her weight increased, his sexual desire for her decreased, and eventually they mutually agreed to sleep in separate bedrooms.

As Jeremy grew, he appeared normal in every way, even without the love and guidance from his parents, but that abruptly changed when puberty started. She knew she needed to talk to him since his father wouldn't, but they were strangers to one another, and he looked blankly at her whenever she'd awkwardly try to begin a conversation. Gilbert generally handled any discipline problems that arose, and Jeremy accepted his punishment without any verbal backlash, but when Millicent began to hear Jeremy talking to himself and answering his own questions out loud, she knew something was terribly wrong. She remembered her mother's lonely voice calling out to her beloved Tom late at night, and many times Millicent herself had witnessed her mother's conversations. Eloise could never be convinced that Tom was not there sharing her conversation with her. She'd retreated into her own mind.

Now she saw the child she'd given birth to acting like

his grandmother had as she slipped into mental illness. Jeremy's friends stopped coming around, and he spent most of his free time alone up in his room. When Gilbert noticed Jeremy's strange behavior, he and Millicent sought counseling for him. They couldn't allow the psychiatrist to suspect that they didn't love their own son, so they acted like any normal parents would, showing concern for their child's physical as well as his mental well-being.

She sighed heavily as she sipped at her iced tea, realizing that the best years of her life had passed her by and she'd never be able to recapture them.

****

Jeremy sat on the bus, staring blankly out of the window. He heard the familiar echoes and tightly closed his eyes for a few seconds.

You almost blew everything! they shouted.

But I didn't, his mind screamed back at them. He popped his eyes back open, then cautiously looked at the other passengers. No one made eye contact with him. They were involved in their own private thoughts. He settled back in his seat as the bus stopped and passengers got off and new ones got on.

It's a good thing we were there to help you keep your cool. Forget Rebecca. She'll never be your girlfriend, they hissed.

Yes, she is! his mind shouted, repeatedly trying to drown out their screeching, hissing voices. He'd concentrate on Rebecca. Thoughts of her brought a smile to his lips. He couldn't wait to see her again. As he willed himself to focus just on her, he chased the demons to the far corners of his mind.

He got off the bus a quarter of a mile from his home and walked across the street to the drugstore. He had the prescription filled, then stuffed it into his pocket and slowly lumbered along the quiet road, enjoying the warm sun on his face. He walked up the curved driveway and around to the back of his house. When he reached the patio, he saw his mother sitting quietly, her expression sad and lost. He watched her for a few minutes, wondering what she was thinking about. Was she regretting the lost years between mother and son that could never be regained? Would she finally give him the mother's love and security he'd lacked for his twenty-two years of life?

He set his backpack down, and she turned with a startled look on her face. "Did you keep your appointment with Dr. Tate?" she anxiously asked.

He felt his anger mount at her lack of a greeting. "Yes," he answered, pulling the bottle of pills from his pocket. "He prescribed these. One pill twice a day."

She nodded as she took the bottle from him. "I'll let your father know."

He thought about pulling up a chair next to hers, but before he could, she abruptly got up and waddled out into the yard. He wanted to shout at her and grab her flabby arms and make her take a good look at him, but instead he silently walked into the house and up to his bedroom.

Chapter Six

"Since when are your conversations with Jeremy confidential?" Gilbert Talbot angrily asked.

Thaddeus Tate rubbed his tired eyes. "Mr. Talbot, I've explained to you that when Jeremy came of legal age he had the right to request confidentiality from everyone, including his parents, regardless of who is paying for his treatment. He never requested that confidentiality until he restarted his therapy sessions with me. I do not have the right to divulge anything he tells me."

"So you're refusing to update me on his mental health?"

"Is he taking his medication twice a day as prescribed?"

"Yes."

"Let's see how that works. Is his behavior causing you concern?"

Gilbert frowned. "He is much calmer than he was, but I've seen this pattern too many times, and he's still living in a fantasy world as far as this Rebecca Walker is concerned."

"I don't think we need to worry about another incident like Julie Howard. Just make sure he keeps taking his medication, and call me immediately if he stops."

"I certainly will, and I trust that you'll alert me if you feel he's regressing?"

"I'll be in touch."

Gilbert furiously set the phone down. He was annoyed with how quickly Tate had hung up without answering his question. He paced around his office, wringing his hands, his gaze finally settling on a family photo sitting on his desk. He picked it up, scrutinizing Jeremy's pose. To the outside world, the Talbot family looked like every other happy and contented middle class American family. He kept the photo on his desk for that reason alone. If it were up to him, he'd have no pictures of his son and wife to remind him of his disastrous marriage, but clients seemed to trust someone when their own family was prominently displayed for all to see. The photo seemed to convey to the world that he had a family of his own to support and was a hard- working man with no personal gains for himself.

Millicent, Jeremy, and he would never be a real family, and the photo was only make-believe. They were miserable, but he'd tried, God knows he'd tried. But by the time Jeremy came along, he just didn't give a damn anymore. The disappointment he'd found in Millicent after their marriage soured him on the whole concept of family.

His mother had insisted all those years ago that he get to know Millicent Bryant. She was the granddaughter of her closest friend, and according to his mother a beauty and quite a catch for any man fortunate to win her heart. Even though he was eight years older than she, he reluctantly agreed to meet her, but only to get his mother off his back. The moment he laid eyes on Millicent, though, he was love-struck. At first she showed no mutual interest in him, but he was patient and wooed her, hoping in time she would soften toward him. He couldn't bear being apart from her.

He sent gifts and stopped by almost every night, knowing she was becoming accustomed to him and enjoying his visits. In time she did warm up to him. He tolerated her prudish ways, knowing her old-fashioned values forced her to save herself for her wedding night. She was ashamed of the circumstances of her birth, but it didn't bother him, only endeared her more to him. He became close to her Nana Em, seeing the warmth and tender care she'd devoted to Millicent. Eloise was another story, though, and he patiently listened to her stories about her fairy-tale romance to Tom Bryant, suspecting that she was so far over the edge she'd probably never come back. His suspicions came true.

He'd been seeing Millicent for almost a year before she'd even allowed him to kiss her lips instead of his customary peck on the cheek. She was beautiful, with sparkling big brown eyes and dark brown shoulder-length hair, which she usually wore tied back with a ribbon. Her figure was almost hourglass perfect, and he often found his eyes shifting to her perky ample breasts. He yearned to see her naked and touch and suckle those breasts, but he never tried. If he made an advance, she would never see him again.

Common sense told him he should give up and find someone else, but his heart wouldn't hear of it. He was strangely drawn to Millicent not just for her beauty, but he admired and respected the way she single-handedly held her family together with no help from her relatives. They treated her as an outsider and were ashamed of Eloise, which finally caused her beloved grandmother to ask them to refrain from any more visits. If he wanted Millicent to be his wife, he would have to include her mother and grandmother in those plans.

When he finally got up the courage to propose

marriage, he was surprised when she didn't hesitate in agreeing to marry him. The wedding night he'd dreamed of and the tender lovemaking he'd planned to share with her was only in his dreams. He practically had to force himself on her, assuming that she had wedding-night jitters and was only scared. Her innocence and virginity endeared her even more to his heart. However, as time wore on, he realized that Millicent wanted no part of sexual intercourse and would lie underneath him totally unresponsive, waiting for him to satisfy himself without showing any passion or desire of her own. He tried to convince her that sexual intercourse was a natural and beautiful part of marriage for a couple to express their love to one another, but she adamantly refused to believe it was anything but humiliating and degrading.

He began reading and collecting men's magazines, and when his desire for a responsive woman became too much, he'd drive around and find a prostitute. He wasn't proud of what he did but rationalized that every man deserved the comfort of an approachable, sexually responsive woman who would match his passion.

When Millicent announced that she was pregnant, he was devastated but kept his feelings to himself. He'd planned to divorce her and give her a nice monthly alimony, but now he was trapped. He couldn't leave her to raise the child alone. That would be an unforgivable act, and he'd face recriminations from society. His public image was extremely important to him. Besides, he feared how Millicent would rear the child. She was deeply depressed during the pregnancy, and her depression seemed to get worse after the birth of their son.

He gently suggested she seek someone professionally to talk to about whatever was causing her unhappiness, but she assured him that she was fine. Still, he worried. He'd seen what depression had done to her mother, and he feared that she had inherited Eloise's mental illness.

His son was an obstacle in his life that he'd neither asked for nor wanted. He tried to muster up some paternal feelings, knowing he should love his own flesh and blood, but he couldn't. Every time he looked into Jeremy's coal-black eyes, he was reminded that this little boy was the reason he had to stay in this loveless marriage. His only release from his frustration was his work and the whores on the strip.

Millicent's beauty seemed to disappear almost as quickly as the weight piled on her once almost-perfect frame. The sight of her bulging body sickened him, and the thought of touching her or making love to her repulsed him even further, so he had no objections when she suggested they begin sleeping in separate bedrooms. He would have completely avoided her and Jeremy, but for appearances sake he shared dinner with them every evening, then either retired to his study to do paperwork or roamed the strip. Sometimes he'd just stop at the strip clubs, sit for hours watching the dancers, and ponder why fate had led him to a cold, unloving woman for his life mate. If only he could turn back time.

He was disappointed and ashamed with Jeremy's short stature and wiry, thin frame. When Jeremy started exhibiting moody, depressive episodes, he knew it was a trait inherited from Millicent's side of the family and desperately sought any measures to keep his son out of the scrutiny of the public eye. He was uncomfortable in his son's presence, but he tried to hide his feelings from the boy. As any father would do, he disciplined him when he did something wrong or didn't do his homework.

Sometimes he felt guilty for shunning him, but he couldn't bring himself to love him. Even though it wasn't Jeremy's fault, he was a product of Millicent.

Gilbert's only consolation came from knowing that eventually Jeremy would leave the nest and carve out his own life. Gilbert would stay with Millicent, but only out of pity. Maybe in time she would figure out what she truly wanted from life and eventually call it quits to this farce they called a marriage. That hope strengthened him.

Millicent seemed to derive contentment with her flower gardens, and he would see an unaccustomed peacefulness come over her face when she was tending her numerous gardens. She had no true human friends and seemed to substitute the flowers for the lack of human contact.

Gilbert sighed as he sat down at his desk and picked up a folder. He hoped Thaddeus Tate was correct in his evaluation of Jeremy. He wouldn't be able to keep any further incidents hushed up as he had with the Julie Howard episode. He'd keep his own eyes and ears open to anything peculiar with Jeremy's actions. He had noticed a quiet calmness about him the past few weeks, and as long as Jeremy stayed on his medication, Gilbert anticipated they'd get through the next few weeks. Once Jeremy graduated from college, he intended to show him the door.

Chapter Seven

Jeremy flashed a smile at Rebecca as Professor Burgess passed out their final exam papers. For the past few weeks he'd hoped she'd speak to him again, but she hadn't. Every morning he arose with anticipation of talking to her, but there wasn't a repeat of any conversation like she'd had with him weeks before. He still felt her touch on him and the scent of her perfume. Her aroma filled his nostrils, and he was immune to any other smell. He'd sent several anonymous letters to her, and he wondered what she thought when she'd read his anguished words of unrequited love. So many times he'd picked up the phone and dialed her number, then quickly hung up when her voice came on the line.

Now their college days were coming to an end, and he worried he'd never see her again. He had to make a move to let her know how he felt about her. He'd written several more letters to her with his identity, describing his heartfelt emotions should they ever become separated, but they remained unsent, hidden in his bureau under his jeans. He was waiting for the perfect opportunity to send them.

He glanced at the essay questions, assured they'd be a

breeze, then picked up his pen and began. Two hours later he set his pen down and picked up his exam. He tossed it on Burgess's desk. Burgess looked at him but said nothing.

Jeremy nodded, then looked over his shoulder as he walked out of the room, seeing Rebecca still bent over her paper.

Thirty minutes later, he sat in the campus bus shelter waiting for his bus to Green Tree.

"Hi, Jeremy, I'm glad I caught you."

He looked up in surprise. "Hi, Rebecca." He smiled nervously as his heart thudded in his chest.

"I never thought I'd finish the essays on time." She pushed a loose strand of hair from her brow. "I suppose you whizzed right through them," she said with a wink.

He laughed, then noticed his bus slowly moving up the street. "That's my bus," he said awkwardly, wishing he could stay and talk to her and take a later bus, but if he did, his mother would have a fit. She watched his every move like a hawk, expecting him home at certain times, and if he were late she'd give him the third degree. If she did it out of concern for his well-being he might be able to understand, but she didn't give a shit about him and was only trying to protect her own reputation from any embarrassment he might cause her. He stood up.

"Wait a sec, Jeremy. I want to invite you to a party this weekend."

His eyebrows went up. "You...you want to invite me?"

She flashed him a smile. "Yes, Jeremy, I want to invite you. I told you that you need to get out, and this is your chance. I'm sorry I haven't had a chance to talk to you for a while, but things have been crazy with finals and everything else going on with graduation preparations."

His face flushed. "I'm not very socially active." His bus

pulled up to the stop and the door opened.

"I'll expect you right here at eight o'clock Friday night. Everyone will be here. It's a pre-grad party."

He nodded numbly as he stepped onto the bus. A grin broke across his face as he plopped into a seat.

****

Later he walked into the kitchen where his parents were sitting at the table with their after-dinner coffee. "It's time for my pills," he said flatly.

Millicent glanced at him, then heavily pulled herself to her feet and waddled to the kitchen cupboard. She shook one of the pills into her pudgy palm and handed it to him. "Wait, I'll get you some water." She filled a glass and passed it to him, standing firmly in front of him and watching with hawk-like eyes as he popped the pill into his mouth and flushed it down with a gulp of water.

"You've been doing well taking your medication, Jeremy."

His eyes briefly met hers. "I'm not a child." He turned to leave.

"Jeremy, wait a minute," Gilbert said.

He faced his father.

"What are your plans after graduation?"

He shrugged. "I'm working on some short stories and a couple of novels. I plan to submit my manuscripts to some publishers."

"I think you need to concentrate on finding a real vocation, Jeremy. You'll be getting a degree in business. You should focus your efforts in that area."

"Whatever you say."

"Are your exams finished?"

He nodded. "Today was the last one."

Gilbert folded his hands together and laid them on the

table. "Monday I expect you to get up early and start looking for work. You should have sought a position months ago. Graduation is Sunday, and I'm certain that your fellow graduates have already secured positions. Get on the ball."

"Whatever," he answered. "By the way, I'll be going out on Friday night. I have a date."

"With whom?" his father skeptically asked.

"Rebecca Walker. She's invited me to a pre-grad party." He saw the look that passed between his parents.

"I thought we'd agreed, Jeremy, that your infatuation with this girl is only a product of your imagination."

He looked into his father's cold eyes. "I know what I know."

"What the hell does that mean?"

He shrugged again. "She asked me this afternoon."

"You haven't mentioned her for weeks."

"I've been busy preparing for finals and graduation."

Gilbert frowned. "I'm sure you're aware that you'll probably never see this girl again after graduation."

He had thought about that and it tormented and disturbed him, but he wouldn't let his father or mother know. Besides, maybe that was why Rebecca invited him to the party. Maybe she wanted to tell him how much she'd miss him and couldn't bear to be apart from him. At the party, they'd sit privately and plan their future together. "Well, I'll be seeing her Friday night," he answered evenly.

****

On Friday night, Jeremy nervously looked through his closet for something appropriate to wear. His palms grew sweaty in anticipation of what the night would hold for him and Rebecca. His adrenalin pumped him up.

Don't go, the demons shouted. *She's going to hurt you.*

Rebecca is no good for you! they hissed.

Jeremy placed his hands over his ears, but the voices only grew louder. "Shut up!" he demanded. "Just shut the fuck up!" He squeezed his eyes shut as his mind became saturated with thoughts and images of Rebecca. The demons felt threatened, but they confused him repeatedly — one minute telling him to stand up for himself, and then taunting him when he did. He couldn't trust them most of the time, but he knew they'd never leave and it was useless to plead with them for release. They embedded themselves in his thought processes, sometimes doing things and then blaming him for it. They were as much a part of him as his legs and arms were. The few weeks of peace he'd had from them had given him false hope, and he felt a peacefulness he wasn't accustomed to. Now they were back and in full swing, stronger than before. He had to keep his guard up and watch them while trying in desperation to hide his real thoughts about Rebecca. *She'll hurt you worse than Julie Howard ever did*, they warned.

"Leave me alone! She's nothing like Julie." He pulled on a pair of jeans, his fingers trembling on the zipper. He felt the familiar bulge beginning to grow, but there was no time. He pulled on a pale blue T-shirt with the college logo emblazoned across the front of it, then grabbed his sneakers and slid his feet into them, tying them tightly. He studied his reflection in his bureau mirror and ran a comb through his tangled hair.

He bounded down the stairs; his father was waiting for him at the bottom.

"Maybe you should stay home tonight."

He shook his head. "I've been staying home for twenty-two years."

"How well do you know these people?"

"Well enough," he lied. "Rebecca's expecting me, and I'm not going to disappoint her. I have to go or I'll miss my bus."

"What time will you be home?"

He shrugged. "When the party's over."

Gilbert's eyes narrowed. "You're not used to parties, Jeremy. You'll feel awkward and out of place."

He laughed. "Not a chance. After all, Father, I graduate on Sunday, and I'll bet you're counting the days until you throw me out on my ass." He looked him squarely in the eye.

Gilbert placed his hands in his pockets. The jangling noise of the loose change and car keys got on Jeremy's already fragile nerves. "Let me give you a ride," he offered.

"No, thanks. I'll take the bus."

Millicent stood uneasily by the door. "Call us if there's any trouble, Jeremy. Be careful...you know how nervous you become in strange situations."

He held up his hands. "Look, I appreciate your concern, and I might even be flattered by it if I thought it was genuine. Unfortunately, I know that all you two care about is your reputations, but not to worry. Tate's little magic pills keep me calm, and I'll cause you no embarrassment tonight. Now if you two don't mind, I have a bus to catch, and my girl's waiting for me."

Don't be a fool! the demons hissed. *Rebecca will break your heart.*

"Shut the hell up," Jeremy mumbled.

"What did you say?" Gilbert eyed him sharply.

"Nothing." He nodded to them then slipped outside into the warm evening. He hurried down the street to the bus stop, relieved that he was the only one there. He glanced impatiently at his wristwatch every few seconds.

It's not too late to go home, the demons called out. *Leave now before it's too late. You don't belong with Rebecca.*

Jeremy steeled himself from the voices of the demons by replacing them with thoughts of Rebecca. The more Rebecca Walker filtered through his mind, the more he felt the demons fighting for control. He was suddenly stricken with a frightening thought. He'd never been on a date before and wasn't sure he even knew how to properly kiss a girl. He needed to practice. He looked around, and still seeing no one, puckered up his lips and pressed them to the back of his hand.

The demons hissed and laughed at his efforts.

"Shut up!" he hissed back at them. He continued kissing the back of his hand as he imagined what Rebecca's full, tempting pink lips would taste like. He shivered. Would she make the first move or should he? How would he know when to kiss her? How would he know if she liked his kiss? He closed his eyes, picturing her pressing her body tightly to his as her need for him grew. His hand would caress her back, then slowly travel down to her buttocks. She would squirm against him, pleading and begging for all of him. He'd finally touch those perfect breasts and feel her nipples harden as he placed his mouth on them, his tongue gently teasing.

He felt his penis harden and as he swelled, he imagined what it would feel like to be deep inside of her. He squeezed his legs tightly together as perspiration poured from his brow.

She'll never want you in that way. Forget it! the demons roared.

CHAPTER EIGHT

Gilbert stared coldly at Millicent. "I want him out of this house before summer's over." His jaw was firmly set. Whenever his jaw was drawn taught, he was serious.

"He needs to find a job first. We can't just throw him to the wolves, Gil. He's not prepared to live in the world on his own." She wrung her hands.

He looked in disbelief at her. "Since when have either of us taken the time or even cared if he was prepared to live on his own? All we've waited for was the day when we could set him out. For God's sake, he's twenty-two years old, and it's high time he supported himself. I've done my duty, and most times I think more than my duty." He looked into her eyes. "Let's tell the truth, Millicent, he was an unfortunate mistake that should have never happened."

Her mouth flew open. "How can you say such a thing? He's our son, and we need to help him."

"Get off it, it's just you and me here right now, Millicent. You can cut the act," he said. "You've never had one ounce of maternal instinct in your body for him, just as I've never been a father to him nor have I cared to be. Neither of us has taught him any values or how to survive in the world, because our only objective has been to raise him and hope someday he moves so far away that we'll never have to see him again." He let his breath out in a rush. He was glad he'd gotten it off of his chest and felt like a weight had been lifted from his shoulders.

Millicent lowered her head in shame. Gilbert's remarks jolted her. "I tried...I really did try to love him, but I couldn't," she cried, her face contorting with emotion. "You do understand, don't you, Gilbert?"

He shook his head. "What I don't understand, Millicent, is how you and I have managed to keep this marriage together." He watched the fear come into her eyes.

"No, Gilbert, you can't walk away and leave me alone," she whined.

"Calm yourself. I have no intention of leaving you, but I won't stand in your way if you want to leave."

"Where would I go? I have no friends. This house is all I have," she said in a frightened, childlike voice.

"I won't leave," he reassured her. "I promised your grandmother I'd always take care of you as long as I lived, but if it wasn't for my promise to her, I would have left years ago."

"I don't know what I'd do all by myself." She rapidly blinked her eyes. "Jeremy seems to be doing much better since he's been taking his medication and seeing Dr. Tate again."

"But how long will he continue taking his medication? Will he continue treatment when he's out on his own?"

"I don't know. I wonder where he'll go when he leaves here or what he'll do."

"He's intelligent and should have no trouble finding a respectable position, but it's his antisocial behavior that bothers me."

"I'm concerned about this Rebecca Walker."

He grimaced. "I don't like the idea of this party, but in a couple of days he'll be graduating and he'll never see any of them again. Rebecca Walker will most likely only become a fond memory to him in the years to come. What I can't figure out is that he's never been a part of their lives or them of his, so why now?"

She raised her eyebrows. "Do you suppose that maybe this Rebecca Walker does care for him? If she asked him to a party, that has to mean something."

He shrugged. "It's most likely an open invitation issued to all of the graduates. She may have just casually mentioned the party and his mind fantasized it into something it's not." He turned to her. "Do you remember when he was five or six and we found all of those skeletons of birds, squirrels, and rabbits hidden behind the garage?"

"What made you think of that now, Gilbert?" She searched his face.

"We both know that wasn't normal behavior. We should have gotten him help then."

She shook her head. "No, we did the right thing. If we'd made a fuss about it, the neighbors and his school friends would have found out and avoided him."

Gilbert cocked an eyebrow. "They avoided him later, but maybe if we had gotten him counseling when he was a child, his life would be different today. He hasn't had any friends in years." He gave her a sharp look. "You have no close friends either, Millicent. Don't you ever get lonely here by yourself all day? You've never been very cordial to the neighbors."

She sniffed indignantly. "Most of them are too snooty for my taste, and I have better things to do with my time than sit around with a bunch of old gossips all day long. I've always been a loner."

"I thought you liked this neighborhood."

"Oh, I do. It's a wonderful place to live, and I'm grateful that the neighbors mind their own business."

"I still think we were wrong in not doing something about Jeremy's lack of compassion when he killed those animals."

"Some things are just the way they're meant to be, Gilbert."

He laughed bitterly. "No, sometimes we get more than we bargained for." He looked down at his hands. "Jeremy's obsession with blood wasn't normal. Most kids would cuddle or protect animals, but our son was fascinated with the sight of blood. Kids at that age cry when they fall and scrape a knee or get a bloody nose, but not him. I'd watch a light come into his eyes at the sight of his own blood on his hands."

"You think that's why he killed those animals?"

"Yes, I think he did it to watch them bleed to death."

She shivered. "He's never been invited to a party before. Do you think he'll call if there's any trouble?"

He frowned. "I honestly think we'd be the last two people on earth he'd call if anything goes wrong." He walked to the bar. "Would you like a drink, Millicent?"

"Gilbert, you know that I never touch the stuff," she indignantly replied.

He poured some whiskey into a glass, then brought it to his lips. "That, among other things."

Her face reddened. "What's that supposed to mean? I've kept a good home for you all these years, Gilbert Talbot, and never once did I complain when you asked me to host dinner parties for your colleagues and friends."

He raised his glass to her. "I am grateful for your social skills. It is the one thing I can always count on from you." He took a long swallow.

"Have you been terribly unhappy, Gilbert?"

He took another swallow of whiskey. "Let's just say, Millicent, that my life certainly took a different direction than I'd planned."

Her eyes narrowed. "It wasn't totally my fault. I tried."

"Why did you marry me?" he bluntly asked.

Her eyes held his. "You offered security."

"What about love?" he demanded.

"I'd grown very fond of you and knew that you were a hard worker and a good man. Nevertheless, most of all I respected you. You never tried to take advantage of me the way most men might have."

He snorted. "You kept your legs so tight together no one could have ever pried them apart."

She sat down on the sofa. "Why are we talking about this now after so many years?"

He walked over to her, then sat next to her. "Maybe we should have had this conversation years ago, Mill." He stared down into the glass he held between his palms, gently turning it.

Her eyes misted. "You haven't called me Mill in years, Gil...since before we married." She bit her bottom lip. "In fact, you were the only one who ever called me that."

His voice softened. "You were so different back then. Slim, beautiful, and always the lady. I knew you weren't in love with me, but I thought once we were married things might get better between us, and I was hoping that you'd grow to love me the way I loved you. I worked hard to give you the kind of home you'd never had but were so worthy of. I truly loved you with all of my being." He set his drink on the coffee table. "I was overjoyed when you agreed to be my wife. What did you think marriage was?" He turned toward her looking into her face.

She rapidly blinked her eyes. "What could I possibly know about marriage? What example did I have? I saw how my grandfather's death left my grandmother in poverty. Then, of course, there's my mother. After my father deserted her and me, she turned into an unfeeling vegetable. That's what I saw marriage do to people."

"But that's not a normal summation. What about happy marriages? I'm certain your grandmother never once regretted her marriage. Your grandfather made her very happy, and when he unfortunately was taken from her much too soon, she cherished the memories he'd given her. That's what kept her going and gave her the inner strength to take care of her family alone."

"But all that hard work to support her family turned her into an old woman before her time."

"She was happy, Millicent, can't you see that?"

She wearily sighed. "My mother was never happy."

"Your mother may never have been happy. She was severely depressed and in desperate need of help."

She looked at him. "I wanted something better for my life than my mother and grandmother had."

Gilbert picked his drink back up and took another swallow. "Have you ever been happy?"

She squinted. "I suppose there have been times in my life I was." She pushed a wisp of hair from her brow. "When I was a little girl, the best times I had were with my grandmother listening to her stories and her beautiful voice as she sang to me. She's the one who taught me all about the beauty of flowers and how to care for them."

"Did your grandmother ever prepare you for marriage

and what to expect?"

"She told me several times that I would someday make some man very happy."

He inhaled sharply. "No, what I mean is did she ever prepare you for what your wedding night would be like?"

She grew uncomfortable. "Sexual intercourse was never discussed in our home."

He set his drink back down and softly placed his hands on her shoulders. "Millicent, look at me." She slowly raised her eyes and met his. "Sexual intercourse is a perfectly natural and normal act between two people. You act as though it's a dirty, vile thing to be avoided at any cost."

She looked away in disgust. "It brings shame to families."

"Is that what you think, Mill?" he asked in a gentler tone. "Do you think that your birth brought shame on your family?"

She bit her bottom lip. "I don't know what I think."

He shook his head. "It wasn't your fault that you were born."

She searched his eyes. "It isn't Jeremy's fault that he was born either."

He thoughtfully scratched his chin. Even though nothing would change between Millicent and himself, he was thankful that they'd had this conversation. It gave him an insight into how screwed up she really was. He realized that as wonderful as her grandmother had been taking over the responsibilities of raising her, not talking about sex had only confused Millicent into thinking sex was so horrible that she never saw it as anything but depraved, and vowed to never partake of it. He knew that this conversation wouldn't bring them any closer to their son either.

CHAPTER NINE

Jeremy bounded off the bus at his usual stop in Oakland. He looked up and down the street but didn't see Rebecca anywhere. He shoved his hands into his pockets.

She's not coming, the demons whispered. *She doesn't want you. Catch the next bus and go home where you belong.*

He ignored them and continued gazing up the street. He took a few paces then stopped, hoping she'd hurry up and arrive. He raised his eyes to the star-studded sky. It was a beautiful night. *A night meant for lovers*, he thought contentedly. He hated standing around, never having had patience when he was kept waiting for anything. After fifteen minutes, he glanced at his wristwatch. He'd give her twenty more minutes tops, and if she didn't arrive by then, he'd catch a bus back to Green Tree. He sauntered a few more paces up the street when a car with tires squealing sped to the curb and abruptly stopped.

"Hi, Jeremy. Sorry we're late. Come on!"

He smiled at Rebecca, who was hanging halfway out of the passenger side window. He rushed over to the car and peered in. The car was crammed full. He recognized the other two girls from creative writing class, and the guys

84

sitting next to them he'd seen around campus.

"Get in, Jeremy," Rebecca said, moving closer to the driver as she half straddled the center console.

He squeezed in and slammed the door shut, then glanced at the driver, remembering his face from history class. Everyone seemed to be paired off except for the driver. Jeremy supposed he was meeting his date at the party.

"Jeremy, I'd like you to meet Nicholas Adams."

"Nice to meet you, Jeremy." Nicholas flashed him a wide friendly smile as he pulled out into traffic.

"Same here," Jeremy answered in a low voice as his gaze traveled to Rebecca's beautiful long, silky smooth legs. She was clad in a pair of khaki shorts and a light pink, short-sleeved pullover, which accentuated her medium-sized, firm breasts.

She introduced him to those in the backseat, and then turned to face him. "I'm so thrilled that you decided to come tonight, Jeremy. We're going to have a blast! This may be the last time we see everyone. After Sunday we'll be spreading out all over the universe," she said in a bubbly voice.

"Um…I wouldn't mind someone spreading out all over me tonight," Brian Chambers said.

"Brian!" Annie Jones exclaimed in mock shock. "You're terrible!"

"And you love it, baby," he grinned.

Rebecca laughed, then playfully tapped Nicholas's leg. "Don't say anything."

"Yes, dear," he said with a laugh as he looked into the mirror, flashing a wide grin at his friends in the backseat.

Cassi Arnold giggled. "No repeat of last weekend, Becky," she warned.

"Tell that to your boyfriend," she giggled. "After all, he started it."

"No way!" Luke Reynolds piped up. "If I recall, it was Nick's idea."

Jeremy didn't have a clue as to what they were talking about, and he squirmed uncomfortably in his half seat as they chatted and giggled among themselves, seeming to forget he was even there. Rebecca touched Nicholas's leg and arm every time she spoke to him. It annoyed Jeremy, and he surmised that she wanted him to show some jealous emotion. That was it–she was trying to elicit some sort of response from him. He knew sometimes girls played games like that just to get their boyfriends green-eyed to prove that they were loved.

You don't fit in with them. They've only invited you to have someone to make fun of, the demons murmured.

He stiffened.

"Are you all right?" Rebecca whispered close to his ear.

He felt her warm sweet-smelling breath on his cheek, which immediately sent a jolting sensation to his crotch. Later he would prove to her how much he loved her. When they were finished making love, she would have no doubt as to how much he worshipped her. "Yes," he nodded, relieved that no one could see his blushing face.

"Jeremy, what are you going to do after graduation?" Nicholas asked.

"I'm trying to land a position with a newspaper."

"Cool...in Pittsburgh?"

"No, I've applied for a couple of positions in upstate New York."

"Great."

"I think Jeremy will someday write a best seller and become a famous author, and we'll all be able to say that we knew him when."

He laughed. "I only wish." He basked in Rebecca's praise, feeling contented that she stood by his decision to seek his living as a novelist. If she weren't planning her future with him, then why would she have brought up the topic of his writing? He settled back in his seat, reassured of Rebecca's love and devotion.

"Here we are," Nicholas announced, pulling into a dimly lit parking lot.

Jeremy had been so engrossed with Rebecca's voice and sitting thigh-to-thigh with her that he hadn't paid attention to their destination. He gazed around at the unfamiliar surroundings. He hadn't actually been to very many places, mostly just Oakland and downtown Pittsburgh or his natural habitat in Green Tree, where he'd lived in the same house for all of his twenty-two years.

Everyone pulled open the doors and spilled out of the car. He heard muffled voices in the distance and caught the drift of popular tunes blaring from someone's boom box. Nicholas opened the trunk, and everyone grabbed blankets and boxes of snacks and headed in the direction of the voices. The path was eerily dark, and a couple of the guys pulled out flashlights to guide their way. When they finally reached their classmates, they set their items down and the girls spread out blankets. Several small campfires were crackling, and Jeremy enjoyed the aroma of the burning wood drifting in the air and filling his nostrils with the pleasing scent.

He stood on the outside of the group, leaning against a tree as he watched the others mingling, laughing, and joking with everyone. He saw one large group roasting hotdogs and toasting marshmallows. Several were crowded around two kegs of beer, and others stood near a table where an assortment of six packs of various brands of beer and almost every kind of hard liquor and mixers were available.

He gazed up at the starlit sky, and even though he knew that one's wish could only come true if one wished on the first star of the night, he made a wish anyway. He needed to secure his bond with Rebecca tonight. He heard snapping twigs and made out Rebecca's angelic face in the dancing firelight as she drew closer to him.

She thrust a foaming cup of beer into his hand. "You do drink beer, don't you?" she softly asked. "There's whiskey, gin, scotch…well, just about anything you can think of if you'd prefer that instead."

He shook his head. "No, beer's fine," he lied. He'd never tasted beer or any liquor for that matter in his entire life, so didn't know one way or the other what any of it tasted like. "Thank you."

"Come over by the fire with us."

"Okay." He followed her, watching as she seated herself on a blanket, and then seated himself next to her. He looked at the cup of beer in his hand and brought it to his lips. Bitterness greeted his taste buds, and he wasn't sure if he liked the taste of beer or not. Luke and Cassi sprawled on the other side of him, and Brian and Annie sat across from him. The crackling flames silhouetted everyone's face, but every so often a clear view was cast. He figured this was what it must be like on camping trips. He'd often longed to experience the trips his long-ago friends talked about taking with their fathers and now understood why they had looked so forward with anticipation to them every summer.

"Having fun?" Luke asked him.

He grinned. "Yeah." He began to relax. Finally, he had

friends, and he owed it all to Rebecca. She wanted everyone to get to know him.

Don't drink that poison, Jeremy. They're trying to weaken you, the demons warned.

Luke threw an arm around Cassi. Jeremy watched as his fingers softly massaged her bare shoulder. He stole a look at Rebecca wishing he were rubbing her shoulder as her head rested on his chest.

Nicholas sat down next to Rebecca and carefully put an arm across her shoulder, drawing her close to him. She rested her head on his chest, then ran her fingertips up and down his arm.

No! he silently screamed. *No, I'm supposed to be the one holding her and touching her*. The demons ridiculed him. *We warned you, she doesn't want you*, they laughed. He gulped down the rest of his beer, forgetting about the bitter taste. He had to quell the rumbling erupting inside of him.

Minutes later, everyone grabbed plates, then passed around hotdogs and hamburgers while they chatted and sprawled on blankets. Jeremy slowly bit into a hotdog as he kept an eye on Rebecca from the corner of his eye. He could barely swallow. His throat constricted. He watched Nicholas run his fingers through Rebecca's silky hair and saw the sparkle in her eyes as the flames from the fire danced in them. His stomach twisted in knots. He had to let her know of his deep undying love for her. She needed to know that she was his only reason for living. He glared at Nicholas, despising him. Nicholas had the type of body every guy wished he had, and of course also had the all-American good looks to go with it, but Jeremy would bet his life that Nicholas didn't share the passion for writing that he and Rebecca did. Intelligence was what had staying power. As Nicholas aged, he'd lose those looks and that perfectly toned body, and what would he be left with—only faded dreams of his jock days. Jeremy at least had the assurance that his knowledge would prove to be worth more in the end.

He became agitated when he heard Cassi Arnold call out to Rebecca. It incensed him to hear the others calling Rebecca "Becky." It was too cutesy, and she was much too sophisticated for such a childish nickname. Once he and Rebecca were permanently together, he would insist to everyone that she only be called Rebecca.

"Hey, Nick, when are the wedding bells gonna ring?" Luke asked.

Jeremy froze.

Rebecca laughed. "We're not even officially engaged yet." She looked at her naked finger. "I don't see a ring here, do you?"

"As far as I'm concerned, we are officially engaged, and the ring is forthcoming," Nicholas announced, then planted a sensuous kiss on her full lips.

The group cheered while Jeremy sat glued to the spot like he'd just been kicked in the stomach. He became dizzy and he took a shallow breath. *We told you she'd never want you*, the demons taunted. *She only invited you to rub your nose in it before she leaves you and Pittsburgh for good. She's nothing more than an obnoxious bitch and a worthless whore!* He bit down on his trembling lip until he tasted blood.

Brian stood up, then walked over to one of the kegs and filled a large plastic pitcher with beer. He grabbed a bottle of whiskey from the table before resuming his spot on the blanket. "Hold your cups up," he said as he began filling them with beer. "Come on, Jeremy. Where's your cup?"

Jeremy reluctantly held up his cup and watched as Brian poured until it spilled over the brim and dripped down onto his hand.

Luke passed around the bottle of whiskey, and one by one they took a large swallow. When the bottle reached Jeremy, he looked at the others, then slowly brought the bottle to his lips and took a large gulp. His eyes watered, then bulged, and he felt like they'd pop right out of his head as the fiery liquid spread down his throat and engulfed the pit of his stomach in a blazing inferno. He coughed deeply as he passed the bottle on to Rebecca.

"Hey, Jer, too strong for you?" Brian snickered. The others laughed. "We only get the best," Brian said. "It's a real man's drink."

"And woman's," Annie added.

They're making fun of you, idiot! Are you deaf? Maybe you like it. Maybe that's all you deserve. Get out of here now before it's too late!

He chugged the beer, then poured himself another.

"Are you all right?" Rebecca whispered. "You don't have to prove anything to anyone."

He wiped his mouth on the back of his hand, ignoring her comment. *Yes, he did have to prove something, but it wasn't to the others. It was to her.*

"Chugalug!" Brian yelled. "How much can you hold, Jer?"

The way Brian insisted on calling him Jer annoyed him. No one had ever called him that before. "It's Jeremy. I like to be called Jeremy," he stiffly replied.

"Yes, sir," Brian grinned giving him a salute. "Jeremy it is. So how much can you hold?"

His head was throbbing, and he was already feeling the effects of the beers he'd rapidly consumed. His hand shook. *Stop before you do something foolish,* the demons hissed. "As much as it takes," he confidently replied, as much to prove his point to the demons as well as to Brian.

"Let's see you do your stuff," Brian prodded.

"Come on, Brian, knock it off. We've all had too much to drink. Let's grab some more food and just have fun," Luke suggested.

Jeremy was relieved for Luke's interference and hoped it would put a stop to Brian's ridiculous challenge.

"No way," Brian insisted. "I want to see what old Jeremy here can do." He carefully pronounced every syllable in Jeremy's name, drawing it out more than was necessary.

Jeremy, annoyed, squared his shoulders. He would show Rebecca what he was really made of. "Tell me when to start."

Brian wiped the back of his mouth with his hand. "How about now?"

Rebecca laid a hand on his shoulder. "Don't do it, Jeremy."

He looked into her bright eyes for a few seconds. The firelight reflected in them made them look like two sparkling emeralds. This was his chance to prove to her and the others that he was as much a man as any other guy here. "I'll be okay," he replied as Brian filled a cup half full of straight whiskey. He picked up the cup.

"First the whiskey, then two cups of beer, and we keep going until you can't take any more. Are you ready?"

"Knock it off, Brian," Nicholas finally butted in. "We're here for a good time."

"It should be Jeremy's decision," Brian answered. "Are you up for it?"

Jeremy felt all eyes on him. He had no choice. He'd look like a wimp if he didn't do it now. He brought the cup to his lips and threw his head back, consuming the drink in two consecutive gulps. His throat smoldered, and he felt like a stick of dynamite had exploded in the pit of his stomach. He picked up one beer, draining the cup, then reached for the second. His head felt detached from his neck. The demons surrounded him. *No more, Jeremy. He's only doing this so he can make fun of you once you pass out.* His stomach lurched violently, and his arms became weak and heavy as if they were no longer an extension of himself but belonged to someone else. "Leave me alone!" he shouted. "I can do it!"

Brian shrugged. "Who are you talking to?" He snickered.

He tried to focus on Brian's face, but it blurrily swam before him. The other faces started swimming in rapid succession around and around and around. Their eyes looked right through him, leering at him as their mouths contorted into horrible-looking gestures. They snickered and whispered things he couldn't hear. *Leave now, Jeremy, before it's too late!* the demons screamed. He scrambled to his feet, his wobbly legs barely able to hold his weight. He stumbled, falling on his side close to the fire, and screamed in agony as a flame licked his right cheek.

"Jeremy!" Rebecca screamed. "Get him away from the fire!" She pulled at his feet.

He felt strong arms grabbing at his legs, tugging at him and dragging his body away from the scorching flames. *What are they doing to me?* he wondered.

Jeremy, go now before they hurt you further! the demons called repeatedly. He pulled himself to a sitting position.

"Jeremy, let me put something on the burn," Rebecca offered.

"I'm fine," he mumbled, forcing himself to his feet. It took all the strength he had to stand up. His stomach heaved, he turned his face from the group and forced his feet to run toward the path. He couldn't throw up in front of them.

*****

"Go after him, Nicholas! He'll get hurt. He doesn't know his way around here," Rebecca cried.

"No, he's just going to spill his guts," Nicholas reassured her. "He'll be back."

"He's drunk for Christ's sake, Nick. What if he wanders down the road and gets hit by a car?"

"He won't go far. He's lucky if he makes it as far as the parking lot, but I'll tell you what. If he's not back in ten minutes, I'll go get him."

"Promise?"

"I promise, baby," he answered, squeezing her hand.

CHAPTER TEN

When his study door opened, Thaddeus Tate raised his eyes. Lily Tate set the steaming cup of coffee on his desk

"Thank you, dear, I was just about to come to the kitchen to pour myself a cup."

She smiled at him. "After twenty years of marriage, I know that at promptly eleven o'clock every night you have a cup of coffee."

He chuckled as he held her hand, giving it an affectionate squeeze. "So I'm that predictable, am I?"

"I wouldn't have it any other way." She kissed his cheek. "Are you going to be working late?"

He tiredly exhaled. "Probably a couple more hours." He pointed to the stack of folders on his desk. "I'm reading my notes from years ago. Something doesn't make sense with one of my clients, and I've got to find the missing link." He frowned. "Have you ever worked a jigsaw puzzle, and when it's almost finished you find there's one piece missing? You keep thinking that maybe the piece was inadvertently left out of the box or was never manufactured in the first place, and the feeling of frustration engulfs you, because you know that it never will be finished until you find that one elusive piece."

"If I know you, Thaddeus, you'll find that missing piece. You're a good and thorough doctor." She looked around the comfortable room. "The smartest thing we ever did was to make this spare room into a study for you. I'd rather have you here at home than downtown at your office half the night."

He patted her hand. "Lily, can I ask you a question?"

"Is it as a psychiatrist or my beloved husband?" she teased.

"Definitely as your husband."

"What is it, Thad?"

"How would you rate me as a husband and father?" He took a sip of his coffee, focusing on her expression. "I want an honest answer."

Her eyes misted. "You're an exceptional husband and father. Marrying you has made me the happiest woman alive. You know that Thad Jr. and Tyler idolize you."

He smiled broadly. "I could have never achieved anything without you by my side. The sacrifices you made for me and the boys went way beyond what many women would do. You are the most selfless woman I've ever known."

"I'd do it all over again with no regrets," she softly said.

"Do you ever miss your career? You know people still talk about what a compassionate but hard-hitting reporter you were. I still watch your old news clips. You were one of Pittsburgh's top TV reporters, and you know as well as I do that eventually you would have been picked up by a national station."

"The awards and accolades were wonderful, but raising the boys and being your wife, Thad, are my greatest achievements in life. And no, I've never had one regret."

"I'm a fortunate man to have you as my wife, Lily."

She walked behind him and placed her hands on his shoulders. "You're so tense tonight," she whispered massaging his shoulders. "What's really bothering you, Thad?"

He sighed. "How can two parents bring an innocent child into the world and develop such an intense dislike for that child that they would mistreat him for over twenty years, and blame him for all of their problems and unhappiness?"

She stopped massaging his shoulders and paused thoughtfully. "Maybe you're treating the wrong person. It sounds from what you've just said that the parents are the ones who need help. I can only wonder what effect their abuse has had on their child."

"That's my dilemma." His breath came out in a rush. "Do I medicate this young man because he refuses to deal with his problems? Is that fair to him?"

"Does he reach out to you?"

"He doesn't reach out to anyone. He doesn't trust people, and I can't say that I blame him. However, lately I have had glimpses to another side of him. I don't think he's even realized that I've seen his vulnerable side, but he let his guard down briefly and I saw the pain in his eyes. Normally his eyes are lifeless and cold, but that day I saw what was really buried in his heart, and he talked more than usual and unburdened a little of the pain he's been carrying around for all these years."

"Maybe that's a good sign, Thad. He trusts you enough to share with you," she said encouragingly.

"I'm afraid he's going to leave therapy before I can make the breakthrough he needs."

"Why do you think he'll leave therapy if he's finally

beginning to make progress?"

"He'll be graduating from college soon, and he's planning to leave the state."

"You don't think he'll continue with therapy somewhere else?"

He shook his head. "He wouldn't have seen me if his parents hadn't insisted he resume therapy. He'd briefly left his sessions and quit taking his medication against my wishes, but his parents had let him do it and now expect me to fix everything as though I'm a magician."

She frowned. "That's a shame, but Thad, you can't force anyone to get help even if you know it's needed. It has to be his decision."

"That's what worries me. I'm afraid he's capable of violence, but with the proper treatment, I believe I can help steer him away from his self-destructive and manic tendencies."

"Maybe he'll listen to you."

"I can only hope I find the right words to convince him to continue treatment. My hands are tied, and I can only sit back and wait. But if he does discontinue treatment, he's a human time bomb waiting to go off the minute someone provokes him."

"This may sound strange, honey, but from what you've told me, I feel sorry for him. I can't imagine not having maternal feelings for T.J. or Tyler."

He nodded. "When I saw the pain in his eyes as he told me how he couldn't ever remember being hugged or kissed by either parent, I knew his grief went much deeper, and he's kept it suppressed all these years as it festered inside of him."

Lily moved to the side of the desk. "I'd love to gather all of those sad and lonely children together and match them with parents who would love and cherish them," she said with tear-filled eyes. "All children deserve to be wanted and loved."

"I know...I know." He looked into her soft eyes, once again thankful for the love she bestowed upon him and their sons.

She put her arms around him, giving him a tender hug, then kissed the top of his head. "Don't stay up too late, honey."

"I won't," he promised. He watched her walk out the door. Her slim figure and beautiful face, along with the graceful way she carried herself, still sent chills through him after all these years. She became more beautiful with each passing day, and no one had to remind him that he was a fortunate man. He longed to call it quits for the night and join Lily in bed, but Jeremy Talbot refused to leave his thoughts.

He looked at the stack of folders and picked up the top one, then slowly opened it and began to read his notes from the first session he'd had with Jeremy shortly before the boy turned thirteen years old.

CHAPTER ELEVEN

Jeremy flung his arms around a tree, grasping it as though he were holding on for dear life. His stomach pitched and churned, the burning sensation blazing all the way up to his throat. He tasted the bile slowly creeping up his esophagus and he opened his mouth, hoping the waste would erupt from his system and he could get on with the party. But all that erupted were wracking dry heaves, making him feel worse than ever. His stomach muscles ached and his throat became raw as the dry heaves consumed him one after another in rapid succession, weakening and sickening him even further. He prayed that he'd just puke his guts out and get it over with. He briefly let go of the tree, but when the ground upon which he stood swayed back and forth, he quickly put both arms back around it to steady himself. His skin grew clammy as perspiration dripped from every open pore. He closed his eyes, but he felt even dizzier so he quickly reopened them.

We told you to stay home, the demons reprimanded him. *Rebecca set you up and now where is she when you need her most? She's with the man she truly loves — Nicholas Adams. She loves Nicholas Adams, not Jeremy Talbot*, they chanted repeatedly.

Tears slid from his eyes as he tried to chase the demons from his thoughts, but he didn't have the strength.

We'll take care of you like we always have, they promised, *but you must promise to never trust another human being. We'll take care of everything for you.*

"But Rebecca loves me," he moaned.

No, they hissed. *She loves Nicholas Adams.*

He dropped his arms from the tree and took a few wobbly steps back. A waft of roasting food drifted by his nostrils. He tried not to breathe in the smells, but the sensation had already reached his stomach, causing it to retch viciously. He bent his head just as the vomit erupted from the pit of his stomach, spewing out of his mouth for the next two minutes. When he was certain there was nothing more to expel, he wiped his mouth on the inside of his T-shirt, then tucked his shirt into his baggy jeans. He took a deep breath of the fresh, clean air, feeling much better, then ran his fingers through his tangled hair. He stumbled and half-fell as he walked, taking calculated steps. He noticed the dim parking lot lights and realized he'd gone in the wrong direction. He was about to turn around and head back in the opposite direction when he made out two silhouettes in the hazy light, their faces obscured from him. He heard fragments of their voices and moved closer, hiding behind a tree on the side of the path as he strained to hear whom the voices belonged to.

"Please find him, Nick," Rebecca worriedly said.

Jeremy smiled. *She is worried about me*, he thought.

"Okay, I will. He can't be too far, but I want you to get back to the others."

Jeremy watched as the two forms moved closer together. She was clinging to him and they were no longer speaking. He knew that Nicholas was once again kissing the sweet lips that belonged to him. He felt a pang go through his heart.

That's who she really wants to be with, the demons said. *We warned you.*

His jaw twitched as anger engulfed him, his blood rushing to his head. He clenched and unclenched his fists. Rebecca's form moved away and he saw her cautiously making her way up the path, the thin ray of light from her flashlight giving her just enough light to put one foot in front of the other. He slid further away from the path and crouched down, employing his hands to slowly make his way through the deepening shadows using the parking lot lights as his guide as he quietly crept along, cautious of the twigs snapping under his feet.

When he reached the edge of the parking lot, he quietly stole between two cars. He didn't have a plan of action until his foot scraped against something. He bent down and picked the foreign object up in his hand. He squeezed the jagged edge of the rock into his palm as his anger intensified, causing him to feel almost out of control. He silently crept closer to Nicholas. Nicholas's back was facing him as he peered down the road, slightly turning his head from left to right. Jeremy held his breath as he turned the sharp edge of the rock outward. He sucked in his breath. He steadied himself and rapidly brought his arm up and with one swift movement slammed it into the back of Nicholas's head. The sharp thud the rock made as it crashed against Nicholas's skull brought a satisfied smile to Jeremy's lips.

Nicholas's hand groped back of his head. He moved his hand in front of his eyes, seeing the blood on his hand before slumping to the ground.

Jeremy gazed, transfixed, on the blood gushing from Nicholas's wound, watching as it seeped from underneath his head and spread out, staining the pavement.

We told you we'd protect you, the demons whispered. *He deserved it for making a fool out of you.*

Jeremy shook his head back and forth.

Pull yourself together, Jeremy. Go back to the group and act as though nothing unusual happened, they instructed.

"Yes, that's what I'll do." He stumbled up the path, composing himself before reaching the others.

"Where were you?" Rebecca asked relieved.

He coughed. "I was sick."

"Well, I'm glad you found your way back." She touched his arm as she let her breath out in a rush of relief.

"No hard feelings, Jeremy?" Brian asked extending a hand.

"No hard feelings." Jeremy shook his hand.

"Did you see Nicholas? He went looking for you."

"No, I didn't see anyone, Rebecca. Where was he?"

"By the car. We thought maybe you went to the car to lie down."

He shook his head. "No, I was by the edge of the woods near the path."

"And you didn't see anyone?"

"No, I went into the woods a little ways so no one would see me vomiting."

Rebecca stood up. "I'm going to go looking for him."

Jeremy noticed her jumpy movements and saw the worry etched on her beautiful face. He hated seeing her so miserable, but once they were together she'd never spend another unhappy moment for the rest of her life.

"He'll be okay," Cassi assured her. "He only had two beers. You know how conscientious he is when he's driving us."

"He should have been back by now, that's all."

"Well, he doesn't know Jeremy's come back," Luke reasoned. "He's probably walking up the road."

Rebecca took her flashlight and started away from the group. "I'm going to see if he's by the car."

"Hold up, Becky, I'll come with you," Cassi said.

Jeremy watched as they walked down the path.

"Want another beer, Jeremy?" Brian asked.

He shook his head. "No, I've had plenty." He flashed him a shaky grin, then nervously placed his hands behind himself, feeling the cool grass between his fingers. He waited, knowing that at any moment Rebecca and Cassi would find Nicholas.

"Well, I'm going to have another," Luke said filling his cup.

Jeremy pulled at the grass, digging into the ground, feeling the moist dirt embed underneath his fingernails. His tenseness increased as he mentally pictured the two women walking down the path. He braced himself and moments later a shrill scream pierced the night echoing throughout the park.

"What the hell?" Luke and Brian looked at one another, then scrambled to their feet as another piercing shriek rang out. Others rose and raced down the path. Jeremy followed Luke, Brian, and Annie. They met Cassi halfway down the path.

"It's Nicholas," she panted, grabbing Luke's jacket.

Luke's flashlight illuminated her face. Jeremy saw her panic-stricken expression and the fear in her eyes.

"What's wrong?" Luke asked in a shaky voice. "What's happened to Nicholas?"

She sniffed. "I don't know. He's lying so still and he's

bleeding."

Luke nodded to his friends. "Come on!" They tore off toward the parking lot, reaching Rebecca who was kneeling next to Nicholas as tears streamed from her eyes. "Please help him!" she cried.

Luke knelt next to Rebecca. "Nick, can you hear me?" He grabbed Nicholas's wrist. "He's got a pulse." He saw the blood seeping from his head. "Oh God! He's got to have stitches." He pulled his T-shirt off and pressed it to the gaping wound. "Nick, buddy, can you hear me?"

Rebecca grabbed Nicholas's hand, enclosing it in both of hers. "Who would do something like this to him?" She kissed his pale cheek. "Why won't he wake up?" She handed the bloody rock to Luke. "This was lying next to him."

Jeremy stood behind the others, staring at the blood soaking the pavement and sopping Luke's T-shirt. A strange sensation rippled through him and he almost laughed but caught himself, knowing he needed to maintain control. As he looked at the fresh blood seeping from the wound, the familiar sensation of power surged through his veins. He felt no sympathy for Nicholas. He got his just desserts for messing with his girl. He watched Rebecca fussing over him, crying and carrying on, and it enraged him. His eyes burned as he stared at her.

She loves him, not you, the demons taunted.

Luke and Brian and a couple of the other guys carefully picked Nicholas up then gently laid him on the backseat of his car. They carefully picked up his head as Rebecca slid in the seat, then cautiously placed his head on her lap as she continued to press the blood-soaked T-shirt against his wound.

Luke and Cassi jumped in the front seat. "Come on,

Jeremy, we'll drop you at your bus stop. Brian, I'll pick up you and Annie as soon as we find out how Nick is."

"We'll catch a ride back, so don't worry about us," Annie said. "Just get Nick to the hospital."

Jeremy slid in the front seat next to Cassi.

"Let us know the minute you hear something," Brian called out.

Luke solemnly waved as he pulled out of the parking lot. No one spoke on the seemingly endless drive to Oakland, the morose silence only broken by Rebecca's muffled sobs.

Jeremy ached to take her pain from her and hold her close, comforting her, but all he could do was sit quietly. He needed to say something soothing to her, but the proper words wouldn't come to his lips.

Luke pulled up to Jeremy's bus stop, and Jeremy hurried out of the car.

"See you later, Jeremy," Luke called.

"Nice meeting you," Cassi said. "I wish the party would have turned out better."

He nodded then peered into the backseat. "I'm sorry about Nicholas, Rebecca," he said with as much sympathy as he could muster.

With red swollen eyes, she whispered, "Thank you."

Jeremy watched the car speed off toward the hospital. He rammed his hands into his pockets as he waited for his bus. He checked his wristwatch. He'd just made it with only a few minutes to spare for the last bus. He watched couples strolling out of the bars. A few came over to the bus stop, gave him a quick once-over, and then quickly averted their eyes when he made eye contact with them. He clenched his fists insides of his pants pockets as he tried to get his rising anger under control.

When the bus arrived, he hurried to a seat in the back and glared out of the window as the demons ravaged his thoughts. They loved his anger, knowing it gave them control.

Forty minutes later, Jeremy quietly slipped into his almost darkened house. A dim light in the foyer guided his way. He snapped the light off before silently creeping up the stairs to the security of his bedroom. Once inside he peeled off his clothes and climbed into his bed. His body ached and he was mentally and physically exhausted, but sleep still refused to come.

The image of Rebecca in Nicholas's arms and his lips on hers kept flashing through his mind, crushing his chest with an unbearable grief. He wondered where else Nicholas had touched her. Had he fondled those perfect breasts or plunged his cock deep within her folds, the place she was saving for his own cock? "No, Rebecca!" he cried as tears slid down his face. "How could you hurt me like this? Did you invite me just to make a fool of me?"

Yes, that's what she did, the demons replied. *She never wanted you.*

His heart broke into a million pieces as he kept reliving the kiss Rebecca and Nicholas had shared. Tears streamed from his eyes.

Let her go. We're your real friends. Concentrate on the blood.

He sniffed, remembering the exhilarating feeling the blood gave him, and slowly his tears subsided. Yes, he had the power to make anyone bleed. If anyone were foolish enough to hurt him, he would make them bleed and then watch as the blood dripped from their bodies, leaving them weak and helpless. A smile crossed his lips as he planned how he would win Rebecca's heart. She would never hurt him again, and they would never be apart, never. "Rebecca, the day will come when we'll be together forever," he promised.

CHAPTER TWELVE

Rebecca sat by Nicholas's bed, tightly gripping his hand. "Nicholas, how do you feel?"

He flashed her a weak smile. "Okay, except for a wicked headache."

Her lip trembled. "I can't believe this happened to you." Tears sparkled in her eyes.

He sniffed, then made a face. "I hate the smell of hospitals. It reminds me of when I was a little boy and my grandmother was dying of cancer. I'd sit in the waiting room for hours while my parents visited her. Every time I went home afterward and threw up because of those smells. It reminds me of death." He let his breath out in a rush. "I hate being here."

She softly ran her fingertips over his cheek. "I'm sorry, honey."

"I wish I would have seen who did this to me." He squinted. "It's weird. I never heard a sound. I was ambushed from behind." His jaw tightened. "If I only knew why this was done to me."

"I'm just as frustrated as you are, Nick."

He squeezed her hand. "I didn't think I had any

enemies, but I must have at least one." He frowned. "Or maybe it could have just been a random attack, but something doesn't feel right about it."

She raised an eyebrow, knowing the frustration he felt. "Whoever did it obviously wasn't after money or a car, because your wallet and car keys were still in your pocket."

His eyes narrowed. "I hope the police catch the cowardly bastard."

She shivered. "It's scary thinking about some nut running around out there attacking innocent people."

"Don't worry, babe, in a couple of days we'll be far from Pittsburgh and we can put this out of our minds."

She nodded, not convinced by his words, but relieved to change the topic of conversation. "It's going to be a wonderful summer, Nick."

"Yes, and an even better autumn," he said with a twinkle in his eye.

She stroked his head. "I can't wait to be your wife, Nick."

His eyes brightened. "I'm going to get you a diamond so big you'll feel like a movie star."

"All I want is you." She kissed his cheek.

"Well, at least I'll be able to graduate with the class on Sunday. This whole thing could have been worse."

"Yes, it could have." She looked at the bandage wrapped around his head. "The doctor had to give you twelve stitches. You lost so much blood!"

"Well, I'm grateful that the rock didn't slam into my temple."

"God, Nick!" Fresh tears trickled down her cheeks. "I can't imagine you..." her voice cracked, then broke.

"Honey, please don't cry." He stroked her arm. "That was a stupid thing for me to say." He squeezed her soft flesh. "I want you to go downstairs and have Luke and Cassi give you a ride home. You need some sleep. The doc says I have to spend the rest of the night just to make sure everything is okay."

"No," she sniffed. "I'm staying."

****

Jeremy opened his eyes, quickly shielding them from the bright sunlight filtering through his bedroom window. He rolled onto his side, then sat up slowly, stretching his arms. A stabbing pain shot through his head. "Shit," he muttered, throwing his legs over the side of the bed as he rubbed his throbbing temples. Gradually he got to his feet. He pulled on a pair of jogging pants and a T-shirt. He slipped his feet into his slippers and padded to the bathroom. He splashed cold water on his face, then brushed his teeth and rinsed his mouth, unable to get rid of the sour taste. He looked into the mirror and noticed his bloodshot eyes as he ran a comb through his hair. He grabbed the aspirin bottle, shook out two tablets, and swallowed them with a large gulp of water, wiping his mouth on the back of his hand as he walked downstairs to the kitchen.

He poured a cup of coffee, sat down at the kitchen table, and only looked up when his parents entered the room. His father threw the morning's paper on the table in front of him and pointed to an article. Jeremy picked up the paper and squinted his eyes, unable to focus. "I'll read it later," he mumbled, tossing it aside.

Gilbert Talbot grabbed the newspaper. "I'll read it to you then," he said in a caustic tone as he adjusted his glasses.

Jeremy yawned as he reached for his coffee.

"*'A brutal attack at High Ground Park leaves college student hospitalized.'* It goes on to say that Nicholas Adams required twelve stitches to his head after a vicious attack by an unknown assailant. Was that the party you were at, Jeremy?"

"Yeah, I was there." He sipped his coffee.

"What time did you get home?"

He shrugged. "I don't know…I guess about two forty-five or so."

Millicent raised her eyes. "Did you see this boy Nicholas at the party?"

"Yeah. He was attacked from behind."

"Do you know him?" Gilbert asked.

"Yeah, he's a friend of Rebecca's."

His father looked skeptically at him. "The report says that Nicholas Adams's fiancée Rebecca Walker found him lying in the parking lot." He paused, waiting for Jeremy's reaction.

"Reporters always screw up the facts." He pushed a strand of hair away from his eyes.

Gilbert pulled out a chair and sat down. "She never calls you, this Rebecca." He folded his hands. "I think you need to see Dr. Tate more frequently.

"What? I've been faithfully taking my medication and going to my weekly sessions. Why do you think I need to see the shrink more often?"

Millicent leaned against the counter. "Jeremy, your father and I are concerned about your feelings for this girl. We think that maybe it's one-sided."

He sneered. "Why would I expect any support from my parents? Of course you can't believe that Rebecca cares for me, just as you couldn't believe that Julie and I were dating."

"You're imagining things again," she insisted. "Dr. Tate can give you something stronger."

"Oh yes! Totally numb my mind so that my thoughts and emotions aren't my own any longer. Turn me into some mindless robot who obeys everyone and only does what I'm told and only thinks what others plant in my brain."

Gilbert slammed his fist on the table. "Dammit, Jeremy! We can't afford to risk everything. You won't get off the hook as easily as you did with Julie Howard."

"Look, I graduate tomorrow, and as soon as I can I'll be out of your lives for good." He looked at his father, then at his mother, but saw none of the sadness that parents normally exhibited when they learned their child was ready to leave the nest, especially when it was their only child. All he saw in their eyes was relief and anticipation at his departure.

"You need to continue treatment," Gilbert said. "No matter where you go, you need to continue seeing a psychiatrist. Dr. Tate has been good for you."

"I don't intend to stay in Pittsburgh."

Gilbert raised his eyes. "Where do you plan to go?"

He clenched his jaw. "To follow my dream."

"And where would that be?"

"New York. I have several manuscripts that I think have good possibilities."

He smirked. "What do you intend to do in the meantime? What if your stories aren't accepted?"

He shrugged. "I'll figure something out."

Gilbert shook his head in disbelief. "Let's get back to this Rebecca."

"Just drop it. You don't believe she and I are going to be together so there's nothing more to discuss." He got up, roughly shoving his chair under the table. He walked out of the room and climbed the stairs.

In his bedroom, he grabbed the student directory from his night side table and flipped it to Rebecca's picture. "We will be together," he said with a smile. "I have everything figured out and under control. We'll never be far apart." He brushed his lips against her image.

****

On Sunday, Jeremy sat with his fellow graduates waiting for the speeches to end. He hadn't been chosen valedictorian or salutatorian, missing by a minuscule amount thanks to Professor Burgess. He knew his final should have received an *A+*, but Burgess only gave him a *B-*. Burgess had had it in for him from the moment Jeremy had stepped foot into his classroom and would never give him the grade he deserved, no matter how deserving his work was. It infuriated Jeremy but at the same time relieved him. He wouldn't have to suffer the humiliation of having to stand up in front of everyone to give a speech. His public speaking class hadn't helped allay his fear of public speaking, and he doubted anything ever would.

He couldn't locate Rebecca in the sea of caps and gowns, but he'd seek her out after the ceremony. He heard his name called for the history award and self-consciously stood until all the awards were given out. After two more long-winded speeches, the graduates rose to receive their diplomas. He listened as the spectators clapped and cheered for their favorite graduates. He heard his name called and awkwardly started across the stage, noticing the distinct silence, the only sounds being nervous coughs and the rustling of programs. He was halfway across the stage when a high-pitched whoop rang out echoing throughout the auditorium. Rebecca's beautiful voice called out "Way to go, Jeremy!" That was followed by Nicholas, Annie's, Brian's, Cassi's, and Luke's voices. His parents had to have heard, and now they would see that he really did have friends. A grin broke over his face as he accepted his diploma.

When Rebecca's name was called, he watched her graciously walk across the stage, hoping his parents were paying close attention and noting her beauty. The clapping and cheering from the crowd was deafening, attesting to her popularity. He clapped until his hands stung.

After the ceremony, he waited outside the auditorium for his parents. Rebecca rushed over to him, flinging her arms around his neck, and kissed his cheek. He cocked an eyebrow when he saw his parents standing a few feet away.

"Good luck, Jeremy. I hope to see you at our tenth reunion," Rebecca said close to his ear, then released him.

Before he could answer, she disappeared into the crowd. He confidently sauntered over to his parents. "I'm ready to leave now," he said smugly.

"Don't you want to visit your friends?" his mother asked curiously. "You may never see some of them again."

"I saw who I wanted to see."

His father shot him a doubtful look. "When is Rebecca leaving the campus?"

"Tonight."

"What will her leaving do to your relationship?"

"We'll work it out." He was damned if he'd let his father ruin this moment for him. Gilbert looked at him with a disbelieving look on his face, but said nothing. Jeremy smiled self-righteously.

CHAPTER THIRTEEN

Thaddeus Tate attentively listened to Jeremy's animated account of his plans. He scribbled a few notes. "Jeremy, from what you've been saying, your entire future hinges on your succeeding as a writer. You need to focus on an alternative. You need a backup plan." He saw him stiffen.

"I do have a backup plan." His eyes shifted. "If my novels don't take off right away, I plan to find work on a newspaper, or maybe as an editor in a publishing or magazine company."

"Do you have anything concrete lined up?"

He let his breath out in a rush. "I'm not worried."

"You need a good job to afford an apartment. You can't just take off, get a job, and then look for an apartment."

Jeremy laughed. "I'll manage."

"New York is an expensive city, Jeremy, and a city you know nothing about. It can be very dangerous to someone who doesn't know his way around."

He threw his hands up. "So I'll explore! I'll learn!"

"I'm afraid you'll be very lonely. You don't socialize much, but at least Pittsburgh is familiar to you. You could seek a position here."

He laughed again. "What do you think it's been like for me most of my life? I know what loneliness and isolation are."

Thaddeus frowned. "I think you need to think things through more thoroughly."

He shook his head. "No, I've already thought it through. That's all I've been thinking about for years…leaving my parents' home."

Thaddeus grew pensive. "Have you heard from Rebecca this summer?"

He smiled broadly. "I've been writing to her."

"Will she be joining you in New York?"

"Eventually. Just as soon as she can get away." He eyed Tate sharply. "It's not easy for her leaving her family. They're very close."

"When are you planning to leave?"

"I'm not certain."

"How are things between you and your parents?"

He laughed bitterly. "Some things never change. They're just anxiously awaiting the day I pack up and leave for good."

"Will you let me know when you decide to leave? I'd like to give you a list of referrals." He watched Jeremy's eyes shift. "You do plan to continue therapy, don't you?"

"Let's face it, doc, what do you think these sessions do for me?" His voice was clipped.

"Why don't you tell me, Jeremy?"

He tensed. "Why must you answer any question I ask you with another question? Can't you just give me a straight answer?"

Thaddeus leaned back in his chair. "All right, that's fair. I hope in these sessions you're learning to get in touch with your feelings and that you are finding it easier to open up and discuss whatever's on your mind with the assurance that what you say stays strictly between the two of us."

Jeremy walked over to the window and looked down at the busy traffic below.

"Do you feel that these sessions are helping you, Jeremy?"

He turned and faced Tate. "I don't know."

Thaddeus saw the preoccupied look on his face. "Why have you continued?"

"To keep my parents off my back," he bluntly answered.

"You need to do it for yourself, Jeremy, not for anyone else."

He exhaled loudly. "The truth is everyone else seems to think I'm some sort of lunatic and need help. Did it ever occur to you that maybe I'm the normal one and they are the crazy ones? How would you feel if your family thought you were nuts? I have to keep convincing myself that I'm not, because if I don't I might eventually believe that I *am* really nuts. That's what they've done to me my whole life, tried to convince me I'm crazy and devised ways to drive me out of my mind."

"No one ever said you're crazy or 'nuts', as you put it."

He became adamant. "That's not how I see it. You can tell by the way people look at you, you can see it in their eyes even if they don't say anything to you. They look at you and watch you like a hawk to see if you're going to attack them or something." He ran his hand through his hair. "I can't wait to get the hell out of Pittsburgh and make a fresh start."

"I wish you well, Jeremy, and I hope you'll stay in touch with me from time to time when you do leave. I'd like to keep abreast of how you're doing. Also, you'll need to have your new psychiatrist get in touch with me so I can get your records to him if you so desire."

He nodded.

"What else have you been doing?"

"I spend most of my time writing. I plan to hand deliver my manuscripts to the publishers when I get to New York."

"Have you saved enough money to even get there?"

He grinned. "Thanks to Daddy Dear's generous graduation gift."

"You've never mentioned his gift."

"He gave me twenty-five thousand dollars in cash."

Thaddeus's eyes grew wide. He'd never heard of a middle class family giving such an extravagant gift to their child. "That's very generous indeed."

He grimaced. "That's what he'd like everyone to believe, when the truth of the matter is, it's just another fucking payoff so I'll get the hell out of his life for good." His body visibly trembled with anger.

Thaddeus cautiously kept his eyes on Jeremy, being careful not to intimidate him. "I'd like to prescribe a new medication to help calm your nerves, Jeremy. It's been proven to be quite effective. It will relieve your anxiety."

"I wouldn't be anxious if others didn't make me feel that way," he snarled.

Thaddeus leaned forward. "You have the power to control your own feelings and emotions. Other people can't make you feel defeated unless you let them."

"Then why the drugs? How can I get in touch with my own emotions if the drugs cloud my mind and thinking?" He looked at him, waiting for a sensible answer.

"What I've prescribed for you, Jeremy, doesn't react in

that way. You know that. If you're feeling differently, it's because you may need something stronger."

"When I was a kid you prescribed drugs that turned me into a zombie."

"Times have changed, and new treatments are being researched every day. Sometimes it takes awhile to match the right treatment to the patient. I try not to use any drugs that will be mind-altering in any way."

Jeremy's eyes narrowed. "But look what those drugs did to me, for God's sake. I was just a kid and they turned me into a freak!"

"You wouldn't open up to anyone back then, Jeremy. You were a recluse, and your parents were afraid you'd harm yourself."

"No, that's a lie! My parents made up stories about me and you believed them. In the beginning, I was honest and told you about the animals, and that's why you believed I'd cause harm to others. You told my parents every little thing I ever told you."

"It is unnatural to harm small animals, and you had a strange fascination with watching them bleed to death. I needed to make sure your obsession with blood didn't make you want to cause harm to yourself or anyone else. The medication eased your compulsion to kill any more animals. Your parents at that time told me that you'd begun harming those innocent creatures when you were about five years old. They thought you'd stopped, but a couple of years later, when your neighbor's dogs and cats began disappearing over a two-year period, they thought you might be responsible."

He rolled his eyes. "Of course they'd think it was me. I'm surprised they didn't call you then."

"Did you do it?"

"Look, that was a long time ago. The past is gone and I'm going to be making a fresh start soon. Let's leave the past where it belongs."

Tate studied Jeremy's noncommittal expression and knew that Jeremy would never give him a straight answer, but in his heart his instincts told him that Jeremy had indeed committed those vicious acts. "All right, but just so you know that those animals had a right to their lives just as you do to yours."

He smirked. "Give me a break! What are you now? Some kind of animal rights crusader?" His eyes sparked. "It still doesn't excuse the fact that I couldn't trust you. You repeated everything I ever said to my parents so I quit telling you anything."

"Because you were a minor, my hands were tied as far as releasing information to your parents. Under the law, I was obligated to inform them of our discussions in your sessions, but the moment you became of age, your parents were no longer able to have access to our sessions without your approval." He watched Jeremy's expression.

He scratched his head. "It doesn't matter. Soon no one will have to worry about what I might do or be afraid of me. I intend to just disappear from everyone's life."

"I think you've still got some unresolved anger you need to deal with."

"Well, sometimes anger is good. It keeps one motivated."

"Explain that to me."

"I think it's self-explanatory," he replied, surprised.

Thaddeus nodded. "Maybe so, but I'd like to hear your explanation."

He sighed. "Well, my anger opens up my creativity and helps me to stay focused and motivated on what needs to be done."

"You told me in our last session about beatings you'd received as a child. I'd like to discuss your feelings about it."

"There's nothing to discuss. It happened, and I've dealt with it and put it behind me."

Thaddeus sensed that Jeremy was bullshitting him, and it angered him. Jeremy was avoiding the real issues that were the cause of his deep-seated problems. He wondered, as he looked at Jeremy, what Jeremy really did have locked away deep inside, hidden from the world and quite possibly even from himself. "Jeremy, how do you feel about hypnosis?"

He laughed. "I've seen it done on TV, but for the most part I believe it's nothing more than a hoax."

Thaddeus was thoughtful for a minute. "Many people have benefited from hypnosis. Sometimes unpleasant episodes from our lives are buried deep inside. Many times the memories are too painful to deal with on a conscious level and the mind blocks it from conscious memory."

"I don't have any problems. Everyone would like me to believe that I do, but I can honestly say I don't."

"I'd like to hypnotize you, with your permission, of course."

He shook his head. "That's too weird for me, doc, no thanks. I'm going to definitely pass on this one."

"It's completely harmless. You have my word," Thaddeus promised.

"No, I don't want any part of it," he said with a note of finality in his voice.

Thaddeus scribbled a few notes. "Jeremy, I'm going to ask you a very personal question."

He shrugged his shoulders.

His eyes stayed trained on Jeremy. "Have you ever had sexual intercourse?" He watched the pink tint slowly creep up Jeremy's neck and reach his face, turning it a bright shade of crimson.

"I don't think that's anyone's business," he indignantly replied.

"Have you and Rebecca made love, Jeremy?"

He became offended. "She's not that kind of girl. She's saving herself for our wedding night."

"You don't see too many young ladies with such high morals today. It's refreshing."

"That's what makes her so special to me."

Thaddeus watched the light come back into his eyes and the calmness that came over him as his facial muscles relaxed. "Have you ever made love to anyone?"

He glanced at the clock on the wall. "Isn't our session over for today?"

"We still have some time." He watched his reaction. "There's nothing wrong with you, Jeremy, if you haven't."

"Just because I refuse to answer, you jump to the conclusion that I haven't?" He rolled his eyes.

"Well, have you?"

"I've screwed hundreds of women," he said sarcastically. "Isn't that what every woman wants? A man who can satisfy her? I'm the best. Give them what they want," he grinned. "Ram your cock up their lily white asses."

"Your sarcasm isn't necessary."

He shoved his hands into his jacket pockets. "If I say no, then you look at me like I'm abnormal. If I say I have, then I'm immoral. I can never win, can I?" His eyes flashed. "It's the same thing over and over. The same thing my parents do to me."

"I'm not your parent."

"But at times you sound just like them. You live your perfect boring lives and don't care how anyone else feels. You just sit in judgment on everyone, especially me. Someday maybe you and my parents will find out that your lives aren't so perfect, and you'll understand how it really feels to be me."

Thaddeus was thoughtful. "Jeremy, what do you mean by that last statement?"

He slowly let his breath out. "Nothing. I didn't mean anything. I'm just sick and tired of having to explain every move I make or every thought I'm thinking. I'm tired of constantly being analyzed."

Tate wrote out a new prescription and handed it to him. "I want you to promise to take these three times a day."

Jeremy stuffed the prescription into his pocket.

"I'll see you next week…all right? The same time."

Jeremy remained silent.

"Call me anytime day or night, Jeremy."

He nodded. "Sure." He quickly departed the office.

Thaddeus's eyes narrowed as he leaned back in his chair. An uncomfortable feeling came over him. Something wasn't right. Jeremy Talbot's moods were swinging back and forth, and he could only hope that Jeremy would get the prescription filled. He also wished in a strange way that Jeremy's remark could have been taken as a threat, but it wasn't strong enough evidence to seek an order to have him hospitalized and evaluated. The uneasy feeling wouldn't release its hold on him and only became stronger.

He'd had the same feeling when Jeremy's parents had first contacted him about their son. Now he wished he would have insisted on hospitalization when he learned from the young boy's own lips how he liked to look at blood as an animal lay dying, watching for hours, then excitedly exclaim how he had the power over their lives and was the only one who chose whether they lived or died. Jeremy fixated on them but would never admit he was the one who caused the injuries that led to their eventual deaths.

Thaddeus recalled his own shock at the boy's enthrallment with blood, but at the time truly believed that medication and therapy sessions were the answer. Now he questioned his original evaluation. As a young man, Jeremy was beginning to exhibit some of the same behavioral patterns he'd exhibited when Thaddeus first got him to open up. He doubted that Jeremy was still torturing animals and now feared he may have already or soon would move on to something else. Thaddeus's only hope was that he could help him before his wrath exploded on unsuspecting victims.

Chapter Fourteen

Jeremy glanced at his wristwatch. It read two-fifteen a.m. He quietly sneaked down the stairs and carefully unlocked the front door, then closed it softly behind himself. He took a deep breath, filling his lungs with the clean, fresh nighttime air. He looked up the street, then stole slowly and quietly down the street. A few cars passed him, their happy occupants returning home, he supposed, from a night out on the town. He continued walking with no destination in mind. Urgency filled him, but it was not an urgency of his own making. They were forcing him to take this journey. They were playing mind games with him again. One minute they told him to avoid people, and the next minute they were forcing him to have contact. He must obey them or the consequences he'd face would be worse than death. At times, though, he did wish for death. Only in death would he finally be free of them.

You know what you must do, the demons whispered. *The first one you see. Become a real man. Tonight's the night to finally prove yourself!*

"Yes," Jeremy mumbled. "Tonight I'll become a man." He passed no one on the deserted street. "Maybe it's too late. I should have come earlier."

No, the demons countered. *If you had come any earlier, it would have been much too dangerous. There would have been too many people around. Wait for the right moment. Trust us, we'll protect you. Do everything we tell you to do.*

He continued on his quest. After stumbling along for five blocks, he saw a playground and hurried through the well-trimmed grass, spotting a bench almost hidden in the shadows. He sat down. His adrenalin pumped as he focused on what lay ahead for him. He licked his lips in anticipation. It was deadly quiet in the playground, but he kept his body as still as he could and heard his own heartbeat, its rhythmic beat in his eardrums. He sat for twenty minutes, then finally stood up and stretched his cramped legs. Out of the corner of his eye he saw a hazy figure slowly making its way through the playground. There was a path that those familiar with the neighborhood used, which was a shortcut leading to the street behind the playground, saving about ten minutes walking time.

Get closer…move slowly, the demons instructed.

Jeremy trembled as he silently moved nearer to the hazy silhouette. His foot hit a twig, snapping it with a sharp crackling noise that caused the unknown person to look in his direction. He froze, even though he knew he was protected by the shadows. The figure was only a few feet from him, and in the moonlight he made out the figure of a young woman.

Get her now, Jeremy. Grab her from behind, the demons called out.

He took a few steps, trying to control his unsteady legs. Another twig snapped. The woman began to run.

Get her…hurry! Take her!

He propelled himself forward, sprinting toward the

woman.

Grab her around the neck, the demons insisted. *Do it now before she gets away!*

He picked up his speed. She glanced briefly over her shoulder as her own speed increased, running as fast as her legs would take her. As he drew near, he could hear her panting and gasping. He reached a hand out and snagged her jacket. She screamed and tried to wriggle free, but he kept his hold on the jacket and she tripped, falling with a heavy thud to the ground.

"Please don't hurt me," she whimpered. "God, please don't hurt me!" she moaned.

Make her keep still, the demons demanded. *Put your hands over her mouth!*

Jeremy clumsily turned her over. He clamped a sweaty hand over her mouth. He stared into her eyes, fascinated as they flitted back and forth. He remembered the animals' eyes when he captured them looking exactly like hers now looked. He was now her captor. She was terrorized, and it sent a powerful surge of renewed energy through him. He was electrified. He controlled her now, her life was in his hands, and it was up to him what her fate would be. He puffed his chest out.

Now's your chance to become a real man. You're the one in control, not her.

"Yes." Jeremy looked at her and smiled. *This is how it will be with Rebecca*, he thought. *Only she won't fight me off. She'll be begging me for it and reaching out for me, pulling my body on top of hers.* He could almost feel Rebecca's nails digging into his back as she begged him to take her. He didn't realize he was drooling until he saw the spittle drip onto the hand he held over her mouth. He removed his hand to wipe it off, and the woman let out an ear-piercing scream.

"Shut up!"

She sobbed. "Please don't hurt me."

He was bewildered. "No, you've got it all wrong. I don't want to hurt you," he said softly as he tugged at her jeans.

"No!" she screamed. "Don't…don't rape me!"

"What?" he asked in disbelief. "I'm not going to rape you. I just want to make love to you." He pulled her jeans down to her knees.

"Please, stop!"

He undid his own jeans and pulled them down. She struggled against him and it angered him. This wasn't how it was supposed to be. She slapped his cheek, then scratched at him with her long fingernails. "Damn you!"

He slapped her right cheek with the back of his hand, and she screamed in pain.

He touched the cheek she had dug into and saw his own blood on his fingers. "Why did you hurt me?" he whispered.

She let out another bloodcurdling scream.

Shut her up! the demons demanded. *She's going to get you into trouble.*

"Please be quiet," he pleaded as he gazed into her eyes, which shined with the tears flowing from them. Part of him pitied her because he knew what it was like to be almost immobilized by fear. He'd felt the same way as a child when the other kids in the neighborhood would taunt him and beat him up because of his small size. He remembered running from them and hiding in fear as they came closer, and when they would eventually find him, they would grab his legs and pull him out, then mock him before beating the shit out of him.

Get on with it!

Jeremy tenderly kissed the cheek he had struck, then moved his mouth to hers. The softness of her lips made him want to keep his lips on hers, but she clamped hers tightly together. As she squirmed, her body rubbed against his, making his excitement grow. She wanted him. He swelled to a full erection, then grabbed his penis and awkwardly shoved it toward her vagina. She squeezed her legs together as he rammed at her, preventing him from entering her. He became enraged. He removed his mouth from hers and she let out another scream. "Stop it!" he ordered. He didn't know how to make her stop that horrible screaming. "Please shut up." He slapped her again.

"Please let me go!" she wailed.

"If you stop yelling, this will be over soon. I don't want to hurt you," he whispered. "I only want to make love to you. If you let me make love to you, I promise I'll let you go when we've finished."

She searched his eyes suddenly crying out, "Oh my God! You're Jeremy Talbot! You live on Hollow Road!"

"What?" He became rigid.

She swallowed hard. "Nothing…nothing."

Jeremy, you're going to get into trouble. She'll tell on you and you'll be locked up for the rest of your life! they hissed. *You know what you have to do!*

"No, I can't!" he insisted.

"Please, just let me go," she whimpered. "I won't tell anyone. I promise."

He released his grip on her.

No, you fool! She'll ID you.

He grabbed her again, pressing his body closer to hers. His penis grew limp. He was embarrassed, but he wouldn't let her know that. He'd think of Rebecca, and that would soon make him swell again.

See what women do to you? They get you all excited and act like they want you, then push you away. They have no feelings and don't care how many hearts they break. Look at her, Jeremy. Remember how you felt when you saw Rebecca putting her mouth on Nicholas's and pressing her body into his? Think of the anger you felt. Hold on to that anger!

His jaw tightened. He wanted to put the image of Rebecca in Nicholas's arms out of his mind. He knew deep in his heart that Rebecca truly wanted to be with him and not Nicholas. He'd tossed and turned most nights, working out a plan so he and Rebecca could be together, knowing that's what she wanted him to do. He was the only one who could finalize their futures together. He hated the demons for tormenting his soul by constantly reminding him about Nicholas and Rebecca, but he couldn't think about that right now. If this stranger told anyone what he'd done tonight, he'd be put away for the rest of his life. He'd lose Rebecca for good. He stared coldly into the woman's eyes. "You know my name and where I live."

"I won't tell. Please trust me. Just let me go."

"I don't know what to do," he mumbled confused.

"Please, just let me go."

You know what you have to do! Do it!

"I don't know how to do it. I don't know what to do," he mumbled again.

"What?" she whispered in a frightened voice.

He looked at her with a bewildered expression on his face. "I didn't say anything."

Use your hands, the demons instructed. *Strangle her like you did the animals.*

He sucked in his breath for a few seconds, then slowly exhaled. She gurgled and he glanced down at his large hands, which were clamped on her pallid neck. Her eyes looked like they were ready to pop out of their sockets. Spittle was oozing from the side of her mouth. He stared into her eyes and they looked blankly back at him, no longer flitting back and forth now, but permanently fixed in one position. He looked closer and was shocked to see the horror in them. He gasped as his hands slid from her neck. Her head fell to one side, and she lay lifeless on the dewy grass. He shook her shoulder but got no response. A thin stream of blood dribbled from her mouth. He stared, mesmerized at the blood, watching as it dripped down the side of her chin.

Get out of here now! the demons screeched.

He looked at his hands again, then quickly pulled his jeans up and backed away from the body, tripping and falling as he ran. He finally collapsed in the grass as a wave of nausea overtook him. He threw up, then lay in the cool grass, calming himself by taking several gulps of air. After several minutes, he pressed the switch on his wristwatch to illuminate the dial. It was three-thirty. He pulled himself to his feet and tucked his shirt into his jeans, then ran from the playground, panting as he reached the sidewalk. He half-walked and half-ran to his house and shakily pulled his key from his pocket, then let himself inside. He leaned against the closed door, trembling in fear. His lungs ached from running, and even though his body was perspiring profusely, he felt icy cold.

You did it. You're safe now.

He removed his shoes and cautiously climbed the stairs. Once inside his bedroom he collapsed on his bed, shaking uncontrollably. His head throbbed as the demons hissed and whispered. He wished they would go away and give him some peace, but that was a dream. They were excited. They would want to discuss for the next several hours what had just transpired.

You did what you had to do, they gleefully chanted. *You would have been caught. You couldn't trust her to keep your identity a secret. If you had let her go, she would have run straight to the police.*

He ran his hand over his face. "Maybe she isn't really dead," he said.

She's dead. You killed her with your bare hands. She gave you no choice. She made you kill her. We've tried to warn you that people will only hurt you if you get too close to them or let them get too close to you. Women love to flaunt their bodies at you and get you all hot and bothered, then they leave you cold, acting like they never wanted you in the first place. Remember what that woman did to you. She would have told everyone that you couldn't even keep an erection, they sneered.

Jeremy bit his bottom lip. "She's dead and I never even got to make love to her. It was all for nothing, and I'm still a virgin."

The demons laughed. *You had your chance. We warned you.*

He became furious. "I should have rammed my dick into her. I should have pumped her so hard my cock would have split her insides!" His eyes narrowed. "Yes, you're all right. It is her fault she died." He clenched his fists. "She deserved to die after humiliating me."

You're powerful, Jeremy. You can determine life or death over anyone you choose. Enjoy your power. Remember the feeling when you slammed that rock against Nicholas's skull? You have so much power hidden within you! Someday everyone is going to give you the love and respect you deserve.

"Yes," he beamed. "No one will ever hurt me again." His thoughts drifted back to the woman in the park. She probably caused so much pain to others, but now he'd stopped her. She'd never hurt another soul. He recalled the look of terror on her face and laughed. Death gave life to him. He smiled broadly. "I can conquer the world! Everybody better watch out."

CHAPTER FIFTEEN

Jeremy got off the bus in Oakland and walked eight blocks to the address he'd been given. He now found himself standing in front of a seedy-looking, run-down building. He was nervous, not knowing what he would find inside. He took a deep breath, then entered the musty-smelling hallway and knocked on the second door on his right. Seconds later a muffled, gravelly voice called from the other side of the door that he had permission to enter.

He cautiously walked into the dimly lit, windowless room. The hazy fog of stale cigarette smoke burned his eyes and assaulted his nostrils. He nodded to the man standing behind a makeshift counter. "I was told you'd have everything ready for me today," he said in a wobbly voice.

The man eyed him guardedly. "And you are?"

"Jeremy Talbot."

He sorted through a packet of envelopes lying on the cluttered counter. "Here it is." He looked at him again. "If you have the cash, your new identity is Nathaniel Cummings, born in upstate New York."

"Good." Jeremy handed him an envelope.

The man peered inside the envelope and carefully

counted the money. "Five thousand cash. For that you get your ID card, social security card, and a birth certificate."

"Are you certain that these will be accepted as legitimate?"

The man laughed, showing off a set of yellow-stained teeth. "It doesn't get any more authentic than these. You'd be surprised how many people come in here ready to start a new life with a new identity. We've never had any problems. Check everything over."

Jeremy looked over the documents. He nodded. "They're perfect."

The man pulled Jeremy's file. "To protect us as well as you," he said as he put Jeremy's file into the shredder. In seconds, there was no evidence that Jeremy had ever been there. "Our business is concluded. If we can ever be of service again, give us a call."

"Thank you." He hurried out of the rancid-smelling building, grateful for the fresh air, or as fresh as the air could be in Pittsburgh.

He walked back to Oakland and caught the downtown bus, sitting quietly until he reached his stop. He got off, then walked the two blocks to Dr. Tate's office.

"How are things going, Jeremy?" Tate asked him the minute he walked into his office.

"Things couldn't be better," he confidently answered. "Everything's on schedule and going as planned."

"You seem to be at peace with yourself," he said with a warm smile.

"I am. I finished another novel. I'm confident this one is just what the big publishers are looking for. I know it'll sell."

"For your sake I hope it does, Jeremy."

"To be honest, doc, the most important thing is my

confidence in myself."

"It's good to hear you speak like this, Jeremy. You have a healthy attitude." He studied him for a moment. "Did you know the young woman who was murdered near your neighborhood a few days ago?"

He shook his head. "No, not personally."

"How did you feel when you heard about her murder?"

He frowned. "I wondered what she was doing out at that time of night. Why was she walking through a dark, deserted playground?"

"According to her boyfriend, his car had broken down. He was returning her home from a party. Since she was only one street away from her home, she told her boyfriend she'd go get help from her father." He sighed. "The boyfriend wanted to go with her, but since the car was stalled in the middle of the street, she convinced him to stay there in case the police came along. When she didn't return after half an hour, he went searching for her, then finally walked to her home shocked to find out that she'd never arrived."

"That must have been quite a jolt," Jeremy answered sympathetically. "Dr. Clark must be going through hell."

He nodded. "Raney was his whole life. She was a beautiful girl...smart and full of promise." He adjusted his glasses. "Murders are rare in your neighborhood."

"I know. Everyone's nervous and more cautious, but they have to realize that the world's changing every day. People need to learn to adjust to these unsafe times. I heard the police were going to grill the boyfriend, Sam Becker, and make him take a lie detector test."

"He's already taken the test, and he passed it with flying colors. He also has two credible witnesses. The occupants of the home he stalled in front of verified that they came out shortly after the car stopped to see what the problem was and stated they remained with him for the entire time he was there."

"Maybe he did it after he left them. They can't pinpoint the exact time of death."

"That's possible, but not very probable. What would be his motive? And where was Raney in the meantime?"

He frowned. "Maybe she was dumping him, and he went crazy and killed her before his car stalled in front of that house. That could be the motive. It happens every day."

Tate kept his eyes focused on him. "Most people don't kill someone they loved because the relationship is ending. If the pain of the breakup is too severe, then usually they try to end their own life, not the object of their affections."

Jeremy didn't like the intensity of Tate's probing eyes. He shrugged. "What do I know anyway?"

"How's the new medication working?"

"Great," he lied. "I feel energetic and ready to take on the world."

"Good." He still kept his eyes focused on Jeremy.

Jeremy averted Tate's penetrating gaze. He felt as though the doctor was looking inside to his very soul. It unnerved him. "I'll be leaving soon," he announced.

Tate raised his eyebrows. "When?"

"In a couple of weeks."

"That explains your excitement then."

Jeremy relaxed, then grinned. "I feel like I can do anything I set my mind to."

****

The following weekend Jeremy wandered Liberty Avenue downtown. He observed the prostitutes on the corners flagging down every car or person who came by, calling out seductively to them. He walked slowly looking at the women with their made-up faces and phony smiles as they wriggled their hips in their much-too-short skirts, promising to fulfill any sexual fantasy. Tonight he would lose his virginity to one of these women. He wished his first time could have been different, but he needed to be experienced for Rebecca. She deserved a man with some skill to satisfy her, and he intended to please her in any way possible by giving her extra special loving care. She deserved it.

He eyed the whores, some old enough to be his mother, others too young to be selling their bodies. After walking a few blocks, a woman he figured to be in her early twenties caught his eye. She wasn't bad looking and in fact, he found her to be quite attractive. Her breasts bulged from her blouse, and her miniskirt showed an abundance of ivory thigh. Her spiked heels gave her added height and as he drew nearer, he saw that she was at least six inches taller than him in the shoes. He smiled shyly at her.

"Hi, Stud," she called out to him in a throaty voice. "I bet I know what a big man like you wants." She winked suggestively as she slid her hands provocatively down her sides, at the same time moving her full hips.

He smacked his lips. "How much?"

She gave him the once-over, then tossed her head back. "For you, big boy, thirty bucks."

"And what exactly do I get for thirty dollars?"

She smiled. "Whatever you want."

"Let's go, then."

"No car?" she asked.

He shook his head.

"Okay, then follow me," she said, leading him to a

building a few doors down. She unlocked the door, revealing an almost barren room that reeked of stale beer, cigarettes, and body odor. His attention was riveted to the king-size bed in the center of the room. She locked the door, then turned to him, running her hands slowly up and down his chest as she unbuttoned his shirt and ran her fingers through his abundant chest hair. "You have such a strong chest," she murmured.

He timidly put his arms around her waist. He was thrilled that finally he was close to a woman, a woman who wouldn't fight him off. It felt so good to hold her, smelling her freshly perfumed body. She put her lips on his, then forced her tongue inside of his mouth. His body tingled when her tongue touched his. Her hands moved to his crotch, and she fondled him through his jeans. He quivered, then moaned as he felt himself begin to grow hard. He pulled away from her, his breath catching in his throat. "You feel so good," he whispered.

She removed her clothes and seductively climbed onto the bed. "What would you like?"

His eyes traveled to her large breasts, then to the dark mound of hair between her legs. He knew the treasure underneath that hair awaiting his throbbing dick. He removed the rest of his clothes and climbed onto the bed next to her.

She leaned over and kissed him. "Now tell me what would make you happy. Would you like me to suck you?"

He swallowed the lump in his throat. "I want to be inside of you."

She placed a hand around his penis, slowly stroking it up and down, then stopped to slip a condom on him.

He could barely hold still as his mounting desire overtook his senses. "I want to be in you now," he moaned.

She rolled onto her back, pulling him down on top of her as she rubbed his buttocks, then arched her back and spread her legs, awaiting him.

He nervously placed a hand on top of her pubic hair, then parted the lips with his fingers, feeling the softness inside of her. He abruptly plunged his fingers in deeper.

"Not so rough," she whispered. "Let me do it." She took his cock and eased it inside of herself.

His breath quickened as he moved a few times inside of her, then rapidly pumped his cock in and out, feeling himself erupt in an explosion that rippled throughout his body. Exhausted, he pulled out of her and rolled onto his back, grinning from ear to ear.

He heard the demons' irritating laughter, but he refused to listen. He'd finally had sex and knew what it felt like to be a whole man. He turned onto his side and looked into the woman's eyes. He wondered if she was as satisfied as he was. He let his breath out slowly, then reached over and touched her arm. "What do you think?" he glowed.

"About what?" Her eyes narrowed.

He propped himself up on one elbow. "About what just happened between us."

She smiled. "It's all in a night's work, sweetie. I don't take it personally."

Jeremy knew that being with him certainly must have held more meaning than with the other men she'd been with. "Well, maybe this time it was just a little special."

"This was your first time, wasn't it?" she asked in a bored tone of voice.

He avoided her eyes. "Why would you think that?"

She sighed. "Honey, I can always tell when it's a man's first time. You're in and out so fast that I barely have time to feel a thing."

"What are you talking about?" he asked, confused.

"Look, just pay me so I can get back to work." She slid off the bed and picked up her panty hose, slipping them on.

He watched as she gently slid them on her curvy legs. "Did I satisfy you?" he asked.

"I told you I never take it personally. You men are all alike, but it's just a job to me," she said.

He slipped off the bed. "What did you mean before about being in and out so quickly?"

She impatiently turned to him, holding her bra in her hand. "All I meant was that you came almost the moment you entered me. Don't take it to heart. That happens to most men the first time, but you'll get better with experience."

He had to be perfect for Rebecca. He'd have to keep practicing until he got it right. He looked at her breasts, then licked his lips. "I'd like to try again." He walked in front of her, forgetting about his nakedness.

She raised her eyebrows. "You want to go again? That'll be another thirty dollars."

He nodded.

She eyed him warily. "I'd like to be paid in advance. That's sixty dollars you owe me."

"No problem." He grabbed his jeans, pulled out his wallet and counted out the money, then handed it to her. He watched as she undressed herself again and climbed back onto the bed.

The demons came out taunting him. *You couldn't satisfy her the first time, so why do you think you can now?*

"Shut up!" he whispered through gritted teeth.

"What?"

"Nothing…I guess I was just thinking out loud."

"Well, come on," she said in the same bored tone of

voice.

The demons laughed. *Come on, she's waiting.*

He pushed them to the back of his mind as he fondled the woman's right breast, squeezing her nipple between his thumb and forefinger. "I'll go slower this time," he promised.

"Ouch, you're hurting me," she said angrily.

"I'm...I'm sorry," he whispered as he put his mouth on the breast and began suckling it.

She put her hands on either side of his head pushing him away. "You're hurting me!" She sat up. "Look, I'll give you thirty dollars back and let's just leave it at that," she said sharply.

The demons chuckled. *You're quite the man. You can't even make it with a whore.*

"Stop it!" He covered his ears with his hands.

She looked at him apprehensively. "Who are you talking to?"

"No one," he quickly replied.

She got off the bed grabbing for her clothes. "I'm sorry, but this trick is over."

"Why?" His jaw dropped.

Because you're a wimp, the demons hissed.

"No, I'm not!" he shouted.

The woman backed away from him. "Look, why don't you put your clothes on and we'll get out of here."

He saw the panic in her eyes and heard the fear in her voice. "You don't have to be afraid of me." He moved closer to her, reaching out to touch her hair. She pulled away from him. "Please don't be afraid of me."

"I need to get out of here." She handed him thirty dollars. "Here."

He shook his head. "No, you keep it."

"But we didn't..." her voice trailed off as she looked him in the eye, then slowly backed away.

"Teach me what a woman likes," he said, stroking her bare arm as he came closer. "Teach me how to satisfy a woman," he pleaded.

"You need to find a special woman—someone you love," she answered feebly. "Then it'll be the way you want it to be."

He laughed sarcastically. "What's love got to do with getting experience? Who could be more experienced than you? This is how you make your living, for God's sake." He raised his hands, gesturing around the squalid room. "Is this the way you want to spend the rest of your life, fucking strangers for money?"

"Why did you come here with me then? It didn't bother you earlier."

"Maybe I've changed my mind," he sneered. "Maybe you don't deserve any better. Maybe that's why you weren't satisfied. It wasn't my fault at all, was it? It was you. How could I relax knowing that I was making love to a slut?"

She quickly put her bra on and with trembling hands grabbed her blouse, buttoning it haphazardly.

He pulled her panty hose from her hands, thrilling at the smooth silkiness of the material. He put one hand inside and touched it with his other hand.

"Please give them to me."

He sneered at her. "No wonder women wear these." He quivered, imagining how it must feel against a pair of bare smooth legs.

She looked blankly at him.

He took his hand out of the pantyhose and rubbed them against his cheek. "So soft," he murmured.

She picked up her skirt and slipped it on, then reached again for her panty hose, but he kept his hold on them as he peered into her eyes. "Do you treat every man the way you've treated me tonight?"

"You're different."

His eyes lit up. "Then you were putting me on before?"

"Believe whatever you want to."

He grabbed her arm, forcing her close as his mouth came crushing down on hers.

She struggled against him until she pulled herself free. "I'm out of here." She ran toward the door, but he clamped a hand on her arm, squeezing it tightly.

"Let go of me, you creep!" she shrieked.

Now you're in trouble again, the demons warned. *We told you not to come here.*

"What should I do?" He cocked his head, waiting for their instructions.

"Just let me go and we'll forget that any of this ever happened," the woman said.

He turned his attention back to her. She looked scared. "Are you afraid of me?" he asked surprised.

She swallowed hard. "You can have all of your money back, just please let me go."

You can't let her go. She'll tell someone about what you've done. Everyone will know that you didn't measure up. You'll be made fun of even more than you are now. Think how your father will ridicule you when he finds out that you can't even make love to a whore, the demons persisted.

"I don't want the money." He looked down at the panty hose he was still holding in his hand.

You have the power over her, Jeremy. She's in your control now.

"Yes," he agreed, pulling the panty hose through his

hands.

She handed him the rest of his money, but he pushed it back at her. "I told you to keep it."

"But you just said yes."

His eyes grew dark. "I didn't say anything. You must be hearing things."

"You've been talking to yourself. Are you all right? Why don't we get some fresh air?" She pulled at the doorknob.

He was quickly at her side blocking the door. "No! Go sit on the bed!" he ordered, seeing the alarm in her eyes. "Now!"

Her lips quivered, and she kept her eyes glued on him as she backed toward the bed.

"Sit down!"

Her mascara was running down her cheeks. He wondered why everyone was always frightened of him. He wished she'd calm down and see what a nice person he really was.

She sat on the bed, folding her hands in her lap.

You've got the power, Jeremy. You control her now, and you know what you have to do.

"I can't do it again," he said in a cracked voice. "There has to be another way."

"Please just let me go. I won't tell anyone," the woman promised.

He rubbed his temples. "I don't know what to do."

Do it now! the demons demanded.

He walked over to the bed and sat next to her, then put an arm around her shoulders, drawing her close as his hand slid under her skirt.

She slapped at his face. "Get away from me!"

He was furious that she would strike him. He clamped

his hands on her shoulders. "Don't you ever hit me again," he warned through gritted teeth, still feeling the heat of her hand on his cheeks.

She squirmed breaking free from him and ran toward the door, screaming at the top of her lungs.

He was immediately behind her, pulling her arm and swinging her backward as he smashed his fist into her face. The tender bones in her nose snapped. She let out a piercing scream. He placed a hand over her mouth, watching the blood seeping between his fingers. He winced as her eyes rapidly moved back and forth in her head like she was having a convulsion. Yes, her fate was in his hands. It was up to him if she was to live or die. But what choice did he really have? If he let her go, she would surely call the police. But could he take her life? He looked at her again. She didn't care anything about him or his feelings. She just cared about getting paid for letting him use her body for his pleasure. She was nothing more than a cheap slut. Most women were, he reasoned—except for Rebecca. He laughed at the woman as power surged through his veins. He took a deep breath, then leaned over and picked up her panty hose. He removed his hand from her mouth, but all he heard were faint moans coming from her throat and the gurgling, choking sounds as the blood continued to gush from her nose. He wiped his bloody hand on the bare mattress.

For a few minutes he watched the blood drip from her nose. Her pallor was deathly white, and the splattering of tears on her cheeks mingled with the blood, then dribbled from her chin. His heartbeat quickened, feeling stronger with every bit that oozed out of her.

Her eyes rolled up into her head, and her body went limp. He ran to the door. He had to get out of here as fast as he could.

No! the demons called to him. *She'll be found, and you'll be arrested and locked away for the rest of your life. Finish her off! You have the power. She made a fool out of you!*

He glanced at the bed, then hurried over to it and bent down over her. He seized the panty hose, then picked up her head by her hair and slipped the panty hose underneath. He let her head fall to the bed, then took both ends of the panty hose. He tied a knot around her throat, pulling it tight as her eyes bulged and blood poured from the corner of her mouth.

Chapter Sixteen

Thaddeus pulled Lily close. "What are your plans today, honey?"

"I've got to run some errands, because I plan to cook you a special dinner tonight."

He raised his eyebrows. "What's the occasion?"

"Well, T.J. and Tyler are camping this weekend, so we have the entire house to ourselves. I don't remember the last time we've had a weekend alone." Her eyes grew bright.

"I'll try to be home early." He tenderly kissed her lips. "I'll definitely be looking forward to tonight." He winked as he picked up his briefcase.

T.J. bounded down the stairs. "Dad, you got a sec?"

Thaddeus set his briefcase back down. "Of course, son. What's on your mind?"

"I've got a few colleges picked out, and I want to go over them with you. I'm trying to get early admission instead of sweating it out next winter."

He patted T.J.'s shoulder as he smiled at him. "Sometimes I wonder where the years have gone. Just yesterday it seems like we were preparing you for kindergarten."

He blushed. "Come on, Dad, you're not going to get all sentimental like Mom does, are you?"

Thaddeus laughed as he noted how his eldest son towered over him. "I'm proud of your hard work," he said, looking into his clear blue eyes. Both of his sons had inherited their mother's looks, and for that he was eternally grateful. "When will you boys be back?"

"Late Sunday night."

"Monday night I promise we'll sit down and look at the pros and cons of each school."

He grinned. "Thanks, Dad."

"Just think, next year we'll have to do it for me," Tyler piped up.

Thaddeus chuckled. "Don't remind me. You boys are growing up way too fast."

Lily looked contentedly at her husband and their sons. T.J., named after his father, and Tyler could have been twins, both with the same fair blonde hair, blue eyes, and husky builds. The only visible difference was that Tyler stood two inches shorter than his brother. She smiled at them, knowing how blessed she was to have her boys. She was equally proud of both of them. They were hard workers and pulled good grades in school, never causing her and Thad any problems. They were all American clean-cut boys, not interested in drugs, drinking, or smoking, instead preferring to work out at the gym and involving themselves in high school sports.

"We've got to get over to Will's," T.J. said, grabbing his backpack. He kissed Lily's cheek.

"Love you, Mom." He threw his arms around Thaddeus, giving him a bear hug. "See ya, Dad."

Tyler kissed Lily's cheek, then hugged his father. "Catch you two later."

150

"You boys be careful," Lily said. "We love you."

"Have a good time," Thaddeus said with a smile.

"Don't do anything we wouldn't," Tyler laughed.

Thaddeus put an arm around Lily's shoulder as they watched their sons bustle out of the house, waving as they rushed, loaded down with their camping gear, down the walk.

"I wouldn't trade them for the world," Lily said with moist eyes. "They're quite a pair."

"They most certainly are." He gave her a squeeze. "I'm looking forward to tonight."

"You never know what surprises may lay in store for you," she said, gazing seductively into his eyes.

"Um…my curiosity is definitely piqued."

She ran her fingertips over his cheek. "Don't work too hard today, honey."

"I plan to save some of my energy for tonight," he promised. "Today actually should be a light workload. The patient I've been concerned about is coming in today, and I sense it's going to be his last session with me. I just hope I can convince him to continue therapy after he moves."

She patted his shoulder. "You're a good doctor, Thad. I'm sure he'll heed your advice."

He sighed. "I can only hope so. I told you he's like a time bomb ready to go off, and I'm afraid he has the potential for violence if he's provoked."

"Can't you have him hospitalized for a complete evaluation?"

"I wish I could, but he has neither said nor done anything that can be taken as a direct threat."

She kissed his cheek. "You've been working too hard, honey. Maybe you can get some much needed rest this weekend."

"I'm going to try. I'll be home by six."

"Good."

He gave her a hug, then picked up his briefcase, and she watched him as he got into his car. She closed the kitchen door, hearing the deadbolt catch, and loaded the dishwasher. She poured a second cup of coffee, flicked on the portable TV, and sat at the table. A special bulletin caught her attention. She listened as the newscaster spoke about another strangulation and how the police now believed the same person committed the murders. A chill went through her. The newscaster went on to report that the murders didn't appear to be targeted to just one area of the city, but went from one of the wealthiest neighborhoods to one of the seediest. The police speculated that they may be dealing with a serial killer and warned that there was no way of knowing where he might next strike. They were issuing warnings to women not to go out alone and to keep doors and windows secured at all times.

Lily shuddered, unnerved by the report. On Sunday she'd warn the boys to make sure they locked the doors from now on when they came in and out. No one would be safe until this monster was caught and put behind bars.

She sighed, then turned her attention to her duties, deciding first to make out her shopping list as she finished her coffee. When she finished the list, she dialed her best friend Marge to invite her to go shopping with her. When she received no answer, she left a message on Marge's answering machine, then stuffed the list into her purse and grabbed her car keys. She kept her mind focused on the special night she'd planned for Thad.

****

Jeremy confidently sat looking at Thaddeus Tate. It would be his last session, and he was elated. He wanted to tell Tate, but the demons thought it would be better to just disappear without telling anyone. When he didn't show up next week, Tate would call his parents and learn that he had gone to New York.

"You seem to be in high spirits today," Tate said.

"I am."

"Any particular reason for your optimism?"

"Rebecca is the reason. Every day that passes brings us closer to the time we can be together."

Tate glanced at his notes. "Jeremy, a few sessions ago you mentioned that you write letters to Rebecca. Do you two talk on the phone also?"

"No."

"Why not?"

He frowned. "My parents would probably listen in on my private conversations."

"You don't seriously believe they'd do that, do you? Besides, how can they listen in on your cell phone?"

He emphatically nodded. "Yes, I do believe they'd figure out a way to hack into my cell phone. They don't trust me."

"So that explains why you write letters instead of texting or e-mailing."

"Exactly. Besides, it's more romantic receiving a handwritten letter."

"Are you certain Rebecca feels the same way about you that you do about her?"

Jeremy became infuriated by the question. "Why would you ask me that?" he sharply demanded. He hated the way the doctor was looking at him.

Tate leaned back in his chair. "Well, it's been some time since you've seen one another, and you don't speak on the phone."

"That doesn't mean she's fallen out of love with me."

"Did she love you in the first place?"

Jeremy clenched his teeth tightly together.

"Did you read the article in the newspaper a few months ago about the attack at High Ground Park? It was the party you attended."

"Yeah, I saw it. What's your point?"

"The article said that Nicholas Adams is Rebecca's fiancé."

He fidgeted. "Why are you bringing this up to me now? Why didn't you ask me about it back then?"

"I thought that maybe the reporter had made a mistake."

Jeremy shook his head. "The reporter did make a mistake, and Rebecca wasn't very happy about it, I might add. She and Nicholas are just good friends and nothing more."

Tate raised his eyebrows. "Jeremy," he began, "what is your true relationship with Rebecca Walker?"

He eyed Tate, his anger rising. No one called him a liar. He had to keep his temper in check. If he didn't, Tate would use it against him. He'd let him play all the head games he wanted, but he'd fight him with common logic. "Excuse me? I've been telling you for months about Rebecca's feelings for me. You never questioned it then, so why now?"

"I did some checking."

"What do you mean, you did some checking?" His nostrils flared.

"I've learned that Rebecca Walker is marrying Nicholas Adams in a few weeks," he calmly announced.

"You had no right to question Rebecca."

"I didn't," he replied.

"Then what the hell are you talking about?"

"I did some checking on upcoming weddings and engagements."

"What gives you the right to interfere in my personal business?"

Tate's voice softened. "Jeremy, I believed what you told me about the relationship between you and Rebecca until you mentioned that you two haven't seen one another for the entire summer." He folded his hands together and rested them on top of his desk. "You aren't working, so why didn't you take a trip to Massachusetts to see her?"

"I can answer that quite simply." His jaw tightened.

"I wish you would."

He briefly closed his eyes feeling the demons come forward. *It's a trick. We told you to stay away from Rebecca.* He cocked his head, then covered his ears as a horrendous headache began. "Just leave me alone," he moaned.

Tate kept his eyes riveted on him. "Jeremy, are you all right?"

He nodded, rubbing his temples. "Sometimes I get horrible headaches."

"Would you like me to prescribe something?"

"No, I don't want any more drugs." He despised the way Tate was looking at him like he was a freak. He sucked his breath in, then slowly let it out. "Now, in answer to your question, I didn't visit Rebecca because her parents, especially her father, don't approve of me."

Tate cocked an eyebrow. "Isn't that the same thing you said about Julie Howard's father?"

His jaw twitched. "I knew you were going to say that, but quite frankly I'm tired of having to explain everything I say or do to everyone." He threw his hands up. "I'm through explaining myself to everyone. I don't give a shit who believes what anymore!" he exploded.

"Please calm down, Jeremy. I'm trying to help you."

"I don't need to calm down. I'll be leaving soon, and no one will have to worry about me anymore. I can't wait until I'm far away from all of you!" He clenched his fists. *You need to keep control. You shouldn't have told him you were leaving. Think before you speak!*

"Jeremy, would you consider going into the hospital for a rest?"

He smirked. "Are you kidding? You'd find a way to keep me there permanently."

"Why do you think I'd do that?"

"Why are you suggesting it then?" he countered.

"I think a rest might do you some good." He scribbled some notes. "You have a lot of repressed anger inside, and I'd like to get to the bottom of it."

"Well, you can just forget it. I don't have any repressed anger inside or outside. I just want to get on with my life with Rebecca."

Tate frowned. "That's the issue I'm trying to help you resolve." He continued staring at him. "You tend to fixate on certain women and imagine they have the same feelings of love for you that you have for them. I think you may be experiencing hallucinations, and your mind has convinced you that events have happened that are entirely conjured up in your mind."

Jeremy choked with laughter. "I don't know where you get these ideas, doc. Rebecca and I will definitely be together. And if you think I'm going to go into the hospital and let my brain be picked apart and brainwashed, you're the one who needs help, not me."

"Jeremy, you have to face reality. Rebecca is marrying Nicholas Adams, not you. She's not interested in you in that way."

He shook his head. "I have nothing more to say, doc. You're way off base and I suppose the only way everyone will know the real truth is when Rebecca becomes my wife."

"Someday I'm sure you'll meet a woman who will love you, but you need to develop a relationship first. It takes time. You can't set your heart on someone and expect to marry her just because you want it. Life doesn't work that way, Jeremy."

"I suppose that you're also an authority on relationships now too." He looked at the picture on the desk. "Every week I come in here and I see your perfect little family, but you never talk about them." He sat down and folded his hands across his chest as he stared into the doctor's eyes. "Come, on, doc. Tell me, are your sons as perfect in reality as they look in that picture—so clean-cut? How about your wife? Do you have that wonderful storybook kind of life? Is everything so perfect in your own little world that you forget that not everyone has that kind of life?"

Tate sat quietly, his eyes still focused intently on Jeremy's.

"How would you feel if something happened to one of your sons or your wife?"

His eyes narrowed. "I would be devastated, which is a normal reaction."

"What if your grief sent you off the deep end?"

"I would seek help no matter what it entailed," he evenly answered. "Jeremy, I know that you didn't have a normal childhood, but you need to resolve those issues. In order to start fresh, you need to come to terms with your past and release that pent-up anger, and accept the fact that your relationship with your parents wasn't a normal relationship."

"What's your point?"

"I want you to go out into the world with a healthy mind, able to cope with the difficulties of life."

He sneered. "I am perfectly healthy in both body and mind." He smiled, listening to the laughter of the demons at Tate's know-it-all attitude.

"You need to stay on your medication."

"I'm fed up with the way you're always pushing drugs down my throat."

Tate cautiously eyed him. "You need more help than I can give you. You aren't living in the real world now, and your relationship with Rebecca is a fantasy you've conjured up in your mind. It doesn't exist," he firmly stated.

Jeremy jumped to his feet. "I'm going to do you a favor by leaving now. If I don't, I fear I may lose my temper." He looked pointedly at Tate. "Or maybe that's your plan. Get me to lose my temper so you can say I threatened you, and then you can have me locked up in the loony bin."

"I am not trying to harm you, Jeremy. My only motivation is to help you, and you certainly have the right to express yourself."

"Do I?" His eyes widened. "Every time I say anything you don't agree with, you want to prescribe a new medication or you accuse me of imagining things when I'm not."

"I'm sorry if you feel these sessions and prescribed medications haven't helped you. That's a sign that you need an in-depth evaluation."

"Maybe if you listened to me once in a while instead of believing my parents' crap all those years ago, you might not have been so one-sided. You had already formed an opinion of me before you even met me." He walked toward the door and laid a hand on the doorknob, then looked again at the picture on the desk then back to Tate. "Maybe someday your perfect life will crumble, and then I'd really like to be around to see how you cope."

"I certainly hope that doesn't happen, Jeremy, but no one's life is without sorrow."

"Only some of us have more sorrow than others. Life has never been fair to me." Before he would allow Tate to answer, Jeremy was out the door. He hated Thaddeus Tate almost as much as he hated his parents. He pictured Tate going home every night to his wonderful wife and sons and sitting down to dinner, enjoying their company. Then later he probably talked to his sons, genuinely caring about what was going on in their lives. It wasn't fair. If Tate knew some of the pain he carried inside of him, he might change the way he treated him. It was up to him to make Tate see the error of his ways. His eyes clouded. Tate needed to see what it was really like to hurt so badly inside that he thought he'd explode.

Chapter Seventeen

Lily spent an hour at the supermarket, then wheeled her groceries to her van and carefully placed them inside. She smiled as she backed out of the parking lot. She intended to make this weekend one Thaddeus would never forget. God only knew if any man deserved to be pampered, it was Thaddeus. Ever since they'd met, he'd been the most giving man she'd ever known.

At first his profession intimidated her, and she'd thought his chosen career would cause him to be stuffy, opinionated, and very analytical. She soon found out that he was just the opposite. He was never preachy, but soft-spoken and compassionate with a refreshing sense of humor. He never tired of listening to her problems and concerns. When the boys were young, he spent many tireless hours explaining to them why he imposed some of the rules he had. He never ended the conversation until he was certain they understood. Whenever they had a problem or were concerned about a friend, they'd discuss it with Thad, assured they wouldn't be lectured, and were shown alternatives and understood the pros and cons. Thad encouraged them to figure out their own solutions, but always stayed close to lend his help if needed.

She pulled the van into the mall parking lot. Last week she and Marge had seen some lingerie and joked about it, but now she decided to purchase it, delighting in the surprise she would see in Thad's eyes when she modeled it for him tonight. She grinned. Yes, tonight would certainly be a night he wouldn't soon forget.

****

Thaddeus' uneasy feeling refused to leave him. Jeremy Talbot had unnerved him, and he wished there was some way he could prove that Jeremy needed to be hospitalized. He was afraid that before long Jeremy would lose total control, and the vengeance he would pour onto his unsuspecting victims would be catastrophic.

He ran his hand through his hair. There had to be a way to get him the help he needed. He was a volcano ready to erupt. He had a gut feeling he'd never see Jeremy again, but he could only hope that Jeremy would heed his advice and seek therapy once he arrived in New York City. He glanced again at his notes, wishing something would pop out at him to prove that Jeremy Talbot was not only a threat to himself but to others as well. Only then would he have the authority to request immediate hospitalization.

****

Lily pulled the van into the garage. She unlocked the kitchen door, then unloaded the groceries from the van.

When she saw the blinking answering machine light, she hit the play button. "We got here okay, Mom," T.J.'s deep voice said. "See you and Dad Sunday night. Remember, Mom, you and Dad are getting old, so behave," Tyler added. She laughed as she listened to the next message. "I'm looking forward to tonight, sweetheart. I'll pick up a bottle of wine on my way home." She smiled as the machine clicked off. She emptied the grocery bags, setting the items on the counter. She picked up her new nightgown and draped it over the back of a kitchen chair. She picked up a carton of ice cream. The doorbell rang, and she set the ice cream on the counter and hurried to the door.

She pressed the intercom. "Yes?" She peered through the peephole, but didn't recognize the stranger. "If you're selling something, I'm not interested, but thanks anyway."

"I'm not selling anything. I have some papers for Dr. Tate."

"He didn't tell me anyone was stopping by. Let me call his office. Maybe you should take them there."

"No, I was instructed to personally bring them to his home. I need you to sign for them. It'll only take a minute." He shifted his weight. "They're marked confidential."

She hesitated as she peered at the young man. "I suppose it will be all right then." She opened the door, and Jeremy stepped inside.

****

Millicent met Gilbert at the door. "What's happened?" he asked. "I got here as quickly as I could."

"It's Jeremy. He's gone."

He raised his eyes. "Gone where?"

She bit her bottom lip. "I don't know...probably New York like he planned. He never said good-bye to us. All he left was this note. It's the oddest thing I've ever read."

Gilbert took the note, read it, and then shook his head. "He says we'll never hear from him again, and as far as we're concerned we're dead to him and him to us. No one will ever hear of Jeremy Talbot again." He looked quizzically at Millicent. "Did you check his room?"

"No. I was out on the patio, and I assumed he was up in his room as usual. I saw him briefly when he returned from his session with Dr. Tate."

"How did he act?"

She shrugged. "Like he always does."

"Let's check his room."

She followed him to Jeremy's room. It had been years since either of them had been inside, because Jeremy valued his privacy and neither of them had had any desire to see how he spent his time in isolation.

"My God! It's a filthy mess in here!" Millicent's gaze swept over the pile of clothes and papers strewn over the bed, dresser, and floor. The dresser drawers were open, their contents spilling out.

"I don't think he planned to leave today," Gilbert stated matter-of-factly. "It appears to be a spur of the moment decision."

"What makes you think that?"

His eyes scanned the room. "Look at the things he's left behind. Wouldn't someone planning to move take his college certificate and his identification?" He picked up the savings account book. "Last week he withdrew his savings."

"I can't believe he'd leave so abruptly," Millicent said, pushing the clothes back in the drawers. "I need to give this room a good scrubbing." She crinkled up her nose. "It's musty-smelling in here."

Gilbert picked up a notebook, scrutinizing it as he flipped through the pages. He stared at the front cover. "This is his high school history notebook. I wonder why he saved this." He turned the pages slowly, and when he was two-thirds through the book, his eye caught something. "Good Lord!" he exclaimed.

"What is it, Gilbert?" Millicent hurried to his side, noticing the sickening pallor to her husband's complexion.

She looked at the page he pointed to, carefully reading the words penned in Jeremy's large scrawl. Her hands shook, causing the notebook to slip. Tears sprang to her eyes. "This is pornographic filth!"

Gilbert swallowed hard. "I'm glad that sick bastard is out of this house. As far as I'm concerned, he *is* dead!"

****

Jeremy gazed around the crowded bus station and casually slipped into the restroom. He splashed cold water on his face, then pulled a pair of scissors from his bag. He grabbed a handful of his hair, cutting the long locks off and tossing them into the trash bin. When he'd cut as much as he could, he plugged in an electric razor, took a deep breath, and began shaving his scalp until all traces of hair were gone. A couple of boys looked at him quizzically as he completed his task. He placed the razor back in his bag, then picked it up and stepped into an empty stall. He quickly removed his clothes, changing into a pair of dress slacks and shirt. He took out a baseball cap and placed it on his head, then replaced his thick, horn-rimmed glasses with a stylish pair of wire frames. He slipped his feet into a pair of loafers and stuffed his old clothing into the bag. He sauntered out of the stall to study his appearance in the mirror. He was pleased with the man who stared back at him. He smiled. He would never recognize himself.

****

Thaddeus pulled his car into the garage next to Lily's van. He picked up his briefcase and whistled jovially as he unlocked the kitchen door. He flicked on the light. He didn't see anything cooking on the stove, so he assumed Lily was waiting until later to have dinner. She was probably upstairs at this very moment, waiting in their bed for him, dressed in something sexy and alluring.

The phone rang and he quickly picked it up.

"Hello, Thad, this is Marge. I've been trying to reach Lily for a couple of hours now but haven't received an answer," she worriedly said. "Is she all right?"

"That's strange, Marge. The boys are on a camping trip, and Lily and I have plans for this evening." He frowned. "Her van's in the garage. Maybe she's in the shower. I just walked in the door when you called so I'll check upstairs."

"She wouldn't be in the shower for two hours," Marge reasoned. "This morning she left a message on my answering machine wanting me to go shopping with her, but I'd already left for Erie to see my sister."

"Maybe she's still shopping and lost track of the time. She probably went with Joan or Sylvia if she couldn't reach you," Thaddeus assured her.

"No, I've spoken to both of them, and neither of them have heard from her today."

"Let me check the house and I'll call you back, Marge. She might be taking a nap," he calmly assured her.

"I'll wait for your call, Thad," she worriedly replied.

He hung up the phone, then walked to the far side of the kitchen and laid his hand on the counter. He felt something sticky and noticed a carton of ice cream melted and dripping down the side of the counter. He looked at the various items set out on the counter. Lily had obviously been in the process of unloading the groceries and had become distracted. She would have never left the food out, especially the perishables, and he wondered if she could have become ill. His heart caught in his throat as he raced to the living room, then searched all of the downstairs rooms, calling her name as his panic mounted. She had to be upstairs. He took the stairs two at a time, his heavy body charging down the hall to the bathroom. He pounded on the door and when he received no answer, he flung it open only to find the room dark and empty. He ran to the master bedroom. His hand trembled on the doorknob as an unexplainable terror gripped him. He panted, his breath coming out loud and shallow. He took a deep breath, then opened the door.

CHAPTER EIGHTEEN

Jeremy took his wallet out of his pocket and looked at his identification. He smiled with self-satisfaction. Jeremy Talbot was dead—gone forever—and today Nathaniel Cummings was born. He settled back in his seat as the bus continued on its way to Boston.

****

Nicholas Adams nervously stood next to his best man.

Luke Reynolds threw an arm around his shoulder. "There's still time to back out," he teased.

"Not for all the money in the world." He peered into his best friend's face. "You know, Luke, I've never said this to anyone before, but I knew I wanted Becky for my wife after our first date."

Luke saw the sheepish expression on his face. "It showed, buddy." He slapped him on the back, then noticed the organist taking her seat. "Here we go, Nick." His eyes beheld Cassi as she slowly came down the aisle, her beauty causing his heart to skip a beat. He planned to ask her to marry him at Christmas. He kept his eyes on her as she took her place, then stole a look at Nicholas to see how he was holding up. His eyes were misty as he watched his bride walk toward him. "She's beautiful, Nick," Luke whispered.

****

Jeremy smiled as he walked into the Zander Realty Company. "I'd like to rent a small efficiency apartment," he announced to the pretty receptionist.

She returned his smile. "I'll buzz Bill Connor. He handles the rentals."

He looked around the comfortable office as she fulfilled her duties. He glanced out the window at the heavy traffic, wondering where Rebecca was at this very moment in time. She could be in any one of those cars speeding by and maybe had even passed him as he walked here. He inhaled deeply. She was close—he could feel it. Her essence filled his senses. It would only be a matter of time now until they were together.

"May I help you?" a deep voice asked.

Jeremy turned around. "Yes, I'm looking for a small apartment to rent."

"I'm Bill Connor. Please step into my office."

Jeremy nodded to the receptionist as he followed Bill Connor into his office.

"I have a number of apartments in all price ranges, Mr...?"

"Nathaniel Cummings."

Connor flipped through a folder. "Where are you employed?"

He smiled confidently. "I'm self-employed."

"What do you do, Mr. Cummings?"

"Please call me Nathaniel. I'm a writer."

"Have I read any of your books? I don't recall the name."

He shook his head. "No, but you will."

"How do you support yourself, Nathaniel?"

"I have savings, and it won't be long before my novels are published."

Bill Connor frowned. "Most of the property owners are strict on who gets in, which is the reason they use our service to list their apartments." He looked at Jeremy. "Quite frankly, Nathaniel, without a steady track record of employment, self-employed or otherwise, you may be turned down. There would be no recourse for the landlord if you failed to pay your rent or broke your lease. Have you tried looking in the newspapers?"

Jeremy cocked an eyebrow. "Suppose you find me something comfortable, and I'll pay six months in advance and throw in an extra bonus for you personally."

Connor thoughtfully scratched his jaw. "I'm sure we can work something out."

****

Rebecca laid her head on Nicholas's strong chest as they danced around the reception hall.

"Are you happy?" he whispered in her ear.

"Yes," she murmured. "It was a beautiful ceremony, just as I always dreamed about when I was a little girl. I've been waiting for this day for a long time."

"So have I, Mrs. Adams." He bent down tenderly kissing her. "The best is yet to come."

"You still haven't told me where we're going on our honeymoon."

He grinned. "It's a surprise."

"Not even a hint?"

"You'll find out in about an hour."

She held him close. "I love you so much, Nick. You're the only man I've ever loved or ever will love."

****

Thaddeus stepped into the room and quietly crept over

to the bed, making out what he presumed to be Lily's form. He wondered why she had the covers pulled up to her chin when it was such a warm evening, then realized she was probably surprising him with some new lingerie and was waiting for him to come closer. He smiled as he reached her, leaning over to plant a kiss on her forehead. He inched closer, then stopped in his tracks as his eyes met hers. She stared blankly at him. He opened his mouth to speak, when the realization came over him that there was no life in those eyes, the eyes he adored.

"No, Lily!" he screamed, pulling the covers from her, then stared in horror at her naked, bruised body. A pair of her stockings was tied in a neat bow around her neck. Dried blood caked the side of her mouth. "God, no!" he shrieked, collapsing on the side of the bed as sobs racked his body. "No, no, not my Lily," he moaned.

After a few minutes he pulled himself from the bed, took a ragged breath, and called the police. He sat back down next to Lily with his head in his hands. His thoughts drifted to T.J. and Tyler, wondering how he could break this news to them. He'd always been thankful that his sons were so close to their mother, but then, Lily had been an extraordinary woman. She definitely had been a rare breed, and he wondered if his sons would ever get over her death. He knew that, for himself, his life would never be the same. Life would no longer hold any meaning without his beloved Lily by his side. It dawned on him that he was thinking about her in the past tense now.

Tears streamed from his eyes as he remembered that just this morning she was planning their romantic weekend together, and now the life had been viciously snuffed out of her.

****

Jeremy set his backpack down and looked around the apartment. It was small but big enough to serve his purposes. He now resided on the tenth floor of the Stafford Tower, two blocks from the college. He was grateful for the convenience stores and delis, or he was certain he'd starve to death. He pulled open the window blinds and looked at the street below. This was it. He was on his own, with no one to tell him what to do or what to think anymore. He heard the demons and sighed tiredly. Maybe someday he'd even be able to figure out a way to banish them from his mind permanently. As long as they stayed, they would make his life with Rebecca difficult. He had to continuously be on guard. Their numbers were multiplying daily, invading his brain and even sometimes now rendering his conscious mind almost useless. He'd find himself doing things against his own will, but the demons demanded satisfaction, and he feared what they'd do to him if he failed to obey them.

He faced the large room. He'd been told that the sofa pulled out into a double bed. An easy chair, lamp, two bureaus, and a desk made up the rest of the furnishings. He pulled his clothes out of his backpack and placed them in one of the bureaus. Tomorrow he'd purchase a computer. He had to have a computer.

He pulled out the sofa bed, then removed his clothing, all except his underwear, and exhaustedly plopped down on the bed. It wasn't as comfortable as the bed he'd slept in for most of his life back in Pittsburgh, but then his sleep had never been sound ever since the demons had moved in, demanding his full attention in the quiet of the night. He hoped, though, that tonight they would give him some much-needed peace. He desperately needed sleep.

****

171

"Dr. Tate, I need to ask you a few questions," Detective Blake Bergan said, looking into the man's glazed eyes.

"Of course."

"First I'd like to offer my condolences on your loss."

Thaddeus swallowed the lump in his throat. "It's a nightmare," he said hoarsely. "I keep telling myself I'm going to wake up from this horrible nightmare at any moment and find Lily sleeping peacefully at my side." He shuddered.

"Can I call anyone for you?"

"No. Thank you. My sons are on their way home. They don't know yet. I didn't know what to tell them." He threw his hands up. "I only told them that their mother had been injured."

"Has anyone made any threats to you or your family?"

"No."

The detective cocked an eye. "You're a psychiatrist. Have any of your patients made any comments that could be construed as a threat?"

"No...no, I can't think of anyone." He glanced toward the door as Marge rushed through. "That's Lily's best friend."

Bergan followed his gaze, watching the brunette, her face contorted with worry, rush over to Thaddeus.

Marge threw her arms around him. "What's happened, Thad?" Her eyes frightfully searched his. "Why are the police here? Where's Lily?"

"I couldn't tell you on the phone." He cleared his throat. "It's Lily," he choked. "She's...she's been murdered."

Her hand flew to her mouth as the color drained from her face. Tears spilled from her eyes. "No...she can't be," she cried. "Why?"

Thaddeus sniffed as he looked at the detective. "I don't know," he moaned.

"When was the last time you spoke to Lily Tate?" Bergan asked Marge.

She wrung her hands. "Yesterday…we talk every day. She left a message on my answering machine this morning, but I was in Erie visiting my sister."

"Did she ever express to you any concerns or fears about anyone?"

"No. Everyone loved Lily. She was the sweetest, most gentle woman you'd want to know. She was so happy and content…one of those people just filled with life." She dabbed at her eyes. "I…I can't believe someone would harm her," she sobbed.

"Dr. Tate, I need you to verify your whereabouts this afternoon," Bergan stated.

Marge whirled on the detective. "You certainly aren't implying that Thad had anything to do with Lily's death, are you?" she asked. "They were the most loving couple on this earth."

He shook his head. "I'm not implying anything. It's just routine questioning."

"It's procedural, Marge," Thaddeus answered, patting her hand. He looked at Detective Bergan. "I was in my office all day. You can check with my secretary, Candace Jermain."

"Did you leave the office for lunch?"

He rubbed his weary eyes. "No, I had a sandwich ordered in."

Bergan nodded. "If I have any further questions for you, I'll let you know." His gaze swept around the room. "This wasn't a forced entry, so we assume that your wife knew her killer." He turned his attention back to Thaddeus and Marge, eyeing them carefully. "If either of you recall anything, please let me know."

"And you'll let me know whatever information your officers find?"

"Yes, Dr. Tate. Again, I'm very sorry for your loss."

"Thank you, detective." He stood up, then turned to Bergan. "I do have one question. Was Lily..." He swallowed the lump in his throat. "Was Lily sexually assaulted?"

Bergan's jaw tightened. "The complete results aren't back yet, but there was semen found on her inner thigh."

"Oh, God," he moaned as he collapsed into a chair.

Marge threw her arms around him as they shed tears for the woman who had meant so much to both of them.

"Dad!"

Thaddeus looked up, seeing the terror-stricken look on his sons' faces as they ran to him.

"What happened to Mom?" T.J. asked in a shaken voice.

Thaddeus squeezed his eyes shut as he drew a ragged breath. "I have some terrible news, boys," he weakly replied.

They searched his face, then looked at Marge, then to the police swarming through the house.

"Dad, what happened to Mom? Where is she? Was there a robbery or something?" T.J. asked.

Thaddeus put his arms around his sons, drawing them close in an embrace he never wanted to relinquish. His chest heaved and fresh sobs tore through him, beginning in his heart and erupting through his brain, tormenting him with the knowledge that Lily was truly gone. His wife and his sons' mother had been unfairly taken from them.

"Dad, where's Mom? Please tell us," Tyler implored in

a small voice. "Why are there police everywhere?"

Thaddeus composed himself as his bottom lip quivered.

"Dad," they pleaded. "What's going on?"

He took a deep breath. "I wish I didn't have to tell you boys this. There should be an easier way." His eyes brimmed with fresh tears. "Your mother has been murdered."

"No!" T.J. shrieked.

Tyler became violently ill with dry heaves and clung to Thaddeus as though he was hanging on for his own life. Thaddeus tightened his grip on his sons.

Bergan stood awkwardly by, watching the family torn apart in their grief. This was the part of the job he despised. He'd been trained and conditioned not to let his emotions get in the way of his work no matter how traumatizing a case became. He tried to distance himself from the victims and their families and conduct his interviews in a professional manner, but there was something about seeing a grown man break down in tortured pain when his loved one was murdered, that ripped his heart out every time. Now as he watched Thaddeus Tate consoling his sons, it was almost more than he could bear.

He turned to Marge, whose red, swollen eyes were brimming with fresh tears. "May I ask you a few more questions?"

She blew her nose as she nodded.

"I need your full name."

She took a damp tissue from her pocket and dabbed at her eyes. "Marjorie Campman."

"Address?"

"Forty-one fifteen Mockhill Lane Road," she answered.

"How long have you known the Tate family?"

"Lily and I met in college in Philadelphia. We've been friends ever since."

"She never mentioned anything to you about any disturbing phone calls or notes she may have received?"

"No."

"Please try to remember, Mrs. Campman. It doesn't matter how trivial you may have thought it to be at the time, or even now." He studied her reactions. "Sometimes these tiny, seemingly unimportant events are the ones that lead us straight to the murderer."

She sniffed. "I'm sorry, detective, I can't recall anything like that. If there was anything, Lily never mentioned it to me." She looked into his eyes. "If you knew Lily the way I did, then you would understand that even if she had received a peculiar phone call or letter, she would have dismissed it and not let it bother her. That's just the way she was. She always saw the good in others and rarely had a disparaging word against anyone. In fact, I can't remember her ever gossiping or joining in any discussion that involved poking fun at another. She truly believed that everyone had a reason for the way they were."

"Thank you, Mrs. Campman, but remember to call me if you do remember anything else."

She nodded. "Detective, do you think this is connected to the other murders?" she frightfully asked.

"At this point I don't know." His eyes traveled back to Thaddeus and his sons. The three sat huddled together, their faces wet with tears and etched with the grief they were suffering.

****

Jeremy marveled at his computer, checking and rechecking all of the connections before turning the power on. He grinned from ear to ear after he signed up for an

176

Internet account, seeing all of the information waiting at his fingertips.

Four hours later, he tossed some notebook sheets of his scribblings on his desk. He picked up the newspaper and scanned the headlines, hoping in time to become familiar with all of the local politicians' names and those in the community with social prominence. This was his new home, where he belonged. Pittsburgh had always seemed foreign to him, never accepting him, but Boston gave him a rebirth he never believed possible. But the most important fact was that Rebecca was here. He inhaled deeply, remembering the light scent of her perfume.

He flipped through the social section of the paper, looking at the beaming faces of the brides-to-be and the new brides. "I'll bet that's how Rebecca will look when we announce our engagement," he said aloud. "She'll impatiently await our wedding night, begging me to take her." He briefly closed his eyes as the images of Rebecca and him making love consumed him. After a few minutes, he reopened his eyes. She was so close now. He scanned the rest of the wedding announcements and abruptly stopped when he saw the names Adams–Walker. His hands shook as he read the wedding announcement. A sharp pain pierced his heart. He gasped for air. "No!" he shrieked.

****

"What do we have here?" Chief Detective of Homicide Kenneth Owens asked, standing over the lifeless form. He bent down taking a closer look. "Shit," he mumbled. "She's just a kid."

"Looks like she was on her way to her dormitory when she was attacked," Detective Gabriel Jackson said. "It looks like she was strangled with her own panty hose."

Owens, a burly man with fifteen years on the force,

eyed Jackson. "Anybody hear or see anything?"

"No. I've got a team out right now interviewing anyone who may have seen her last night."

"Okay, seal off the area. Then we'll need to talk to the victim's friends, classmates, anyone who knew her."

"I've got it covered," Jackson said. "The body's going to be picked up and transported to the morgue in a few minutes. We found her purse with the contents intact from what we can tell, with a couple of credit cards and over a hundred dollars in cash, so that rules out robbery. Her Student ID lists her as a sophomore at State College."

Owens shook his head in disgust. "Has the next of kin been notified?"

He nodded. "They're on their way and should be here sometime tonight. She's from Wisconsin."

"Okay," he sighed. "I'm going back to the station to see if there are any leads. Get the area sealed off, and don't let anyone near here."

CHAPTER NINETEEN

Nicholas stroked Rebecca's soft cheek, loving the feel of her silky smooth skin. "How does it feel to be together in our own home and our own bed?" he asked.

She smiled and let out a contented sigh. "I don't think there are words to express how I really feel, Nick." She pulled his face down to hers and brushed her lips against his. "You are my dream come true."

He grinned. "I love you so much, Beck." He propped himself on an elbow and gazed into her eyes. "I sorted all the mail. You're quite a popular woman."

She laughed. "I thought today I'd get started on the thank-you cards." She put a finger on his lip, gently tracing an outline with a fingertip.

"Good…I'll give you a hand." His eyes narrowed. "Honey, I need to talk to you about something."

"What? You're so serious."

"This *is* serious, Becky. You must have received a dozen anonymous cards and letters while we were on our honeymoon."

She sat up straight. "Who's doing this, Nick?"

He saw the fear in her eyes. "I don't know. This psycho

seems to know where you are all the time. It was bad enough all summer long, receiving them at your parents' house, but now they're coming to our apartment. I thought maybe they'd stop after our marriage."

"I have no clue who it could be," she said in a shaky voice.

"There's more."

"What?" Her eyes widened.

"The letters all summer long were postmarked Pittsburgh, but these today are postmarked from Boston."

"So...so he's here in Boston. He could be anyone." She put her arms around Nicholas, holding on tightly.

He felt the tremors in her body as he protectively put his own arms around her. "We need to talk to the police."

****

Jeremy clicked on his e-mail and read the brief message as a smile broke over his face. "Yes!" he ecstatically shouted, pounding his fist on his desk. He read the e-mail again. "This is it!" he grinned.

****

Detective Blake Bergan grabbed a cup of coffee, then sat back down at his desk. He wearily ran a hand over his face, rubbing his tired eyes as he looked at the stack of files on his desk. Any murder even remotely similar to Lily's Tate's was here. He'd hoped the Tate case would be an open and shut one and the murderer would soon be caught, but that was before he saw the similarities between the Raney Clark case and Sandy Williams, the prostitute who was murdered shortly after. Lily Tate had been murdered in the same way the others were. He had run into a dead end. The Adams girl had been sexually molested, but Sandy Williams and Lily Tate had been raped. A few suspects had been brought in, but the DNA didn't match.

He scratched his head. Just as quickly as the murdering spree had begun, it had abruptly ended. He'd questioned everyone who even remotely knew Lily Tate, but no one had a clue whom her murderer could be. They all agreed that Lily was a tenderhearted woman, loved by all that knew her and apparently didn't have an enemy in the world. She let someone she trusted well enough to enter her home, then was brutally raped and murdered by him. *But who and why? What was the killer's motive?* he wondered as he turned on the computer. He punched in a password, then ran a check for murders around the country comparable to these three. He typed in the information he was looking for and waited for the cross match. After a few seconds, the screen filled with the most likely matches. He scanned the list for twenty minutes, carefully searching for any victims who were strangled with an article of their clothing. After a few more minutes, he stopped staring at the screen. He typed in a few more phrases, then waited. When the screen loaded, he looked at the exact comparisons. "Here it is," he called to his partner.

Detective Gary Benson hurried to Bergan's desk, stooping over as his eyes rapidly scrutinized the information on the computer screen. "God, Boston's had four of the same types of murders in the past two months."

"What does that tell you?"

"Ours stopped and Boston's began."

Bergan eyed the younger man. "Are you thinking what I am?"

He nodded excitedly. "I'm one step ahead of you. I'll call Boston."

****

Thaddeus pulled another file from his filing cabinet, sighing heavily as his fatigued eyes read through the contents of the folder. He scowled. There had to be something a patient had said that might lead him to Lily's killer. Lily would have never allowed a stranger inside. She knew her murderer. He was certain of that fact. He realized how futile his efforts really were since Lily didn't know his patients and they certainly didn't know her. Nothing made sense anymore. All he knew was that the police didn't seem to be getting anywhere so he would continue to grasp at any straw he could. He was afraid Lily's murder investigation would eventually wind up in a folder marked *Unsolved*. He couldn't stand the thought of Lily's killer never being caught. He also knew that the more time that elapsed, the harder it would be to solve her case.

He slammed his fist down on his desk, trying to fight back the tears but knowing deep in his heart that it was useless. His tears would never dry up. Lily had been his world from the first moment they'd met. She was his best friend, lover, wife, and mother to his children. *How could he face the rest of his life alone?* He covered his face with his large hands as the tears poured from his eyes. *Who hated her so much that he would take her life and leave him without his love, and his sons without their mother?* he wondered. His sons acted strong for his sake, but he knew that's all it was—an act. He saw the pain in their eyes and heard it in their voices. They'd been like troupers, helping him through the funeral preparations and then the funeral, holding him up when his legs gave way at the sight of Lily's snow-white casket being lowered into the ground.

He'd never believed in an eye for an eye, but now he felt the same pain many of his patients had felt after losing a loved one to a vicious crime. He listened and gave them suggestions for dealing with their grief, and now he understood the haunting loneliness that had invaded those once happy hearts. Life would never be the same for him or T.J. and Tyler. T.J. had gone off to college as planned, and Tyler involved himself in every activity he could in his high school senior class, but nothing could ever ease the pain of losing Lily. He looked at the clock, which read eleven p.m., then at the door, half expecting Lily to appear with a steaming cup of coffee for him.

****

Gilbert Talbot finished packing Jeremy's things as Millicent stood silently by, watching him stack the cardboard boxes in the attic, all except for one box which he left aside. He wiped his hands on the back of his pants, then stood up. "I want to take this box downstairs."

"Why? It only contains Jeremy's journals."

His eyes narrowed. "I want to read them. I need to know for myself just how sick he really is. You remember the notebook we found with that pornographic filth?"

Her face reddened. "I remember. We already know what's in those journals, so why do you want to read them?"

"Maybe there's a clue somewhere."

She looked at him quizzically. "A clue to what?"

He shrugged. "I don't know...to the way he was, I suppose," he said.

"But it's just fiction, Gil. You can't base anything on those stories."

"But is it all just fiction, Millicent?"

CHAPTER TWENTY

Jeremy stretched his legs as he sat at his computer, typing the final edits for his novel, *Revenge*. His publisher, Jake Truman, wanted to meet with him next month to set up the publishing schedule for the two sequels Jeremy had already completed and submitted. Next month he'd finish the edits on those novels. The advance he'd received for the three novels would keep him content, but he chose for now to live meagerly instead of packing up and moving to a new apartment or home riddled with material luxuries. Maybe someday he would, but not yet. He suspected that eventually Rebecca and Nicholas would buy a house as most newlyweds did. He'd wait and find a home nearby where he'd be able to be close to her all the time. He needed the closeness of her. She belonged to him, and he waited for the day they would be together.

Every night he walked near her apartment, but she never saw him. A few times he even took a taxi to the suburb where she worked, waiting in the shadows outside the large building and catching a glimpse of her as she hurried out of the complex to her car. She looked radiant and beautiful, and he longed to come out of the shadows and reveal himself to her, but he couldn't, not yet. But someday the time would be right.

When his thoughts ripped him apart with images of Rebecca and Nicholas making love, the demons called for revenge on her, but he refused and looked for a woman to satisfy his sexual yearnings. Something always seemed to go wrong, though, with the demons making him seek the blood of the women instead, the blood that gave him power. It wasn't his fault the women died. He knew that. If they'd only do what he asked, but they refused, instead becoming frightened of him. Now with his new identity, and especially his writing success, he couldn't let any of them identify him, so the demons stepped in and silenced them. If the women weren't wearing panty hose, their bras or another garment was used to choke off their horrible voices, voices filled with nothing but terrible lies about him. He'd never used a weapon—his large hands were the only weapons needed.

His publisher wasn't pleased when he refused to have his photo on the dust jacket of his book and refused all interviews that involved him actually being there. He finally convinced Truman that he suffered from anxiety attacks, and the older man eventually conceded but was then overjoyed when Jeremy's mysteriousness resulted in even more advance orders. Nathaniel Cummings was becoming a notable name in the literary world. The advance reviews praised the talent this bright author possessed, matching his writing styles to some of the most famous. The only downside to his success was that no one could ever know that Jeremy Talbot was the man behind the novels. He yearned for the world to know, but that was impossible. When Rebecca and he were finally allowed to be together as they were meant to be, he intended to tell her and let her share in his happiness, as he knew she would want to. But until that time, his secret would remain his own.

He picked up the letter he had typed earlier and neatly folded it, then placed it in an envelope. Every day he wrote a letter to Rebecca, and every night he mailed it. He smiled, wondering what her reaction was as she read each letter describing his love for her. He grabbed his jacket and placed his baseball cap on his head before leaving the apartment.

His stomach rumbled, reminding him that he'd had no nourishment for several hours. He slowly walked down the busy street filled with mostly college students, and occasionally glanced in the windows of the various eateries. He found most of them to be jam-packed at this hour of the night and continued walking until he happened upon a quaint little café called Gretta's. He peered into the window seeing students, some with books propped up on the tables as they studied while downing a snack, and others chatting nosily together as the jukebox blared in the background. His eyes settled on a pretty redhead who hurried from table to table, quickly clearing them off only to have them rapidly refilled. The café looked full, so he was about to leave and find another restaurant when he spotted a solitary booth near the front counter. He stepped inside, slowly sauntered over to the booth, and then slid into it.

He looked around the bright room, listening to a song blaring much too loudly from the jukebox for his taste. *So, this was what he'd missed for the last four years of college.* He wondered if Rebecca had inhabited places such as this and surmised that she most likely had. He recalled his first conversation with her, realized that she had probably encouraged him to socialize on campus so she'd run into

186

him in a place like this and have an excuse to slide in the booth next to him, her thigh close to his. He picked up a napkin and wiped the sweat from his brow.

The redhead appeared at his booth. "I'm sorry you had to wait. What can I get you?" she breathlessly asked.

He smiled up at her, noticing her name tag. "Just a cup of coffee for right now, April."

She returned his smile. "Coming right up."

He watched her as she walked behind the counter and poured his coffee, then quickly grabbed a menu and brought both back to his table.

He slowly slipped his coffee as he kept an eye on April. She was slender, almost underweight, with clear blue eyes and a warm, friendly smile.

Ten minutes later, she returned with the coffeepot and topped off his cup. "Are you sure you wouldn't like a piece of pie with your coffee, or some cake? Everything is freshly baked on the premises."

He grinned. "You've convinced me. What do you recommend?"

"Our apple and cherry pies are very good. We also have chocolate cake and Boston Cream pie."

He tapped his chin. "Everything sounds delicious, but I think I'll go with the apple pie."

"Plain or à la mode?"

He laughed. "One small scoop."

"Be right back."

He leaned back in the booth, watching her as she cut the pie and topped it with a large scoop of vanilla ice cream. Her hips swayed gently as she walked back to his booth and set the plate in front of him.

"Do you attend college?" he asked.

"I go to Boston State. You?"

He took a bite of pie. "This is great! No, I don't attend college."

"Are you from Boston?"

He shook his head. "No, I was born and raised in upstate New York."

"What brings you to Boston…a job?"

"I'm a writer."

Her eyes widened. "Wow! What do you have out?" she enthusiastically asked.

He smiled as he took another bite of pie. "Nothing yet, but soon. I've just signed a contract."

"That must be so exciting."

"Yes, it is."

"So your writing brought you here?"

"In a sense." He set his fork on the side of his plate. He cocked his head as the demons came to the front. *She's nice, Jeremy. Later you can watch her blood oozing from her eyes and nose, then the corner of her mouth as you tighten her stockings around her throat.* His eyes narrowed as he looked at April, then to her long, slender, stocking-clad legs.

"Is something wrong?" she asked.

He shook his head. "No, I'm sorry, I just became distracted for a moment. Writers tend to do that from time to time," he said with a laugh, inwardly fighting to banish the demons to the back of his mind.

She smiled. "I'd better get back to work and let you finish your pie in peace."

"I've enjoyed your conversation, April."

"Maybe I'll see you again."

He nodded. "That would be nice." He picked his fork back up.

"What's your name? I'll look for your book. If you will, I'd like you to sign my copy as soon as it's released," she said shyly.

"My name's Nathaniel Cummings, and I'd be honored to sign a copy for you."

"Thank you, Nathaniel. Well, I have some customers waiting."

His gaze swept over her as she walked back to the counter. The sensuous curve of her legs forced his eyes to travel up to the short hemline. She was tempting…so very tempting. He licked his lips as he thought about the moist treasure between her legs, wondering if she'd ever given anyone the pleasure of entering her.

Chapter Twenty-One

Blake Bergan picked up the phone. "Thank you for getting back to me. I think we may have a link between your recent spree of murders and three unsolved ones here."

"What do you have?" Kenneth Owens asked.

"All of the victims seemed to be strangled in the same manner."

"You don't have any suspects?"

Blake let his breath out in a rush. "No, the murders ended as quickly as they began. The odd thing, though, is when they ended here they began in Boston."

Owens was quiet for a few seconds. "So what we have to figure out is, if this guy is one and the same, why he left Pittsburgh and traveled here and how he chooses his victims." He pulled on his chin. "Were the victims similar in any way?"

Blake stared out of the window as the sun slowly began its descent, leaving an eerie semi-darkness in its wake. "The first victim was a young woman from a prominent neighborhood, the second a prostitute, and the third a psychiatrist's wife, a middle-aged woman. We're looking into all unsolved murders to see if there is any correlation."

"Were all the murders committed away from the victims' homes?"

"All except the last woman, the psychiatrist's wife. She was strangled in her bed in the late afternoon." He exhaled noisily. "There was no sign of forced entry, and we've surmised that she knew her murderer."

Owens squinted. "How can you be certain? It could've been a solicitor or a delivery man."

Blake shook his head. "No, Thaddeus Tate has a tight security system, and Lily Tate personally knows all of the delivery men."

"Who's to say that a delivery man isn't suspect?"

"We've run checks, and everyone has an alibi and an up-to-date log book. Lily Tate would have never opened her door to a salesman or anyone unknown to her."

"You said her husband is a psychiatrist. What about a patient with a vendetta?"

"No, Thaddeus Tate's gone through every file in his possession and has come up empty."

Owens leaned back in his chair. "We still don't have anything concrete that can definitely link your murders to ours."

"I think you're wrong about that," Blake quickly replied. "The similarities are uncanny."

"It could be some nut who read about the murders in the papers."

"No, my gut instinct tells me that these are not copycat murders. This is the same guy, and the only difference is the location. We're trying to determine why he left Pittsburgh and traveled to Boston."

Owens looked up to see Detective Gabe Jackson in the doorway. He motioned the officer into the office. "I'll get back to you, Detective Bergan. Let me know if you come up with any further information." He set the phone down, then turned to Jackson. "Do you have something?"

He nodded. "It might be nothing, but I think it bears checking out."

"What is it?"

"I've just finished taking a statement from a newlywed couple. It seems the wife has been receiving anonymous gifts, cards, and letters for several months." He cleared his throat. "It started when she was a student in Pittsburgh and has just recently intensified."

"And you think this has something to do with the murders?"

He shrugged. "I know it's a long shot, but it's the best lead we've gotten so far."

"Where is this couple?" Owens asked.

"In the conference room. I asked them to stick around in case you wanted to talk to them."

"Tell them I'll be right there."

Five minutes later, Owens walked into the conference room. His eyes quickly swept over the young couple. "I'm Detective Owens," he said, extending his hand. "Detective Jackson tells me that you've been receiving threatening letters."

"Yes," Nicholas quickly replied. "My wife has been receiving cards, gifts, and letters for quite some time."

"Have you yourself personally received any?" Owens asked, eyeing him carefully.

"No."

"Tell me about the letters."

He took a deep breath. "At first Becky, my wife," he said, squeezing her shoulder, "ignored the letters. She didn't tell anyone when she first started receiving them."

He looked at the young woman. "Why didn't you tell anyone, Becky...may I call you Becky?"

"Yes, of course." She twisted her hands. "I knew that Nick and I would be graduating from college and leaving Pittsburgh for good, and I figured they would just stop. Besides, in the beginning they were harmless. I figured it was just a guy with a crush on me. He never signed his name, so I had no idea who the author of the letters could possibly be." Her voice was tense.

"What happened when you left Pittsburgh?"

"The letters, cards, and gifts continued to come. They came to my parents' home, so I figured whoever was sending them got the address from the college directory."

"But it started getting more extreme," Nicholas broke in, "with letters coming every day. When Becky and I married, the letters started coming to our apartment. It wouldn't have bothered us, except that they weren't forwarded, and our address wasn't publicized. We're still not listed."

"With the Internet it's easy to obtain addresses."

"I suppose," Nicholas conceded.

Owens thoughtfully scratched his chin. "Becky, can you think of anyone who may be doing this?"

She shook her head. "No, last spring I just started getting them one day in my student mailbox. As I said, I thought they'd eventually stop, but now they're postmarked from Boston. Whoever's sending them is in this city."

He saw the fear in her eyes. "When did you notice they were postmarked from Boston?"

"About the middle of September."

Owens shot a look in Jackson's direction. He sensed what the younger man was thinking—the same thing he was. The murders ended in Pittsburgh and began in Boston at that same time. "Do you have the letters?"

"Not all of them. When I first started receiving them, I threw them away. After I told Nicholas what was going on, we began saving them."

Nicholas pulled a neatly tied stack of letters from his jacket pocket. "We have a lot more at home, but these are the more graphic ones." He handed them to Detective Owens, then leaned back in his chair, putting a protective arm around his wife.

Owens felt Nicholas's hand tremble as he handed him the letters. "Would you two like anything? Coffee or a soda?" He set the letters on the table.

"Coffee's fine," Nicholas replied.

"Yes, thank you," Becky said as a weak smile briefly appeared on her full lips.

Gabe Jackson turned to Owens. "I'll get it. Be right back."

Owens picked up a letter and read the contents aloud, then picked up another. His eyebrows rose. "This guy is certainly obsessed with you, Becky." He skimmed through a few more. "He only mentions you indirectly, Nicholas, and only when he's referring to how crushed he is at finding out that Becky has married you."

Nicholas grabbed Becky's hand and held it tightly. "That's why I insisted to Becky that we come down here. He's making indirect threats, but I'm not sure if they're directed at me or Becky," he said.

Owens frowned. "The letters tend to ramble on, and most times they don't make any sense at all…at least not to me." He looked at Becky. "By the way he writes, does that give you any possible clue to his identity?"

"No, I have no idea whom it could be."

"You need to be on guard with everyone. This is more than just an obsession. According to this letter, he's making plans to claim you for his own."

"I don't know who this could be," she said in a shaky voice. "It's almost like he knows everything I'm doing. He knows when I leave for work and when I return." She shuddered.

"Think back to your last few months of college. Did anything unusual happen, or did you have a confrontation with anyone?"

"No." She looked at Nicholas. "There's no one I can think of."

Jackson entered the room and set two steaming Styrofoam cups of coffee in front of the couple, then took a seat across from them.

Owens pushed the letters toward him. "Read these and see what you make of this guy."

Jackson read a few of the letters, then shrugged. "This guy is totally infatuated. He's a classic stalker."

"But most stalkers don't hurt their victims, do they?" Rebecca whispered.

Jackson slowly let his breath out. "Sometimes they do."

"But why me?"

Owens' eyes softened as he looked at her. "No one knows why these people fixate on anyone. It could be your hair color, your voice, or any number of things." He shrugged. "Maybe you smiled at him. It's usually something quite innocent on the victim's part that the stalker has conjured in his mind to mean something more."

"Do you think these letters could be from a rejected boyfriend?" Jackson asked.

"No, Nicholas is the only one I dated in college."

Jackson's eyes narrowed. "Nicholas, do you recall any

remarks made about your wife...you know, maybe someone joking around with you in the locker room? Could a comment have been made that, at the time, you may have taken as just a joke?"

He slowly shook his head. "No, nothing comes to mind."

Owens leaned forward. "So you two finished out your college days with nothing unusual happening and returned to Boston?"

Rebecca shook her head. "No, not exactly. Right before graduation, Nicholas was attacked while the graduating class was having a nighttime picnic."

"Was the attack serious?"

"I had several stitches in my head and had to be briefly hospitalized."

"Tell me more about this attack," Owens said.

Jackson took notes as the couple spent the next twenty minutes describing the night Nicholas was ambushed.

"This Jeremy Talbot whom you stated had disappeared and that you went in search of, was he a good friend of both of you?"

Nicholas raised his eyebrows. "No, I wasn't fond of him and only invited him along to make Becky happy."

"I felt sorry for him," she quickly said. "No one ever spoke to him, only picked on him, and he's very nice once you get to know him. He's an introvert with a dream to become a writer, and I think he'll do it someday," she added.

"Could this Jeremy Talbot be the author of these letters?"

Becky laughed. "No, I don't believe it could be Jeremy. He's very shy, and I can't picture him writing the filth this pervert has," she said, glancing toward the letters.

"What do you think, Nicholas?" Owens asked, carefully observing him.

He shrugged. "I doubt he did it, but he gives me the creeps just the same."

"If you get any more of these letters, I want you to bring them in immediately. In the meantime, please be careful, and if anyone says anything that appears suspicious, contact us immediately. This sounds like an unbalanced individual we're dealing with."

"There's nothing you can do?" Nicholas asked.

Gabe Jackson folded his hands. "We need something concrete to go on, but we're going to run a check on your friends just to be on the safe side."

Becky's brow furrowed. "We don't want our friends to think we're accusing them."

"They won't even know we're doing a check," Owens promised. "We'll just see if there's anything in any of their backgrounds."

She swallowed hard. "Thank you, detectives."

****

Blake Bergan listened intently to Detective Owens. "I'll have a check run immediately on Jeremy Talbot and get back to you." He set the phone down and looked at Gary Benson. "Find out everything you can on a Jeremy Talbot. I'm going to call Thaddeus Tate to see if Talbot rings a bell with him."

"It would be nice if this was the lead we've been waiting for."

Blake thoughtfully rubbed his jaw. "I'm not getting my hopes up, but it's the first break we've had."

"I'll get the background check started."

Blake dialed Tate's office and quickly informed the secretary that he needed to speak with the doctor immediately. Seconds later, Tate's voice came over the line.

"Do you have some information about Lily's murderer?" he asked expectantly.

Blake wished he could tell him they did. "We're still working on leads. I need to ask about someone who may have been a patient of yours."

"I can't give out any information without the patient's consent."

"Is there some way we can work around this? I need to know if the name Jeremy Talbot means anything to you. It's extremely important."

He hesitated. "I understand that Jeremy Talbot now resides in New York City."

"Are you certain?"

"That's where he planned to go. Is Jeremy in some sort of trouble?" Thaddeus asked.

"He could be. His name has come up recently, and I'm trying to get some background information on him." He paused. "What types of behavioral problems did he have? Was he a drug user? Did he have violent tendencies?"

Thaddeus sighed. "You understand, detective, that I can't violate a doctor-patient confidentiality."

"I understand. I'm trying to make a connection between Jeremy and a young woman he'd gone to college with."

"Has Jeremy done something illegal?"

"That's what I want to find out. I'm checking with several of the woman's college classmates. Do you know if Jeremy was dating anyone before he left Pittsburgh?"

Tate hesitated. "According to him he was, but I have my doubts."

"Can you tell me how long he'd been seeing you?"

"I never said that he had been," Thaddeus answered evenly.

Blake ran his hand over his chin, feeling the stubble. He was tired and not in the mood for games. "Let's just cut to the chase, Dr. Tate. I know that Jeremy Talbot was a patient of yours. If he ever exhibited bizarre behavior, it would be very beneficial for me to have this piece of information."

"I did see him." Thaddeus slowly let his breath out. "Jeremy Talbot's parents brought him to me when he was a young boy. I've been treating him off and on up until the time he left the city."

"Do you think his parents would give you permission to release some information?"

"I can't answer that, detective, but even if they did, I would only be able to release his files up until the time he reached the age of consent."

Chapter Twenty-Two

Millicent stiffly sat next to Gilbert, every once in a while stealing glances at Detective Bergan. Finally, she spoke. "My husband and I have agreed to give Dr. Tate permission to release Jeremy's files to you."

Blake nodded gratefully. "Thank you both for your cooperation." He looked in Gilbert's direction. "Would you mind answering a few questions, Mr. Talbot?"

"No, of course not," Gilbert replied without emotion.

"Where is your son now?"

Millicent clasped her hands tightly together as she looked at Dr. Tate.

Gilbert's jaw tightened. "We have no idea where Jeremy is. We're assuming New York City," he answered.

Blake looked at Thaddeus. "Dr. Tate, were there any unusual things you noticed about Jeremy when you first began counseling him?"

Thaddeus looked at the couple, then back to the detective. "Jeremy was an unusual child. He appeared to live in a world of his own, and when he did talk, it was about not feeling wanted or loved by his parents. He talked about not fitting in at school and being bullied. But he was bright and hoped to make a career as a writer."

"Did you believe him when he said he wasn't loved by his parents?"

"They obviously cared about his well-being or they wouldn't have brought him to me." He cautiously stole a look at Gilbert. "I knew Jeremy wasn't physically abused as I never saw a mark on him. And he always had clean clothes and appeared well fed. What I did learn, though, was that he was a very unstable child in dire need of help."

Blake became intense. "What do you mean by unstable? Was he mentally unstable?"

"I believe so."

"In all the years you counseled him, did he ever mention having girlfriends?"

"Yes, twice…once in his senior year of high school and in his last year of college."

"We ran a background check and found out that he has a sealed record. Mr. Talbot," he said, turning his attention back to Gilbert. "What's in that report?"

Gilbert ran his hand through his hair. "Jeremy became obsessed whenever a girl showed the slightest act of kindness toward him. He'd blow a simple gesture way out of proportion and imagine the gesture to mean more than it did." He folded his hands and placed them in his lap. "We had thought he was getting better, but…" He shook his head. "He stalked a girl in high school." He looked at Millicent. "After he'd gotten out of that mess, he seemed to calm down, until his senior year in college when he became obsessed with a fellow student."

Millicent pursed her lips. "He…he's always been an odd boy."

Blake raised his eyebrows. He eyed Millicent carefully. "Do you know the name of the girl?"

"Rebecca Walker," she said quietly. "Jeremy became upset when his father and I gently asked him if this young woman truly cared for him, or if he was only imagining that she did as he had with the girl from high school."

Blake's heartbeat quickened at the mention of Rebecca Adams's name. "What was his reaction?"

"He became verbally abusive toward us."

"Is Rebecca Walker the same woman who eventually married Nicholas Adams?"

Millicent's eyes narrowed. "I wouldn't know anything about her marriage. What I do know is that Jeremy was supposedly invited to a pre-graduation party last spring, and that happened to be the same night that Nicholas Adams was attacked at the party by an unknown assailant."

"Yes," Gilbert added. "I showed Jeremy the newspaper article about the attack. I brought his attention to the fact that the article stated that Rebecca Walker was the fiancée of Nicholas Adams. I assume that Rebecca Walker eventually married Nicholas Adams."

"How did Jeremy react when you showed him the article?"

"He became incensed, accusing the press of printing false information. He insisted that Rebecca Walker was his girlfriend."

Blake frowned. "There's a strange connection here," he said, scratching his jaw.

Thaddeus looked at the Talbots, then at Blake. "Can you share the connection, detective?"

"I'm working on some leads with Boston, and Rebecca Walker Adams has been the victim of a stalker since her senior year of college," he stated. "She continues to be stalked."

"You think it's Jeremy?" Gilbert asked.

"That's what we're trying to determine," the detective replied.

Gilbert's jaw nervously twitched as he eyed his wife. "I need to show you something," he said uncomfortably. He got up and walked quickly from the room. Blake watched him leave, then focused on Millicent. Her face flushed a deep red as she looked at Thaddeus, then at Blake.

"We found some journals Jeremy had been keeping. We didn't find them until after he'd gone," she said.

Thaddeus stiffened. "Can we see the journals?"

"I believe that's what my husband has gone after."

Gilbert walked back into the room with the notebooks. He looked at Millicent, seeing the fear in her eyes, the same fear he felt. Jeremy's journals painted an abusive and unstable upbringing by his parents. He'd documented every incident he could remember, and accurately and morbidly described his feeling of excitement at the sight of blood and the power he derived from it. He'd also filled book after book with vivid details of his imagined girlfriends and sexual unions with them. Other notebooks were filled with bizarre fiction encompassing the most gruesome forms of murder Gilbert could ever imagine. With shaky hands, Gilbert handed the notebooks to Blake, then sat down again next to his wife. He removed his glasses and wiped them with a tissue before putting them back on. Beads of perspiration dotted his forehead.

****

Jeremy slipped into the booth with a broad smile as April quickly made her way over to him. "Nice to see you."

"It's always nice to see you, April," he replied with a wide smile.

"What can I get you tonight, Nathaniel, besides coffee?"

she asked brightly. "Are you hungry?"

He nervously fiddled with a napkin. "I'd like to ask you something."

Her eyes filled with concern. "Of course, Nathaniel. You know you can ask me anything."

He gazed at her. "How long have I been coming in here now?"

"Over a month." Her eyes met his.

He nodded. "I've grown very fond of our conversations these past few weeks. I look forward to my nightly visits here, just to see you."

She grinned noticing his increasing nervousness. "Are you trying to ask me out, Nathaniel?"

He looked down at his hands.

She blushed self-consciously. "I'm sorry, I just assumed—"

He looked back up at her. "Yes," he answered in a low voice. "I'd like very much if you'd go out with me."

She squeezed his hand. "I'd like to, very much."

****

Thaddeus flipped through the pages of the notebooks, every so often stopping to read for a few minutes. Gilbert watched the various expressions appearing on the doctor's face, ranging from sympathy to horror. He wondered if Tate was thinking Millicent and he had done those horrific things to Jeremy. Would the doctor believe the words written by an obviously disturbed young man? Or would Tate assume they had nothing to hide since they relinquished the notebooks in the first place.

Millicent sighed heavily. "As you can see, Jeremy was an extremely ill child," she feebly explained. "He was a handful from the minute he was born."

Thaddeus eyed her sharply. "Did you know about his

204

obsession with blood?"

"I had no idea. We—" She looked at Gilbert.

He cleared his throat. His eyes met Tate's. "We knew for a very long time that our son was prone to erratic behavior, and that's why we brought him to you," he said accusingly. "We trusted his mental well-being to you, Dr. Tate."

Thaddeus returned Gilbert's cold glare. "I did everything I could to help him, but he always came back to his feelings of being unwanted."

"We've always been concerned with Jeremy's well-being," Gilbert defensively avowed.

"But did you love him?" Thaddeus demanded. "It goes beyond just providing the necessities of life. Did you make him feel protected and loved?"

A lone tear slid from the corner of Millicent's eye. "I tried," she whispered in a broken voice. "I really tried."

Gary Benson, who had kept silent during the meeting, now turned to Blake. "Look at this." He thrust the notebook at his partner, stabbing his finger at a passage. "No one knew any of this—except the murderer!"

Blake's eyes filled with revulsion as he read the paragraph. He cleared his throat, then held up the notebook. "This is a confession to the murders of Raney Clark, Sandy Williams, and Lily Tate."

Thaddeus gasped. "Jeremy murdered my wife?" he moaned. "Why?"

Millicent's eyes darted back and forth in her head. She grabbed Gilbert's arm as her heavy body swayed unsteadily. She opened her mouth to speak, but nothing would come, rendering her speechless as though her voice had dried up.

"Pull yourself together, Millicent," Gilbert ordered,

cautiously watching the detectives. "Jeremy's mindless ramblings don't prove anything. These notebooks are only works of fiction, and I refuse to allow my son to be implicated in these murders!"

Benson's eyes widened. "Are you blind? Have you read them?"

Blake leaned back in his chair. "Mr. Talbot, if you've read these books, which I'm certain you have, then you know that your son has described in vivid detail facts about these murders."

Gilbert grunted. "I don't believe it. Jeremy most likely wrote those stories based on information he'd picked up from the news. That's all."

"Jeremy expressed in his own words the power the sight of blood gave him. He described facts that only the police could know," Thaddeus said as he looked at Benson for confirmation.

"No one, not even the press, knew some of the details he vividly described in his writings," Benson replied. "We'll be requesting these notebooks as evidence."

Gilbert grew anxious. "Jeremy might be disturbed, but I will not believe he's capable of murder."

"What if he did it, Gilbert?" Millicent moaned. "He won't stop. It'll be an obsession just like those young women were."

Blake ran a hand over his chin. "Mr. Talbot, these notebooks will enable us to have your son arrested for the murders of Raney Clark, Sandy Williams, and Lily Tate."

Thaddeus looked at Bergan and opened his mouth to speak, but before he could utter a word, made a choking sound as he clutched wildly at his chest, gasping for air before slumping to the floor.

Chapter Twenty-Three

Jeremy inhaled deeply, then stood back in the shadows. After ten minutes Rebecca came out of the house, followed by Nicholas. Jeremy's jaw tightened as he watched Nicholas gently take Rebecca's elbow and protectively slip her arm in his.

He moved further back in the shadows as they passed, seemingly oblivious to him. He clenched his fists into tight balls, then abruptly turned on his heel and headed in the opposite direction.

He walked into Gretta's and over to the counter. "A cup of coffee, please," he said.

"I'm glad you're here, Nathaniel. I was hoping you'd stop in," April said uneasily.

"Is something wrong, April?" He sat down on a stool.

Her bottom lip trembled. "The murders, Nathaniel. Nowhere is safe anymore. The police don't know where he'll strike next. Haven't you been listening to the news? Everyone is on edge. I won't feel safe until that monster is caught."

He saw the fear in her eyes. "Yes, I have, and that's why I've come to safely escort you home," he said, smiling warmly.

"Thank you," she whispered, relieved. "My shift ends in about twenty minutes." She poured him a cup of coffee. "Will you be able to wait?"

He smiled again. "Of course. I'll just sit here and read the paper."

"Thank you," she said, patting his arm. "I feel so safe with you."

Jeremy sipped at his coffee, then picked up the newspaper. Occasionally he glanced at April as she bustled around the café, waiting on customers and wiping tables. He beamed contentedly. Everything any man could possibly want was his — money, fame, power and women — everything was his for the asking.

Except for Rebecca, the demons taunted.

He frowned. She *was* his. He was never far from her. His plan was set in motion. Time was on his side. He hated watching the way Nicholas had touched her. He had no right to put his filthy hands on Rebecca. She belonged to him, not Nicholas. In his heart he didn't blame Rebecca for her marriage to Nicholas. She had to have been forced. She was waiting for Jeremy to claim her. He would come to her like a knight upon a white horse, and they would ride off into the magical world he intended to show her. It was just a matter of time now. He closed his eyes, fantasizing about his life with Rebecca, when he felt a gentle hand on his arm.

"I'm ready, Nathaniel."

He opened his eyes, then slid off the stool and helped her into her coat. He silently escorted her from the café.

"You're very quiet tonight, Nathaniel. Is everything going okay with the new novel?" April asked. "I loved *Revenge*, and can't wait for the sequel."

He squeezed her elbow and for the next twenty

minutes talked about his work in progress. When he'd finished, they were standing outside of her apartment building—a large brownstone with beautiful columns leading into the main lobby.

"Would you like to come up for a cup of coffee?" she offered.

"That would be nice, April," he replied, following her inside.

Once inside her apartment, April scooped her kitten, Scootchie, into her arms. "She's grown since you've last seen her," she said with a laugh.

Jeremy tenderly stroked the calico feline's soft coat, enjoying the sensuous feel on his fingertips. "Yes, she has."

Scootchie purred, then leaped out of April's arms and scurried to the bedroom.

April motioned Jeremy to the sofa, then hurried into the kitchen to fix the coffee. Minutes later she handed him a steaming cup. "It's instant," she confessed, seating herself next to him.

He laughed. "Instant is fine. That's all I drink at home."

She cleared her throat and looked uncomfortably at him. "I enjoy spending time with you, Nathaniel."

"I enjoy your company too, April." He saw the strange expression that crossed her face. "Is something wrong?"

She hesitated as she stared into her coffee cup, then raised her eyes to his. "We've been seeing one another for quite a while now, and I don't know what type of relationship we really have." She set her cup on the coffee table. "You've never kissed me or made any advances toward me. Are we just friends, or are we building something more together?"

He set his cup next to hers, then took her small hands in his. "April, you must know by now how much I care for

209

you. You've become so important to my life." He sighed. "I've always been a loner and never gave much thought to developing friendships with too many people, but your friendship has enlightened my life. I wish I could give you more, but right now, with my career taking off, I don't have the time I would want and need to nourish a relationship that is anything deeper than friendship. Do you understand?"

"I understand," she quietly replied.

"April, I need you in my life." He stared into her eyes, seeing the embarrassment there. "This has nothing to do with you—you are a beautiful, intelligent young woman. I would never do anything to jeopardize our friendship."

"Please don't explain, Nathaniel." She smiled weakly. "I do understand the constraints on you right now."

"Thank you, April." He picked up his cup again. "I sense, though, that this serial killer has gotten everyone's nerves on edge."

She let her breath out in a rush. "It's frightening, and the police can't seem to find him. He could be anywhere at any time. He could be on the same bus as me, maybe has come to Gretta's, or he could even be living in this building for all I know. Now all the hype is that he's possibly originally from Pittsburgh because there were a series of murders there that match the details of the ones committed here." She trembled. "No one will be able to feel safe again until he's caught."

"He'll be caught when he wants to be caught," Jeremy replied.

April frowned. "What do you mean?"

"I meant that he'll slip up eventually. They always do."

We won't let you slip up, Jeremy, the demons hissed.

****

210

Thaddeus lay back on his fluffed pillows, looking distastefully around the drab hospital room. "I'm getting out of here in a couple of days."

Blake Bergan nodded. "Good. You gave us quite a scare."

Thaddeus laughed. "I gave myself quite a scare." His eyes grew serious. "Have there been any leads in Jeremy Talbot's whereabouts?"

Blake's forehead creased. "No. It's almost like he's disappeared into thin air. We've got APBs issued all over the country, but not one solid lead." He shook his head. "Still, the murders in Boston are mounting."

"You're convinced the murders in Boston are connected to those here?"

"Yes, all evidence points to the same person." He squinted. "And from what we read in those notebooks, my gut tells me it's Jeremy Talbot."

"I don't understand how Jeremy Talbot is able to elude this manhunt. It seems irrational in my thinking that someone hasn't seen him. He's not the type to just blend into a crowd." His eyes narrowed. "What about credit cards, bank accounts, or his social security number? Surely there has to be a record somewhere of some activity."

"Nothing. We've drawn a blank. He's obviously using a forged or stolen identity. But it's only a matter of time before we get him."

"Hopefully before any more innocent victims lose their lives to him."

****

Kenneth Owens scratched the stubble on his chin as he sipped a lukewarm cup of coffee.

"You look like hell," Gabe Jackson said as he threw a folder on the desk. "Did you even go home last night?"

"Yeah, but I couldn't sleep so I came in early." He stretched his arms and nodded at the folder. "What's that?"

"Results of the samples taken from Freddie Jones's body."

"And?" Kenneth cocked an eye.

He frowned. "They match the samples taken from the others."

"Dammit! How is this Jeremy Talbot eluding us? What are we missing?"

"He's always one step ahead of us. We've got to catch him, and soon. The city's becoming paralyzed with fear."

"I know, and it doesn't help with the heat we're taking because of the media hype."

Gabe slammed a fist on the table. "He's making a fool out of us, and he's using the media to do it." He pulled a picture of Jeremy Talbot from a file. "Look at this wimpy geek! Now how in hell can someone who looks like that hide from us? Someone must have seen him somewhere." He pointed to the window. "He's out there laughing at us. Sometimes I almost think he's right in the room next to us, then the minute we turn around, bam, he's off and running again." He punched a closed fist into his palm to emphasize his point.

Kenneth scratched his jaw. "We've got to protect Rebecca Adams. He knows her every move, so we know he's never far from her."

Gabe rolled his eyes. "I doubt we'll get the okay for around the clock police protection. The last time we did, Talbot never showed, not even once, though the letters and cards continued."

"It might have worked if the rookies assigned to the detail hadn't been so obvious." He smirked.

"All I know is that something better break soon."

"Have you been keeping in close touch with the Adams'?"

"Yeah, in fact, I talked to them last night. They're getting ready to move into their new home. I don't think they have much faith in us anymore though." He frowned. "But they do have a fresh stack of letters for us."

****

"Nick, the house is *so* beautiful!" Rebecca bubbled. "I can't believe it's really ours! It's so much more than I ever dreamed our first house would be." She affectionately squeezed his arm. "In a month we'll be moving in," she squealed.

He picked her up in his strong arms and twirled her around. "You deserve the best, Becky," he said tenderly. "I want you to always feel safe and secure." He checked the locks on the doors and windows. "I'm having the security company install an alarm system next week."

She touched his cheek. "He won't find us here, honey."

He shook his head, unconvinced. "I'd like to believe that, but he's somehow managed to track us down no matter where we go or what we do."

"This might sound strange, Nick, but I don't believe Jeremy Talbot would ever hurt me."

"I wish I felt the same," he stiffly replied.

CHAPTER TWENTY-FOUR

Jeremy stood outside of April's apartment building. The light from her window meshed in with the others, looking like a tiny speck surrounded by the illumination shining from the other windows. *That's how we all look*, he thought. *We're nothing but little specks all running around in this vast universe.*

He was deeply flattered that April found him worthy of her love. He still wasn't quite used to the new him and wondered if he ever would be. Even though he had changed his outward appearance, he knew that his inward self would always remain the same, all of the insecurities embedded into his soul forever.

If his heart hadn't already been given to Rebecca, April Hillard definitely would have a chance for his affections. She was a beautiful, fun-loving, vibrant woman, and he would forever cherish her friendship. But friendship was all he could ever offer her. As long as she continued her friendship with him and caused him no ill will, then he would allow no harm to come to her. She took away some of the loneliness he felt, and he didn't want to lose that.

Why don't you just do her in? the demons insisted. *You*

know how you crave to touch her. She wants you, Jeremy. She practically spread her legs for you tonight. All you had to do was take what she offered. Or are you afraid that you're not man enough – that's it, isn't it? They laughed.

"No!" he shrieked, covering his ears with his large hands.

A young couple passing by looked strangely at his odd behavior. The man hurriedly grabbed the woman's hand and quickly led her to the other side of the street.

Jeremy glanced at their departing backs, then removed his hands and stuffed them into his pants pockets. He slowly walked down the street with head bent low. His head began to pound around his temples. The headache was coming back. He swallowed hard. In a moment, the intense pain would almost blind him. He needed to get back to his apartment before the impending torture rendered him immobile.

****

April washed the coffee mugs and set them on the drain board. She bent down to pet Scootchie, who purred contentedly at her before running off to explore another room of the apartment. She sighed as she picked up her English Lit book, then settled herself at her kitchen table. Her mind refused to focus on her lesson, instead forcing her to turn her full attention to Nathaniel Cummings.

She felt foolish for practically throwing herself at him earlier. The embarrassment would stay with her for quite some time, she was afraid. He might even be romantically involved with someone else. After all, in the months she'd known him he'd never invited her to his home, even though she'd hinted several times for an invitation. But then, she reasoned, if he wasn't interested in her, why had he asked her out in the first place? She sighed again. Maybe it was only for companionship. All she knew for certain was that in the months since they'd met, she found herself hopelessly drawn to this peculiar man. His creativity and self-imposed discipline fascinated her. His long hours in total isolation were something she herself would never have been able to endure. She needed to be surrounded by people.

Several times her friends had questioned why Nathaniel never appeared with her at various social functions. She'd invited him but was always adamantly refused, his excuse being how large crowds made him uncomfortable. Her friends didn't understand his reasoning and gently tried to persuade her that maybe he wasn't the man for her. But their words couldn't deny what was in her heart—she'd fallen in love with him. She only hoped that maybe someday he would feel the same way about her. But if all he was able to offer at this point was only friendship, she would make certain she was the best friend he could ever hope for.

****

Jeremy stumbled onto a park bench. He panted, drawing sharp ragged breaths in as the pain in his head increased. The demons screamed and taunted him unmercifully. *Go back to April's apartment*, they insisted. *You know what she wants. Give it to her! After you do, you'll see that she's like all the others. She'll laugh at you. She's not your friend, Jeremy. She'll hurt you. Women bring nothing but pain. You're doing the world a favor by eliminating them one by one.*

"No!" he screamed. "April is my friend!" Hot tears streamed down his pallid cheeks. "Please leave me alone," he cried.

CHAPTER TWENTY-FIVE

Kenneth Owens stood over the partially clad body. A beige colored bra was neatly tied around the woman's broken neck. "Shit!"

Gabe Jackson walked over to him. "There's nothing here."

Kenneth looked down the alleyway, then sighed. "Are there any witnesses? Anyone hear anything unusual last night?"

"No." He looked at the body. "Just the guy who found her this morning. He's giving his statement right now."

"Talbot strikes again," Kenneth angrily retorted.

"When we catch that bastard, I'd like just five minutes alone with him."

Kenneth saw the fire in his partner's eyes. "Yeah, me too."

"I'd love to strangle the life right out of his body the way he did these women."

"We'll get him, Gabe," Kenneth vowed. "If it takes the rest of my life, we'll get him."

****

Jake Truman folded his hands, then rested them on top

of his desk. "Nathaniel, your next novel is due to come off the press in two months. I think it's important that you do a book promotion tour."

"My first novel has done very well in such a short time." He shrugged. "How are the advance orders for the new novel?"

"They're pouring in," he admitted.

"I'm selling books for you and making you a lot of money."

He looked skeptically at Jeremy. "The book tour will increase sales further."

"I've already given you my reasons why this tour is a bad idea. I'm not a public speaker. Large groups of people make me uneasy."

Truman was thoughtful for a moment. "If it's a matter of stage fright, then I'm sure something could be prescribed for you—"

"No! I do not believe in medications," he firmly stated. "I don't trust drugs. I need my mind clear and focused at all times. Any in-person interviews or television appearances will only be a detriment to my career. As you can attest, I express myself on paper much more eloquently than I ever could in person." He tapped the edge of the desk. "Look at the online interviews I did. They were very well-received."

Truman frowned. "Okay, I won't pressure you anymore at this time, but my gut instinct still tells me that you're hurting your career."

"We'll see," Jeremy replied. "I think my talent as a writer will take precedence over my ability as a public speaker." He smiled. "Who knows? Maybe I'll start a new trend. This mysterious author who doesn't grant interviews in person will intrigue people. I believe that it'll sell even more books in the long run."

Jake Truman gave him a stern look. "We'll try your angle, Nathaniel, but if it doesn't work, you'll go out on tour before the next book is released. Do we have a deal?" He extended a hand.

Jeremy nodded his consent. "It's a deal." He shook his publisher's hand.

Later, Jeremy sat at his computer, revising the last chapter on his novel. When he finished, he leaned back in his chair and stretched his cramped limbs. He was pleased with his work. His fans wouldn't be let down, and he was well on his way to fame and fortune. The words Professor Burgess had once said to him made him smile. He had proved that pompous idiot wrong. He could make it without showing his face in public. He fantasized about signing a copy of his book for Burgess, but that was impossible. Even if no one else knew about his success, he did, and soon Rebecca would as well.

****

Blake Bergan looked around the immaculate office. He thanked Candace Jermain for the cup of coffee she set before him and watched as she left the office, then focused on the large desk. "So, this is where Jeremy Talbot sat when you held your sessions with him?"

Thaddeus Tate let his breath out in a rush. "I should have delved deeper into his psyche. He was a kid in pain, and I ignored his obvious cries for help by believing every damned word his parents said about him."

"You can't blame yourself. You did what you thought was best at the time."

Thaddeus slowly shook his head back and forth. "No, if I would've listened to what that young boy had told me back then about the abuse from his parents, I may have been able to help him." He ran a hand over his eyes. "If I had, then maybe now we wouldn't be dealing with all of these murders."

"You had no way of knowing what Jeremy would do. Even if you did, that's no assurance that you may have stopped him from committing these murders."

"Shortly before Jeremy left Pittsburgh, he showed me scars on his body. Those scars weren't self-inflicted." He propped his head in his hands. "He wanted me to suffer as much as he was. He asked me once how I would feel if I lost someone close to me. I'll never get over losing Lily. I go through the motions, but life just doesn't mean the same without her."

Blake looked sympathetically at him. "How are your sons doing?"

"College keeps them occupied, and they're both attending out of state, so I really only see them during their breaks." His eyes glistened. "I know that the reason they don't come home often is because they can't face being in the house without their mother. They'll always be haunted by her death."

Blake had come to admire and respect Thaddeus Tate and wished he had some words of comfort to offer the man, but he knew there was nothing he could say. Thaddeus Tate was a broken man. He also knew that the shock of Lily's murder had been a contributing factor to his heart attack. Now as the detective looked at the man, he saw a shell of who Thaddeus Tate used to be. His once portly body was replaced by sagging skin, brought on by rapid weight loss. His eyes were dull, as though the life had gone out of them, and in a sense it had. Lily had been his life. That was obvious from every conversation he'd had with him.

Blake took a gulp of coffee. "How well do you think

you knew Jeremy Talbot?"

Thaddeus laughed bitterly. "I don't think he ever allowed anyone to get close enough to know him at all. He didn't trust anyone." His eyes narrowed. "Just between you and me, detective, I believe his parents are as much responsible for the murders as he is for not reporting the unusual things he was doing as a young child. Instead, they ignored it and verbally and physically abused him, compounding his fragile mental state. He disassociated from the world. That was the only way he could protect himself."

CHAPTER TWENTY-SIX

Rebecca cheerfully hummed a popular tune as she hung the living room drapes. She stood back to admire them. Nicholas's jeep pulled into the driveway and she smiled. She couldn't wait to show him what she'd accomplished while he was at the supermarket. The back door opened and she heard the rustling of grocery bags as he set his purchases on the kitchen counter.

Nicholas walked into the sun-drenched living room. "Looks like you've been busy," he said appreciatively as his gaze drifted over the new drapes. "They look very nice."

She glanced at him as her bottom lip began to tremble and tears silently rolled down her cheeks.

He was quickly at her side, wrapping his strong arms around her. "What's the matter, honey?" he asked.

"Nothing," she answered, swiping at her moist eyes. "I'm just so happy."

He laughed softly. "Sweetheart, you deserve to be happy."

Her eyes searched his. "Do you think we'll ever be free of Jeremy Talbot?"

"The police will get him. You're safe now. There's no way he knows our address."

She pulled an envelope from her back pocket and with a trembling hand gave it to him.

"What's this?" He took the letter out of the envelope and slowly read the words. "He's sick!" He looked at Rebecca.

She pointed to the envelope. "Look at the address, Nick."

He turned the envelope over. "How the hell did he find our address?"

****

"I'd like to purchase a house," Jeremy informed the realtor.

Tim Simons studied him for a moment. "Do you have a particular price range in mind?"

Jeremy smiled. "No, but I have a particular house in mind."

The man's thin lips curved slightly upward. "Which of our properties are you interested in?"

"The house I want isn't for sale, but I'd like you to make the owners an offer they can't refuse."

Simons' eyes narrowed. "I'm sorry, but I don't believe our company will be able to help you, Mr. Cummings." He started to rise.

"I could make it worth your while. There would be a nice bonus for you personally."

He sat back down. "Why is this particular house important to you?"

"It reminds me of the house I used to live in as a boy in upstate New York. There's not another one like it in the entire city. Call it sentimental reasons."

Simons rubbed his chin. "I don't know. I'll need some time to think about it."

Jeremy studied him as he took a cashier's check from

223

his breast pocket, holding it in eye range of the man. "Maybe this will change your mind. This is the personal bonus I was referring to."

Simons' eyes widened in surprise. Jeremy saw the greed in the man's beady eyes. Inwardly he laughed as he realized that money truly could buy almost anything.

"What's the catch?" His tightly drawn lips became moist with perspiration.

"You don't have to commit murder," Jeremy joked. When he saw the look of horror in Simons' eyes, he quickly added. "I'm joking of course. I'm a fiction writer. There's no catch, but I would like to keep this transaction strictly between us. The owners can't know who the purchaser is."

"Why?" he asked skeptically.

"I'm a very private man, and since I am becoming a well-known author, I'd like to keep as much privacy as I can."

"We have some lovely homes that may be better suited to a man of your means," Simons quickly said.

"I'm a simple man by nature, and this is the house I want. Nothing else will do."

He nodded. "I'll see what I can do, but I can't promise anything."

"Offer them twice as much as the house is worth." He placed the check back into his pocket. "When we close the deal, this check is yours."

****

"Look at this!" Nicholas raged. "That psycho jerk sent this to our home!"

Kenneth Owens read the letter as Gabe Jackson looked over his shoulder.

"How'd he know we'd moved?"

"He's obviously following you," Gabe said.

"That's quite apparent," Nicholas replied sarcastically. "What exactly are the police doing to catch him?" He threw his hands up. "I can't believe this! My wife is a walking target. Are you just going to sit back and wait until she becomes one of Talbot's victims?" His body shook with rage and fear combined.

"Calm down, Nicholas." Kenneth ran his hand through his hair. "We're doing everything we can possibly do. You've installed the security system, haven't you?"

He nodded. "Before we moved in." His nostrils flared. "You'd better hope you catch him before I do!"

Gabe laid a hand on his shoulder. "We'll get him. I promise you."

"He wants my wife. His sick mind thinks she belongs to him. I'm not going to sit around and wait for him to make his move."

"I know it doesn't seem like we're doing anything, Nicholas, but believe me, the entire country is searching for him. It's only a matter of time before he slips up," Kenneth stated.

"He's managed to avoid being caught so far, so please forgive me if I don't take much comfort in your words."

****

Thaddeus walked through the forlorn rooms of his house, ghosts of past joys held in this house flooding his mind as loneliness engulfed him. He could almost see Lily entering the room, a radiant smile on her face as she held her arms out to him. A tear slid from his eye. "God, Lily, I miss you so much!" he moaned. "I can't survive anymore," he cried.

When his tears subsided, he washed his face. His sons were due home shortly and he didn't want them to see him like this. It had been four months since T.J. and Tyler had last come home for a visit. He knew it was hard on them, and he saw the strain in their faces as they looked silently at the vacant seat at the dining room table. Thaddeus had attempted to get them to open up about their feelings, but whatever it was locked deep inside of them, they weren't ready to share — not yet. But he kept a watchful eye on them when they were home for the obvious signs of depression. He worried endlessly about them.

He knew they hadn't accepted their mother's death just as he hadn't. Since Lily's death, he'd been unable to sleep in the master bedroom and had moved his things to the guest bedroom. He hadn't stepped inside what had once been the room he and Lily had shared their love in — he couldn't bear to. He knew he had to clean out the room so he'd finally asked Marge to come over next week and sort through Lily's things. He couldn't do it.

He stepped into his office and looked at the stack of folders piled on the floor in a corner. Jeremy Talbot's life was displayed in those numerous files. He'd read and reread them several times, looking for anything that would give him some insight to Jeremy's murderous spree. He'd always known that he was like a volcano ready to erupt, but he'd felt that Jeremy's rage would be used against his parents or turned on himself if it ever did explode. At least the medication calmed things a bit, but he wondered if Jeremy had continued medication after he'd left the city. Jeremy's hatred toward his mother had warped his mind against women — all except for Rebecca Adams. He speculated about what had made her so special to him. He couldn't even hypothesize at this point if Jeremy would cause harm to the only woman he professed to love. In many ways Jeremy fit the profile of a serial killer and stalker, but in just as many ways he did not. He wondered where he was and what he was doing. He prayed that some innocent young woman hadn't moved him into her home, not knowing what this man was capable of.

"Hi, Dad."

Thaddeus turned to the open door. "T.J., it's good to see you!"

T.J. lumbered over to him, throwing his arms around his neck. "How are you feeling, Dad?"

Thaddeus saw the concern in his eyes. "As good as new," he exuberantly exclaimed.

T.J.'s eyes revealed the pain he was desperately trying to conceal as he looked around the office. "Tyler will be here shortly. I talked to him this morning."

"Good…good. Is there anything special you two want to do this weekend?"

T.J. grew uncomfortable and shifted his weight from one foot to the other. "We want to talk to you about some things, Dad."

"What is it, son?"

He slowly let his breath out. "I'd rather wait until Tyler gets here."

Thaddeus nodded. "Okay, but is everything all right in school?"

"Everything's great," he smiled.

The front door slammed. "Anybody home?"

"Your brother's here," Thaddeus said with a laugh. "In here, son!" he called.

Tyler appeared in the doorway and stood next to his brother. He gave Thaddeus a bear hug. "It's good to see you, Dad." He slapped T.J. on the back. "How's it going?"

"I've aced my psych test."

Thaddeus raised his eyes. "I should hope so!"

The boys laughed.

"Are you two hungry? I thought we could go out to dinner."

T.J. and Tyler exchanged glances. "Would it be okay if we just order a pizza or something tonight, Dad?" T.J. asked.

"Of course. Whatever you boys want." He looked sharply at them. "Is everything all right?"

"We just want to talk to you, Dad," Tyler said.

Thaddeus frowned. "You know you can tell me anything."

****

Gilbert Talbot put down the evening paper. "He's made the front page news again."

Millicent sighed heavily. "The hype will die down eventually, Gilbert."

"You don't have to go out into it every day," he reminded her. "I can't even get a damned cup of coffee without someone gawking at me or asking me how I feel about my son being a serial killer."

"It'll die down in time," she repeated.

He emphatically shook his head. "How can it? Haven't you been listening to the news?"

"It's not our fault," she insisted. "We tried to get him help. Thaddeus Tate is the one who is to blame."

"How can you say that?"

"We did the best we could do with him."

Gilbert frowned. "Did we?"

****

Thaddeus wiped his mouth on a napkin. "Okay, boys, you've been way too quiet all through dinner. Now tell me what's on your minds."

T.J. looked down at his hands. "We're worried about you, Dad. This house is so big for you."

He shrugged. "I have the cleaning service come in once a week. I do know how to cook, you know." He smiled. "Don't worry. I can take care of myself. You two have enough to worry about with your finals coming up."

Tyler scrutinized him. "I'll level with you, Dad."

Thaddeus raised his eyebrows. "I wish you would."

"T.J. and I are worried about you since the heart attack. Mom's death has been rough on all of us." He gulped and rapidly blinked. "We don't want you to blame yourself for Mom's death."

He squinted. "I never have blamed myself."

T.J. exhaled loudly. "Dad, you don't have to say the words, it's in your actions. You had no way of knowing Talbot would do this."

He swallowed hard. "Is that how I've been acting?"

He nodded. "Yes. We loved Mom too, but sometimes we feel that since she died, you have too." Tears filled his eyes. "You've shut us out completely without meaning to. We need to talk about Mom. It's time. She's been gone for a long time, and now that she's gone there are so many things we want to know about her. I can't speak for Tyler, but that's the only way I can cope with her death right now."

Tyler nodded. "I feel the same way, Dad. I want to know everything there is to know about Mom."

Thaddeus was silent for a few minutes. "I'm sorry, boys. All I've tried to do was protect both of you."

"You can't protect us from death, Dad," Tyler said quietly. "Is that why all of mom's things are still in her closets? As much as I wish she could, she's not coming back, Dad."

Thaddeus ran a shaky hand over his eyes. "Would you boys like to help me sort through some of your mother's things?" His eyes filled. "You're right. It's time."

****

Jeremy turned off the TV. He was the top news story again. He put his hands behind his head. *How stupid can everyone be?* he wondered. *Jeremy Talbot doesn't exist anymore.*

CHAPTER TWENTY-SEVEN

Present Day

Jeremy moved away from the window. Rebecca would be in Pittsburgh next weekend. She planned their reunion at the exact place they'd met. *How like her to be so romantic,* he thought. He'd forgive her for everything that Nicholas had forced her to do, including giving birth to those two brats.

The demons surrounded him. *Don't go,* they warned. *It's a trap!*

"No!" he shouted. "She loves me. We'll finally be together the way we were meant to be."

****

Julie Howard relished the familiarity of her bedroom. "You haven't changed a thing," she beamed, looking at her mother.

"I couldn't," she quietly answered. "Your father and I are grateful you could come home for a few days, honey. You know how fond your grandmother was of you." Tears sprang to her eyes. "Her only regret was not being able to spend much time with you these past fourteen years."

Julie threw her arms around her mother's neck. "She understood why my visits were so infrequent, didn't she,

231

Mom? Surely she knew how much I loved her."

Her mother patted her back. "She knew, Julie, but it didn't make your absence any easier on any of us, especially when we learned that Jeremy Talbot was responsible for murdering all those women here and in Boston. We worry so much about you." She shuddered. "Who would think he was a serial killer?" She hugged her tightly as though she were afraid to let go. "We should have pressed charges on him back then."

"We had no way of knowing what he would evolve into, Mom. They'll catch him," she said, masking her own fear for her mother's sake.

"I hope so," Mrs. Howard answered, unconvinced.

Julie squeezed her mother's hand. "I'd better get a shower."

She nodded. "Yes, we have to be at the funeral home at six."

"It'll be okay, Mom."

She nodded again, then left the room.

Julie took a leisurely shower, then dressed and joined her parents downstairs.

"Julie, I need to speak to you," her father solemnly said.

She raised her eyebrows. "What is it, Dad?"

He frowned. "I want you to be extra cautious while you're here."

She looked hesitantly at him. "I'm always cautious, Dad." She assumed his worry had to do with his mother's sudden death in a car accident and the realization of how quickly a loved one could be snatched from you in the blink of an eye.

He tenderly laid a hand on her shoulder and looked into her eyes. "I know you're a grown woman, but I can't help but worry since the police believe that Jeremy Talbot may show up in Pittsburgh this weekend."

Her eyes widened as her heart suddenly lurched. Her throat dried out. "Here?" she whispered. "Why would he come back here?"

"The police called while you were in the shower. They're warning everyone he may have a vendetta against."

She slowly shook her head back and forth. "I don't believe it. It doesn't make sense that he would come back here after all these years. That's insane." She saw the anxious look that passed between her parents. "Is there something else you're not telling me?"

"Julie, the police believe that Jeremy may now be tracking down everyone whom he believes ever wronged him." He wrung his hands. "God only knows how many women he's murdered."

"But why this weekend?"

"It's the tenth year anniversary of his college graduation."

Her eyes narrowed. "Okay, let me get this straight. The police haven't been able to track down this monster for the past ten years, and now they believe he may show up this weekend and waltz right into his class reunion as though nothing has happened?"

Her father frowned. "I know it doesn't make any sense. All I know for certain is that whether or not the police have information they're not releasing to us, we need to take every precaution. I don't want you going anywhere alone. Promise me."

"I promise, Dad."

"I doubt he'll even give Julie a second thought since he's been obsessed with this Rebecca Walker Adams for the past ten years," her mother quickly interjected.

"Just the same, I won't rest until he's caught." He studied his daughter's reaction. "You can't hide your fear from your family, Julie. We know how Jeremy Talbot has destroyed your peace of mind ever since that incident in high school."

She fidgeted. "Yes," she confessed. "My life hasn't been the same, and I don't think it ever will be while he's out there roaming free." She smiled weakly. "But I have grown to love California almost as much as I love Pittsburgh."

Her father's face relaxed. "Maybe someday you'll find a man you can trust. I know it's been difficult for you as far as relationships are concerned."

"Maybe someday you'll even give your father and me a grandchild," her mother said with a wink.

Julie smiled. "Uh-oh, is this going to be the speech about how my biological clock is ticking? I do have time...I'm only thirty-two."

Mrs. Howard lifted an eyebrow. "We can hope, can't we?"

Julie's eyes filled. "I was going to wait for a more appropriate time to tell you, but, yes, I have met someone special. We've been seeing each other for almost eight months now. I didn't want to say anything until I was sure where the relationship was heading." She bit her bottom lip. "I wish Gram could have met him. He wanted to come with me."

"Oh, honey, we're so happy for you." her mother said. "You should have brought him with you."

"I don't want you to meet him at such a sad time."

"We understand. Does this special man in your life have a name?" her father asked.

"Bill Parker. He's a forest ranger."

Her father nodded approvingly. "I'll look forward to

meeting him."

"Maybe in the not-too-distant future we'll be hearing wedding bells," her mother replied.

****

Jeremy smiled as he snapped his overnight bag shut. In less than forty-eight hours, he and Rebecca would be together, finally. He grinned, anticipation welling in his chest. He picked up his bag and exited his house. The taxi he had ordered was waiting for him.

He placed his bag in the back of the taxi, then settled himself inside next to it. He punched in April's work number on his cell phone. "Hello, April," he said to her voice mail. "I've got to go out of town for a few days and will be in touch when I return." He clicked off the phone, then settled back in his seat for the remainder of the ride to the airport.

Later in his hotel room, he ate a solitary dinner of steak, a baked potato, and a green salad. He looked out the window at the view of downtown Pittsburgh, observing how nothing much seemed different, yet everything changed so much in his ten-year absence. Pittsburgh, his birth city, still held no roots for him, not that Boston did either, but with Rebecca he would finally have the roots he longed for. They would move far from everyone they'd ever known, and both their lives would begin fresh, as fresh as the love they would finally be able to share.

He walked over to the mirror, studying the reflection that stared back at him. The man in the mirror was a stranger. He was attractive, with natural-looking blond hair and eyebrows, and the contact lenses he wore gave the illusion of a pair of beautiful clear blue eyes. The neatly trimmed beard and mustache gave him an air of distinction.

Three hours later he stood outside the Curtis Funeral

Home, watching as the mourners exited the building. He saw Mr. and Mrs. Howard still looking as pompous and self-righteous as he remembered them. Julie walked a few steps behind them, and he kept a close eye on her as she stopped to briefly chat with an elderly woman.

Julie hadn't changed much, he noted, except to become even more beautiful than she already had been. She still wore her hair long and loose. Her girlish curves had matured into the figure of an alluring woman. It would be exciting to seek the jewel between her legs and unlock the joyous wonders within. He licked his lips, then quickly remembered what she had done to him. She'd had her chance. His heart now belonged to only Rebecca.

The demons laughed. *Julie Howard was the beginning of your downfall. Don't ever forget that. She played you for all you were worth! She made a fool out of you and your love for her.*

"Yes," Jeremy whispered. "Now she must pay. The past needs to be closed before Rebecca and I can live together in peace." He hadn't known about the death of Roberta Howard until he'd read it on his computer, along with the rest of the daily Pittsburgh news, which was delivered to his e-mail every morning. He marveled at his good fortune. How auspicious for him that Julie would be in Pittsburgh the same weekend as his college reunion. Now he wouldn't have to track her down in California.

"It's a sign," he said. "Destiny is preparing the stage for mine and Rebecca's permanent union."

****

Professor Jeffrey Burgess finished reading the last page of *Revenge 5*. He set the book on the coffee table, completely satisfied with the outcome of the murder mystery. As an avid murder mystery fan, he'd been spellbound with Nathaniel Cummings' ability to pull a reader into the story without the reader realizing he'd been hooked. He admired the author's style and flair with words. Cummings was indeed a rare talent.

Ever since he'd read the first novel, he'd been haunted with the familiarity of the author's technique, wondering where he'd read his work before. He picked the book up and turned it over. As usual, there was no photograph on the dust jacket, and a very vague author biography stating only the man's birth state and his love of writing. He thought it odd that Nathaniel Cummings had been published for almost ten years now and still no picture on any of his books. He'd read once that Cummings was an eccentric man who refused to grant interviews or have his privacy invaded, and that he chose to live in seclusion. *He certainly is an ambiguous man*, Jeffrey thought. He racked his brain trying to remember where he'd read this man's work prior to his novels. He wouldn't be able to rest until he found the answer.

CHAPTER TWENTY-EIGHT

Millicent Talbot wearily sank onto the sofa. She picked up the remote control and flipped through several channels, finally settling on a cooking program.

Gilbert sat across from her reading his newspaper and every so often offered an unasked comment on the world's events.

The ringing of the doorbell startled them both, but not for the obvious reasons. No one ever called on the Talbots, especially since their son was the focus of a nationwide manhunt. Gilbert had even taken an early retirement to avoid the constant harassment he received everywhere he went. The curious looked at him with pity in their eyes, others with hatred, seeming to blame him for bringing a cold-blooded murderer into the world. The media had hounded him relentlessly until he felt pressured into going to his employer to seek a solution. His employer was only too happy to grant his request of an early retirement, and he supposed that they too were becoming uncomfortable with his unwanted publicity and were relieved with his offer to leave the company. In the end, he graciously accepted the more than generous retirement package they offered. They rarely went out anymore except when necessary. They'd been forced into a life of seclusion.

He peered at Millicent over the top of his newspaper. "Who could be calling at this time of night?"

"Probably reporters since the news thinks Jeremy will show up in Pittsburgh this weekend because of his college reunion," Millicent said.

"I doubt he'd ever come back here. I'll get rid of whoever it is." He set his newspaper down, then walked to the door with Millicent at his heels. "Who's there?" he called through the double bolted door.

"Mr. Talbot, I have some information about your son, Jeremy."

"I'm not interested. Please, just go away and leave us alone. I'm fed up with you media types. You people have done nothing but destroy our lives!"

"I'm not a reporter or from any media contact."

"Well, whatever it is you're after, I'm not interested, so please go away and leave us be."

"Do you know where your son is?"

"I haven't seen him for over ten years, and I don't care to ever again. Furthermore, if I had any inkling as to his whereabouts, I would immediately pass that information on to the police. I'm sure you're aware of the fact that he is wanted."

"I know where he is."

Gilbert froze. He looked at Millicent, whose skin tone had turned ashen. "Then you need to quickly give that information to the police," he replied.

"I'd like to talk to you first. It's important."

"Just go away," Gilbert insisted. "I have nothing to say and certainly nothing I want to hear from you about Jeremy. He can rot in hell!"

"I'm a close friend of his. I think you'll be interested in what I have to tell you about your son. I promise I'll only take five minutes of your time. You need to hear me out. It's in your best interest."

Gilbert looked questionably at Millicent. She shrugged. "Only five minutes," he said, opening the door. "Then you get your ass off my property."

****

"He's out there somewhere right now. I can feel it," Blake Bergan stated. "He's closer than we think."

Gary Benson set a fresh mug of coffee in front of him. "What makes you so sure?"

"Call it a hunch. It's the ten-year reunion of his college graduation this weekend. If he still has an ax to grind with anyone from the class, he'll show up. Besides, Rebecca Adams is here in Pittsburgh—without her husband."

Gary's jaw dropped.

Blake eyed him. "Don't worry, she's well protected."

"What about Thaddeus Tate and the Talbots?"

"Thaddeus is in Seattle for a few weeks. Wouldn't the capture of Jeremy Talbot be a nice welcome home gift for him? We're going to send someone over to watch the Talbot house. All we can do now is sit back and wait for Talbot to make his move, then we'll nail his sorry ass."

Gary leaned forward. "It's been ten long years. The minute we knew it was Jeremy Talbot, I thought we had him. I never dreamed it would take all these years, ten long years of him making fools of us all."

"I'm glad I'm single, or I believe my marriage wouldn't have survived." He nodded at Benson. "But you managed to court a very beautiful woman and ended up marrying her. So give an old bachelor like me some advice. How do you manage with this crazy schedule?"

Gary laughed. "Lots of good loving when I get home. And it doesn't hurt that she has as many crazy hours as I do in the law firm. We complement one another."

"I'll keep that in mind the next time I decide to ask someone out. After her obvious qualities, I'll make sure she has a job with odd hours."

Gary grinned. "It helps."

Blake exhaled loudly. "It's going to be a long weekend. Are you ready to join the reunion festivities?"

"I've been waiting ten years to get that bastard."

****

Gilbert suspiciously eyed the young man. "Something about you seems vaguely familiar. Have we met before?" he sternly asked.

He grinned. "You don't recognize your own son, Father?" He tipped his cap to Millicent. "How've you been, Mother dear?" His eyes swept over her frame. "Still have a weight problem, I see."

"Jeremy?" Millicent clutched her chest. "Where…where have you been all these years?"

"Writing novels. Certainly you've head of Nathaniel Cummings. He's a world-renowned literary genius. Very mysterious and eccentric from what I hear." He glared at Gilbert. "Of course, you never held much stock in my writing abilities, now did you? Didn't you once say that I needed to find a real job?" He smirked. "I make more money in a year than you've made in your lifetime!"

Gilbert wiped the sweat from his brow. "Why have you come back now?"

"To take care of some unfinished business. Besides, it's my ten-year college reunion. Rebecca and I have a big weekend planned."

"Rebecca? But Rebecca is happily married with two

young sons," Millicent protested. "Certainly you must know that."

"Shut up about Rebecca," he barked. "You don't know anything. She's never been happy since we were torn apart. She's been patiently waiting for me all these years."

"Jeremy, you need help. Please call Dr. Tate. He's helped you in the past."

His eyes flashed. "I don't think Thaddeus Tate would want to speak to me, as much as I would love to tell him how skillful a lover his wife was. I'll never figure out what she saw in a fat slob like him." He smacked his lips. "Am I shocking you, Father?"

Millicent fearfully gripped Gilbert's arm. "Jeremy," she hoarsely whispered. "Did you murder all of those women here and in Boston? We can get a lawyer. You can plead insanity. You do know that the police are looking for you, don't you?"

"You didn't recognize me. For ten years no one has, so I doubt the police will either. He glared at her. "I had no choice with those women. Their own stupidity got them killed. They asked for it."

Gilbert's mouth dropped open. He removed Millicent's hand from his arm, then quickly turned on his heel and dashed to the telephone. As his hand closed around the receiver, he felt the phone being torn from his grip.

"I told you and Mother to get in the real world. Too bad you don't have cell phones." Jeremy kept his focus on Gilbert as he ripped the phone wire from the wall, then instantly turned his attention to Millicent, who had a trembling hand on the doorknob. "Don't even think about it," he warned.

"Get out!" Gilbert demanded.

Jeremy laughed. "Oh come on, Father. I thought that

you, Mother, and I could have a nice little visit. We'll have our own reunion. After all, ten years is a long time to be separated. Haven't you two ever wondered or cared about what had happened to your only child?"

Millicent swallowed hard. "What do you want from us?" she weakly asked.

He coldly eyed her. "To kill you, what else?" he calmly replied. He walked closer to her.

She kept her death grip on the doorknob, but his icy cold hand clamped down on her arm. He motioned to Gilbert. "Sit on the sofa." His fingers dug into Millicent's fleshy arm until she relinquished her hold on the doorknob. "That's better," he said. "Now get over there and sit next to him."

"Why are you doing this?" she moaned. "We're your parents, for God's sake! We gave you life!"

He sneered. "That's a good one, Mother. When did you two ever give a fuck about me? Not since my earliest memory. You made my life a living hell." His eyes flared. "Now I'm going to give you a taste of what you've both done to me!"

****

Rebecca smiled. "I wish you were here, Nick. It's not going to be the same without you. I should've stayed home with you, or at the very least, you should have come to the reunion. After all, everyone will want to see what the most handsome jock in college looks like today."

He laughed. "They'll all envy me when they take a look at you. I want you to relax and have fun, honey. I wish I was there too, but the doctor says at least one more day in bed for Ricky."

"How's he doing? I shouldn't have left him."

"Becky, he'll be fine. He's playing cards right at this

moment with Riley. I promised the boys that tonight I'll bring the TV into the bedroom and we'll watch some videos together. We're going to have a real men's weekend, with no woman around to tell us to pick our socks off the floor or to clean up the house."

She chuckled. "I don't know what I'd do without you, Nick."

"I couldn't do any of it without you, Becky. You've been through so much these past ten years with that psycho Talbot stalking you. At least you can breathe a little easier this weekend without having to constantly look over your shoulder."

****

Jeremy cocked his head. *Do it now, Jeremy, take all that pain and give it back to them. They never loved you. You were a mistake! Do it!* "Yes," Jeremy answered. "Yes, you two hated me from the moment of my conception." His eyes traveled to his mother. "You thought you had a gem between your legs." He laughed. "But dear old Dad here found his jewels between the legs of the cheap whores he fucked every night when you thought he was working late at the office."

Gilbert jumped to his feet. "Get out of here now, you dirty bastard! You're no son of mine!"

Jeremy stood menacingly in front of him. "I'm not afraid of you," he said quietly. "Now sit your bony ass back down."

Gilbert pushed past him. "I'm getting you the help you need."

Jeremy placed a heavy hand on his father's thin shoulder. "You're not going anywhere."

Gilbert pushed his hand aside. "How dare you!"

"How dare I?" His eyes smoldered as he placed both hands around his father's neck. "Do you know how easily I could snap your scrawny neck…just like a pencil?"

Millicent screamed. "Gilbert, please sit back down!"

Jeremy turned to her. "Nice show of compassion for your husband, Mother, but it's a little too late."

****

Nicholas answered his cell phone. "Hello," he said, eyes riveted on the movie he was watching with his sons. With his free arm he absentmindedly ruffled his son Ricky's hair.

"This is Detective Kenneth Owens."

He removed his eyes from the TV screen. "What can I do for you, detective?"

"We have reason to believe that Jeremy Talbot may show up in Pittsburgh this weekend for the reunion. I want to alert you and your wife in the event you may be attending."

Nicholas's jaw twitched. "Can you hold on a minute? I want to take this call in another room."

"Of course, I'll hold."

Nicholas looked at his sons. "I'll be right back, boys. I have to take this call."

"Okay, Daddy," they answered in unison.

Nicholas walked to the master bedroom. "I'm sorry for the wait, Detective Owens. Why do the police think that Talbot will show his face in Pittsburgh?" he nervously asked.

"That would be the perfect opportunity for him to make his move."

"It doesn't make any sense. He's been in Boston all these years, as far as we know. He'd be a fool to go back to Pittsburgh."

"Are you and Rebecca planning to attend the reunion?"

Nicholas scratched his head. "No, I'm staying home.

Our son isn't feeling well. Becky went to Pittsburgh this morning. I thought it would be good for her to get away for a few days."

"Where's she staying?" Owens asked.

"With some old college friends of ours—Brian and Annie Chambers."

"Please give me the address and I'll notify the Pittsburgh authorities."

"He's made no threats to harm Rebecca. All his cards and letters ever say is how much he loves her and is waiting for the day when they can be together. In all these years he's never made a move to hurt her. We've gone on with our lives and are just waiting until the day we hear he's been arrested."

"Detective Jackson and I have been going over Talbot's pattern. He's always one step ahead of us where your wife is concerned. He knows every move you two make or are planning to make. We strongly believe that he may follow your wife to Pittsburgh."

****

Jeremy looked around the living room. He walked over to the dangling phone wire and snapped it out of the phone. "Tie her up!" he ordered.

"You're insane," Gilbert retorted.

Jeremy laughed. "Maybe it's genetically passed down from my parents." His eyes blazed. "I'll give you ten seconds to do it or I'll do it myself!"

"No, please, Jeremy, we can work this out," Millicent panted. "I...I—" she broke off sobbing.

"Shut up!" He grabbed Gilbert and pushed him roughly toward Millicent.

Gilbert nervously held the cord in his hand. "I'm sorry, Mill."

CHAPTER TWENTY-NINE

Cassi threw her arms around Rebecca. "It's so good to see you! I've missed you so much!"

Rebecca hugged her. "I've missed you too, Cassi. Where's Luke?"

"He's gone off with Brian. I think they're reliving their old jock days. They're both disappointed that Nicholas wasn't able to attend."

"I know. I felt guilty coming without him." She sighed wistfully. "It's not the same without him here."

"We'll have to get together soon and have our own reunion," Annie suggested. "After all, our kids should get to know each other better. Who knows, they may become good friends like we have," she said with a grin.

"That's a great idea!" Rebecca smiled. "We should definitely plan something for late summer. The guys would love it." She looked at her two friends. "Who would think we'd all be married to our college sweethearts and have little clones of Nicholas, Luke, and Brian running around?"

Cassie laughed. "It is odd that not one of us has given birth to a girl."

Annie winked playfully. "I'll bet the guys planned that

too."

"How is everything, Becky?" Cassi asked. "I mean, with everything in the news about Jeremy Talbot. How are you handling it?"

Rebecca drew a deep breath. "I'm terrified, but I don't let on to Nick how scared I really am. I think he knows though, because I can't hide anything from him." She looked around the campus. "Sometimes it's hard for me to actually believe that Jeremy is capable of committing such horrifying crimes."

Annie's facial muscles tightened. "Who would imagine him to turn out to be a cold-blooded murderer?" She trembled. "It's uncanny, remembering the picnic at High Ground Park."

Rebecca nodded. "I know. Ever since we've found out the truth about Jeremy, I've wondered if he was the one who attacked Nicholas that night."

Annie's brow puckered. "The odds would point to him, since you know that he is obviously the one who's been sending all those letters to you."

"He's never threatened me." She flashed a weak smile. "It's a relief to know that I'm far away from him, for a few days anyway."

****

Jeremy shoved Gilbert toward the kitchen. "Go on," he ordered.

"What are you going to do to him?" Millicent screamed.

He shot his mother an icy look. "You'd better shut your mouth right now," he warned. "Move!" He placed his hands on his father's bony back and pushed him roughly, almost knocking Gilbert off balance.

Jeremy pulled open cabinets and drawers, finally grabbing a roll of duct tape and some twine. Gilbert's eyes

248

narrowed. "What are you going to do?"

He ignored the question as his gaze swept around the room, then settled on the knife rack. He pulled out a butcher knife seeming transfixed on its sharp shiny blade.

Gilbert's eyes widened with fear. "No," he choked. Perspiration ran down the sides of his worn face.

"Get back in the living room."

Gilbert stumbled into the room, his body quivering as he made his way to the sofa.

"Don't hurt us," Millicent pleaded. Her eyes focused on the butcher knife in her son's hand. "No!" she shrieked.

"Shut your mouth!" He unrolled a long piece of duct tape and cut it with the knife, then walked over to her and stood menacingly in front of her. "You don't listen, do you Mother?" He put the tape over her mouth and watched as she tried to work the tape loose. He laughed, turning to his father. "At last, silence. Doesn't it feel wonderful, Father? Bet you wished you would have thought of this years ago."

Gilbert's eyes darted back and forth. Jeremy noticed that they looked like tiny little marbles rolling around in his head. "Just leave, Jeremy. We won't say a word. No one will know that you're in Pittsburgh."

"I don't make deals." He stared at them for a few minutes. "Untie her."

Millicent's eyes became calm. Gilbert nodded, relief flooding through him. "Thank you."

Jeremy sneered. "Oh, don't thank me, Father. The fun is just about to begin."

****

Blake Bergan strolled around the campus, keeping his eyes peeled for any sign of Jeremy Talbot. He looked at a trio of attractive women laughing and chattering, spotting Rebecca Adams among them. He scanned the groups surrounding her but saw no sign of Talbot. He watched Benson making his way through the crowd.

****

Julie Howard hugged her parents. "Don't wait up for me. I'll be fine."

Her mother's brow creased. "Please tell Mindy to walk you to the door when she drops you off."

She rolled her eyes. "Mother, please stop worrying." She gave her another hug. "I'm no longer allowing Jeremy Talbot to control my life. He's haunted me for fourteen years, and now I'm putting an end to it. I'm not going to fear him any longer."

Even though she wanted to believe her last statement, it wasn't true. She would always fear him, but she needed to get some control back in her life. He'd taken so much from her, but ever since she'd met Bill, she was slowly regaining her trust in men again, instead of living in her own little cocoon afraid of the world.

Her father sighed heavily. "Why don't you and Mindy visit here? I think it will make your mother feel better."

"I haven't seen her in years, Dad. She's invited me to meet her family."

"I understand, but I want you to promise us that you will give us a call when you're on your way home."

She laughed. "Dad, I feel like I'm sixteen again and hearing your lecture before going on my first date."

He squeezed her shoulder. "Just be careful, honey."

"I promise."

Mindy's car pulled to the curb. "Hello, Mr. and Mrs. Howard," she called from the opened window.

They waved as Julie hurried to the car.

****

Gilbert handed the phone cord to Jeremy.

"Get over here," Jeremy motioned to his mother, who was stretching her cramped limbs.

She put her hands to her mouth and gently endeavored to loosen the tape.

"Leave the tape on," he ordered. He cut another length of tape and placed it over Gilbert's mouth. He turned to Millicent. "Now tie him up."

Millicent reluctantly took the phone cord and wrapped it around Gilbert's upper body, pinning his arms tightly to his sides.

When she finished, Jeremy pulled on the cord, then tightened it. Gilbert winced. "Now tie his feet together." He cut a piece of twine and handed it to her, then watched as she secured his feet.

The demons surrounded him, hissing excitedly. He was too tired to fight them off anymore. *Do it, Jeremy. Take the knife and cut them to little tiny pieces. Make them bleed! Every drop of blood that flows from them will be your revenge!*

Jeremy closed his eyes, then popped them back open. The headache was back with an intensity that almost caused him to vomit. He rubbed his temples. *Do it now before it's too late!* He stared coldly at his mother. "Get over here." he said, motioning to her with the knife. "Now!"

****

Jeffrey Burgess sipped a glass of wine as he ran a search on his computer. After an hour of ineffective searching, he gave up trying to find any information on Nathaniel Cummings. The man remained a mystery.

He skimmed through his set of *Revenge* books, looking for any clues that would help him learn where he'd read this man's work previously. As he skimmed familiar sections of the book, recognizable slices of prose popped out at him. He grabbed a notebook and pen and rapidly wrote down the familiar passages. He wondered why these books seemed to jog his memory.

He took a sip of his wine and as he set the glass back down, the thought struck him to check his files. Over the years he'd saved the essays and stories that had shown literary promise, with the hopes that if the authors ever became famous he could take even a small amount of pride in knowing that he'd helped guide them.

He pulled some folders from his desk drawer, scanning through the contents of his former students' prose and tried to recall the student. He wondered how many of them had actually chosen writing as a career. Once in a while, a former student would send him a clip of a published article or short story published in a literary magazine, but he'd never known any of them attaining best-selling status with a book.

He grabbed a folder marked "Jeremy Talbot." He leaned back in his chair, remembering the pathetic young man. He had to concede, though, that Jeremy was a talented writer, even though Burgess had never told him. He hadn't liked Talbot. He rubbed him the wrong way. He was an odd man, was so unkempt and timid that Burgess didn't believe the literary world was something Talbot could ever cope with, no matter how good his writing was. Burgess prided himself on his appearance and well-spoken language. He believed it was as important to be able to carry on a conversation as it was to put those same thoughts on paper. He'd lose respect for anyone in a moment if he'd read them and was taken with their prose, only to find out that in conversation he or she was a bumbling idiot, barely able to talk in complete sentences. That was the way he remembered Talbot, tripping and stumbling over the eloquent prose he'd composed while alone.

Burgess liked to push his students to the edge. Those few dedicated souls who had the drive and ambition to stick it out learned not only the basics of good storytelling, but also how to motivate themselves. He read through some of the essays and short stories written by Jeremy Talbot, then suddenly stopped and grabbed his notepad. He compared the passages he'd copied from *Revenge* to a couple of short stories. His eyes bulged when he saw that the passages were the same, word for word. His pulse raced as the awareness came over him that Nathaniel Cummings was actually Jeremy Talbot, the most sought after man in the country.

Chapter Thirty

Julie Howard stepped out of Mindy's car and waved to her friend as she drove off. When she saw the bright light shining in the living room window, she laughed to herself. She expected to see the night-light in the small entrance porch, but not the living room light. She filled her lungs with the fresh nighttime air as she looked up gazing into the star-studded sky. A light breeze rustled the branches of the large oak tree that stood in the front lawn. A branch gently tapped the bedroom window. Julie watched it for a few seconds, remembering how that same branch had tapped the window when she was safely tucked in bed every night. She knew every inch of that tree, having climbed it when she was a child and her mother gently coaxing her down.

She missed Bill. She could barely wait to show him off to her parents, knowing they would wholeheartedly approve. She wished her grandmother could have met him, but in a strange way she felt that she would. She saw a bright twinkling star. "Good night, Grandmother," she whispered.

For the first time in a long time, she felt truly happy

and contented with her life. She'd been despondent when she'd left Pittsburgh, but California had become her home now, and meeting Bill made everything right again. She felt safe and secure in his love. His wonderful sense of humor and gentleness made her fall even more in love with him.

She strolled up the walk to her house, lost in her thoughts about Bill. Suddenly a large hand clamped over her mouth. She struggled against her attacker, gnashing his hand with her teeth as she furiously kicked at him. Then she was dragged backward, away from the sidewalk. "No" she tried to scream as he continued to drag her to the secluded, darkened backyard.

****

"I need to talk to someone immediately," Jeffrey Burgess said to the desk sergeant. "It's about the Jeremy Talbot case."

Sergeant Daniels suspiciously eyed him. "Jeremy Talbot?"

"Yes. I believe he's been using an alias all these years, and that he's really Nathaniel Cummings."

Daniels looked skeptically at him. "Do you know how many people we get in here claiming to have information about Jeremy Talbot?" He chuckled. "We even had one guy claiming to be Talbot." He propped his elbows on the counter. "Now tell me why I should believe you?"

"I'm serious, dammit!" Burgess stated. "Lives are in danger, so please let me speak to whomever is in charge of the investigation."

****

Blake Bergan signaled Gary Benson and walked to a distant corner.

"What's up?"

Blake's jaw tightened. "There's a new lead. It looks like

Talbot's been using an alias for the past ten years."

Gary's eyebrows shot up. "An alias?"

He nodded. "The famous writer Nathaniel Cummings."

"What?" Gary asked as his jaw dropped. "Do you know what kind of heat we're going to take by fingering Nathaniel Cummings? We could be facing a lawsuit here if it's not him."

"I said the same thing, but there's irrefutable evidence."

He cocked an eye. "If it's true, then it only stands to reason that he's altered his appearance to match his new name. Which would mean that for the past ten years he's been making a fool out of everyone. He's been right under our noses."

He nodded again. "Yes, but unfortunately no one seems to have a photograph of Nathaniel Cummings, so we have no idea what he looks like."

"The party's wrapping up for tonight." He shook his head. "We wouldn't know Talbot if he was standing right next to us," Gary said disgustedly.

"We've got to alert Rebecca Adams about this new development and give her full police protection."

****

Kenneth Owens nearly dropped the phone. "You're telling me that Jeremy Talbot is Nathaniel Cummings?"

"Yes. We're putting out an APB on Nathaniel Cummings as we speak," Blake Bergan said. "I'll be in touch."

Owens set the phone down, slowly shaking his head from side to side as he turned to Gabe Jackson. "You're never going to believe this."

****

"Do you know the occupant of the house next door?"

Nicholas squinted. "No, just some eccentric guy who

lives alone." He rubbed his sleep-filled eyes. "What's going on?"

Owens laid a hand on his shoulder. "You're not going to believe this, Nicholas. May we come in?"

"Sure." He motioned Detectives Owens and Jackson into his home.

****

Jeremy kept his hand clamped over Julie's mouth. "I'm only going to say this once," he hissed close to her ear, "so you'd better pay close attention." He tightened his hold on her thin waist. "When I remove my hand, if I hear so much as a peep out of you, I swear I'll not only kill you, but your parents as well." He guardedly removed his hand.

"Please don't hurt me," she pleaded. "If you want money, here's my purse."

"I don't want your money."

"What...what do you want?" she choked.

"What any red-blooded man would want from a beautiful woman like you," he whispered.

She squirmed against him. "No, please, don't rape me," she moaned.

He laughed softly. "I wouldn't call it rape. I'm only claiming what you promised me all those years ago." He turned her until she was facing him. "Isn't anything about me familiar to you, Julie?"

She frantically shook her head back and forth. "Who are you? You've got the wrong woman."

"I don't think so." He caressed her waist. "I have the right woman," he said self-righteously.

"I don't know who you're looking for, but it's not me," she cried. "Please just let me go."

"You made a fool out of me." His eyes grew dark. "After you told me you were my girl, you denied it to

257

everyone."

"No!" she screamed pulling away from him.

"You can't escape me," he said as he clasped his hand back over her mouth. "I warned you not to scream. Now I'm going to have to punish you," he calmly said.

Her eyes brimmed with tears and he felt them after they slowly descended down her cheeks, wetting his hand. "We could have had the world, Julie. I've become rich and famous. Now I belong to another. You had your chance." He sighed. "You shouldn't have told those lies about me."

She stiffened.

"Now it's time for you to pay for your past mistakes, but first I intend to have a taste of what you once promised was mine."

****

Jake Truman furiously threw the door open. "What's this all about?" he demanded. "I don't see why this couldn't have waited until morning. It's three a.m., for God's sake!"

The detectives stood impatiently on the threshold. "It's concerning an author from your publishing house."

His eyebrows rose skeptically. "Has something happened?" he asked in a calmer voice.

"May we come inside, Mr. Truman?"

"Yes, of course." He led them through his spacious foyer to the living room. "Please have a seat." He gestured to the matching leather sofas.

After they were seated, Gabe Jackson pulled out a notepad. "We've got some questions for you."

He cocked an eye. "What's happened?"

Kenneth Owens folded his hands and placed them on his lap. "Do you know Nathaniel Cummings?"

His face paled. "Has something happened to

Nathaniel?" he anxiously asked. "He's our best-selling author."

"Tell us everything you know about Nathaniel Cummings."

He grew pensive. "Nathaniel is a very complex man, sharing little of himself with anyone, I'm afraid. He refuses public appearances and interviews. If his books hadn't sold as well as they have, then I would have been forced to pressure him into the public spotlight."

"What do you know about his personal life?" Gabe asked. "Does he ever speak of a family or girlfriend...anything of that nature?"

"He's never mentioned anyone to me. I told you, he's a very private man." He eyed the detectives. "What's this all about?"

Kenneth handed him a paper. "Please read this." He looked at Gabe as the man read. When Jake was finished, he shrugged his shoulders. "What's your point?"

"Now read this," Kenneth said handing him another paper.

He read the second paper, then held them in his hand and flashed Kenneth a quizzical look. "Is this some kind of joke?"

"Would you say that these two passages are identical?" Gabe asked.

"What's going on?" he demanded, losing all patience.

"Mr. Truman, do you recognize these passages?"

"What is this, an interrogation? Of course I recognize these. They were written by Nathaniel Cummings." He frowned. "What am I missing here?" he asked. "Obviously you have a point, or you wouldn't have asked me to read this same passage twice."

"These were written by two supposedly different

individuals."

He jumped to his feet. "That's impossible! Is someone plagiarizing Nathaniel Cummings?"

Kenneth looked evenly at him. "Ten years ago these words were written by Jeremy Talbot for one of his college creative writing classes."

"I don't believe you! Are you telling me that Nathaniel Cummings plagiarized Jeremy Talbot's work? That's impossible!" His eyes darkened. "What's even more ludicrous is your assumption that Nathaniel Cummings even knows Jeremy Talbot."

Kenneth carefully chose his next words. "What if I told you that Jeremy Talbot and Nathaniel Cummings were one and the same?"

"I'd say that you've been working too hard, detective. I've seen photographs on the news and in the papers. They are two very different men."

"Can you give us a description of Nathaniel Cummings?" he asked. "We're having a difficult time locating a photograph of him."

"We'd like you to come down to the station where our sketch artist can work up a composite," Gabe said.

The color drained from the man's face. "You believe that Jeremy Talbot has taken on the alias of Nathaniel Cummings and has committed all of these murders?"

Gabe looked at the papers in the man's trembling hands. "We need your help, Mr. Truman."

CHAPTER THIRTY-ONE

Blake Bergan studied the Talbot file. "Was there anything suspicious reported around the Talbot home last night?"

Gary Benson raised his eyes. "No. There's nothing unusual in the report."

Blake ran a hand over his tired face. "The composite should be coming over any minute. We're close now, Gary. He'll never get out of this. We'll finally get that son of a bitch."

"It won't be too soon for any of us." He looked up when he saw Lieutenant Macon making his way toward them. He watched the lieutenant's stony-faced expression as he reached the desk. "Lieutenant?"

Lt. Macon slowly shook his head. "Julie Howard was murdered last night. In her own backyard."

"Son of a bitch!" Blake's facial muscles tightened. "Talbot?"

He slowly nodded his head. "Her bra was tied around her neck. She was raped."

Gary slammed his fist on the desk. "Dammit!"

"What about the Talbots? A security detail was

requested. We should have requested one for Julie Howard too."

He grunted, his slightly overweight body showing the pressure of his job. "I've gotten the okay to tighten security, but last night there was only one car assigned and it was for the Talbots." His eyes narrowed. "I haven't been able to contact them. I thought you might want to get over there and check out the situation. The detail didn't report any suspicious activity."

"We're on our way," Blake said, grabbing his jacket.

****

Jeremy inched his way around the darkened basement. He peered around a corner, seeing that it led to the laundry area. He stayed huddled where he was, watching as a tenant walked to a washing machine, her basket overflowing with clothes. After she loaded the washer and started the machine, she glanced around the dimly lit room and then left. Jeremy slowly let his breath out as he quickly hurried through the room to the door on the far side. Once safely in the storage area, he breathed a sigh of relief. He gazed up and down the row of neatly caged bins. After every five bins there was a small alcove, and he slowly walked to the first where he was safely hidden from view to anyone who may open the door. He would stay hidden until he could safely make his way to Annie and Brian Chambers' apartment. He'd been relieved last night upon discovering that the security door in the old building was easy to pick. He could freely go in or out of the building.

It's a trap, the demons warned him. *She's not worth it!* Jeremy put his hands over his ears, trying to shut them out. He wanted them out of his life now. His head began to pound. "She'll be mine!" he hissed.

****

Blake tapped the patrol car window. "Anything going on?"

The officer in the driver's seat rolled his window all the way down. "Nothing much. No one in the house has so much as stirred this morning."

"Have you observed anyone coming to the house?"

"No. It's been quiet."

He looked at the house. "It's such a nice day...seems strange that no one's come out." He spotted a newspaper lying on the perfectly manicured lawn. "Now that's really strange," he said, checking his watch. "We'll make sure everything's all right inside."

He motioned to Gary, and they slowly walked up the sidewalk, their eyes focused on their surroundings. When he reached the door, Blake knocked. After a few seconds, he knocked again, louder this time. He turned to his partner. "Something's not right. Why aren't they answering the door?"

"Let's check out back," Gary said.

They walked to the back of the house. "Nothing out of the ordinary here," Blake said looking around. He stepped onto the back patio. The blinds were drawn tight. He knocked and waited for a full minute. "Let's go try the front door again."

They made their way back to the front of the house. Blake knocked on the door again. "Mr. and Mrs. Talbot," he called.

Gary cupped his hands around his eyes and peered into the window next to the door. "I can't see a thing."

Blake motioned to a small window at the top of the door. "I wonder if we can see in the window. Let me find something to stand on." He looked around the porch, finally spotting a stool holding a large potted plant in the far corner. He quickly removed the plant, then pulled the stool to the door. "Give me a hand." Gary held the stool as Blake stepped onto it. He stretched his body until he was eye level with the window and peered through it.

"See anything?" Gary asked.

Blake moved his eyes to the right, then suddenly stiffened. "Radio Lt. Macon. Tell him to get backup down here!"

****

Kenneth Owens and Gabe Jackson walked through the sparsely furnished rooms of Nathaniel Cummings' home.

"For the money this guy has, he certainly isn't into material possessions," Gabe observed.

Kenneth walked to the window in the computer room, gently pulling the curtains apart. The Adams home was in full view. He imagined Jeremy standing at this very window, watching the comings and goings of Rebecca Adams.

"Ken, check this out!" Gabe exclaimed. "This guy is obsessed. There must be thousands of pictures of Rebecca Adams in here!" He shut the file, then pulled open one that had Rebecca's name prominently printed on it. He took out some folders and opened one.

Kenneth looked over Gabe's shoulder as they read the contents. "Look at the dates. It's a personal diary of Rebecca's life, with everything chronologically detailed." He glanced around the rest of the room. "How the hell could he have watched her every moment of the day?"

Gabe pulled open another drawer. "Look at these." He pointed to a number of dated videotapes. He walked over to the window and ran his hand around the sash.

"What are you looking for?" Kenneth asked.

"Just a second." His hand touched a thin wire. "I don't

believe it! He thought of everything. He has a camera embedded into the window frame. It's not obvious from the outside or to the naked eye unless you know what you're looking for." He let his breath out in a rush. "He must have trained the camera on the house every second of every day."

Kenneth frowned. "Let's go through the rest of these files. He knows more about Rebecca than she probably knows about herself."

Gabe flipped through the pages of a notebook. "Listen to this, Ken." He raised his eyebrows. "Jeremy Talbot is dead. No one will ever learn the truth about his demise and eventual reincarnation as Nathaniel Cummings. Well, almost no one. Rebecca will know the truth when we are finally reunited."

Kenneth was thoughtful for a moment. "Have you read any of the *Revenge* books?"

"I've read them all. Why?"

"Something's been eating away at me, and I've finally figured out what it is."

"And?"

"In every one of the novels, the main character has a vendetta against some woman, and the woman always ends up strangled."

"So you don't think any of the murders were random?" Gabe asked.

"No, I think most of them were random. His rage overcame him, and those murders were to satiate him while he waited to seek revenge on his main target."

Gabe's eyes narrowed. "Don't most writers keep notes on novels they're currently working on or plan to write?"

"That's my understanding."

"What if his work in progress tells us who his next

victim is?"

****

Lt. Macon motioned to Blake and Gary. "The composite came through right after you two left the station."

The detectives studied the sketch. Blake scratched his head. "What a complete transformation. I'd have never known or thought the man in this picture could be the same man known as Jeremy Talbot."

"Do either of you remember seeing anyone who resembled him last night?" the lieutenant asked.

"No," Gary answered, "but thank God we'll have something concrete to go on at the reunion dinner dance tonight."

Lt. Macon motioned to the door. "Let's see what's in there."

Blake watched the two officers move away from the dismantled door. He looked at his partner, then took a deep breath as he stepped over the threshold.

****

April gently patted Scootchie as she flipped through the channels on the TV, finally settling on an old romantic tearjerker movie. She settled back on the sofa, trying to focus on the movie, but her mind wandered to thoughts of Nathaniel. Over the years he'd become her closest friend and confidant. Even though in the beginning she'd longed for something more with him, she was satisfied just to be a part of his life as their friendship flourished and grew. She was aware that a part of her would always love him in a way she had no right to, and that was the one reason she hadn't pursued an interest in another man, instead throwing herself into her work as a paralegal in a prominent firm. The hope would always remain in her heart, though, that one day Nathaniel would come to her and profess his love for her.

A late-breaking news bulletin flashing across her screen caught her attention. Nathaniel's face appeared seconds later, and panic filled her. "Oh, no," she said aloud, worried that a major catastrophe had befallen Nathaniel. She turned the volume up and heard the newscaster announce that a major manhunt was underway for Nathaniel Cummings, who was formerly known as Jeremy Talbot.

Her body went rigid and her heart froze. "There has to be a mistake," she mumbled repeatedly. The cruel, heartless murderer the newscaster was describing was not the Nathaniel she knew and loved. Nathaniel Cummings was a kind, gentle, witty, compassionate man. Not this monster they were talking about.

CHAPTER THIRTY-TWO

Blake took a few steps into the entrance hall, then looked to his right just as he had when he'd peered into the window. He cautiously moved closer. He drew a deep breath. A hand, palm up, partially between the entrance hall and the door to the living room caught his eye. His adrenalin pumped as he glanced over his shoulder at his partner. He reached the living room doorway and stopped cold. Millicent Talbot's lifeless, horror-stricken eyes stared up at him. He covered his mouth with his hands and gagged, feeling the vomit gurgling up his throat.

"Oh, God!" Gary exclaimed in horror. "They've been gutted!" He looked at Blake, who was battling a case of the dry heaves. He laid a hand on his shoulder. "Why don't you get some air? I'll check out the rest of the house."

He shook his head. "No," he choked. "I'll be okay." He swallowed hard. "I wasn't expecting to see anything like this."

"He's never used a weapon before," Gabe said.

Blake looked at him. "But how do we know it's Talbot who did this? It could've been someone who wanted revenge on the Talbots. What better time to commit murder, knowing that the blame would be placed on Talbot."

Lt. Macon's face was ashen. "This is one of the most brutal murder scenes I've ever seen." He looked at the blood-splattered walls, then cast his eyes once again to Millicent's body. He bent down to take a closer look. "Check this out." He pointed to her neck. "It looks like a piece of twine tied in a little bow around her neck." He turned to Blake and Gary. "Get this place sealed off right away."

****

Kenneth Owens wiped the perspiration from his brow. "This has got to be one of the most gruesome murders I've ever heard of."

"I wonder why he didn't just strangle them like he did all of those women?" Gabe asked.

"I don't know. Who knows what's going on inside his sick mind?"

Gabe bit his bottom lip. "I can't imagine anyone slicing his own parents like that. According to the report, he took his time making each cut." He shuddered. "The suffering they must have endured at his hands." He shook his head. "It makes you wonder what was going through their minds knowing their own son was going to murder them."

Kenneth picked the report up again. "He straddled his mother in order to make a vertical cut from her diaphragm to her pubic bone, then made two more cuts to open her abdomen."

Gabe's complexion turned as white as the sheet of paper Kenneth read from. "What a sick bastard."

"After he disemboweled them, he cut their hearts out and laid his mother's heart on his father's body and his father's heart on his mother's body." Kenneth swallowed the bile in his throat. "I pity the officers who walked in on that one."

"I talked to Blake Bergan. He and his partner were the first on the scene. He said this is one crime scene that will haunt him for the rest of his life. I've never heard anything like it. Talbot made the cuts like a surgeon."

"He knew what he was doing," Blake said. He most likely did a lot of research." He continued studying the report. "He attacked his father from the left side and made a horizontal cut from left to right." He looked at Gabe. "He strategically planned out every move with his parents. The report says they believe his mother was the first to be murdered."

"And he obviously made his father watch." He shook his head. "We've got to get that bastard. Has anyone spotted him in Pittsburgh?"

"No," he answered solemnly. "Last night a previous high school classmate of Talbot's was found strangled. Julie Howard."

"Damn! Nicholas Adams must be going nuts with this latest news."

"I've been assured that Rebecca is being well protected."

"Didn't they tell us last night that the Talbot's were being protected?" Gabe noted.

Kenneth let his breath out in a rush. "Yeah," he replied rubbing his jaw. "His last book never mentioned revenge on his parents, nor did any of the notes we saw on his work in progress, but do you remember the notes on his newly published book?"

Gabe nodded. "The Howard girl was the first girl he'd stalked back in high school. He said she'd pay for what she'd done." His jaw tightened. "He changed the names and a few details, but if anyone had been paying attention to the novels, it was all laid out for us. He had a good laugh on all of us."

Kenneth gave him a quizzical look. "He had a question mark next to the question, 'Should the only woman I've ever loved and am destined to spend my life with also have to die?'"

Gabe slapped his forehead. "God! He is so sick!"

"Who knows what he's thinking. He's too far gone at this point, I'm afraid. He wrote all of those torrid, passionate pages filled with love for Rebecca, but if she refutes his attempts and pushes him away, who knows what he might do? If she convinces him that she truly does not feel the way about him that he does about her, he may just go off the deep end and kill her too."

"We'll get him before he gets the chance," Gabe promised.

Kenneth rubbed his tired eyes. "We don't have any choice."

****

Nicholas squinted. "God, Rebecca, I'm so scared. Maybe I should fly out there."

Rebecca's voice was shaky. "The police are watching Annie and Brian's building. I'm protected."

"I'd feel better if I was there with you, honey," he said softly. "Dammit, Becky, I can't believe he's lived right next door to us all these years and we never had a clue." He coughed nervously. "At any time he could have—"

"Don't, Nick. I don't want to think about what he could have done," she answered as her trembling hand gripped the phone. "I can't believe he's the reclusive Nathaniel Cummings."

"Well, you did say that Talbot was a talented writer

who would go far," he said quietly.

"I never dreamed he had so much evil inside of him. I only tried to show him some kindness."

Nicholas's voice grew soft. "I know, honey. If it hadn't been you, it would have been some other girl. The same thing as that Julie Howard. She only tried to show him some human compassion."

"And she's dead now."

****

Jeremy stole through the storage area and reached the door at the end of the corridor. He slipped inside the boiler room. He'd be safe here. All he had to do was wait. It wouldn't be long now. *No one is keeping Rebecca away from me*, he angrily thought.

****

Rebecca tossed her head. "I don't know how I'm supposed to feel," she said, wringing her hands. "It's like a bad dream or a horror movie. You know the minute it's over everything will be all right again, and you continue on with your life."

Cassi and Annie exchanged looks. "You befriended him, Becky, because that's the kind of person you are. You act as though everything is your fault," Cassie said. "It's not, sweetie. None of us knew how mentally unstable he was."

She ran her hand through her hair. "I should have gone to the authorities when I first began receiving those letters and gifts."

"But what good would that have done? You didn't have any idea who was sending those to you, and no threats were made. Besides, it was close to graduation and you assumed once you left Pittsburgh they would stop." Annie looked evenly at her.

"Why did he become so fixated on me? I never said one thing that could have been misconstrued as a come on."

"You didn't have to," Cassie said evenly. "His mind did that for him."

"I remember the very first time I'd ever spoken to him. He was shocked that I even acknowledged his presence. The look in his eyes was so bright and happy, just like a child's." She threw her hands up. "I can't believe he's the same person who murdered all of those women and his parents." She shuddered. "How could anyone murder their own parents…especially in such a brutal way?"

"We may never know," Annie replied. "But rest assured he'll be caught, Becky. Now that the police know his new identity, it's just a matter of time."

"I'd never have recognized him. And to think he lived next door to me and Nick for all these years." An icy chill ran up her spine.

Cassie scowled. "It's so sad, because he's a phenomenal writer, and he's really quite attractive looking now. Just imagine the life he could have had."

"What a waste of a life," Annie said disdainfully. "He had everything he ever wanted."

Rebecca shook her head as she stared at her two friends. "Not everything…he didn't have me."

****

April paced back and forth. "You've got the wrong man," she said heatedly. "You don't know Nathaniel like I do. Why are you on a vendetta to destroy him?"

Kenneth scowled. "This man that you keep insisting is so wonderful has viciously murdered countless women and his own parents. We have the right man."

"I don't believe it," she adamantly replied. "Nathaniel couldn't have committed those murders. He's the kindest, warmest, and gentlest man I've ever known. You're targeting him because of his writing. He has a wonderful imagination."

"Miss Hillard, Nathaniel Cummings is Jeremy Talbot," Gabe calmly said. "I know all of this must come as a shock to you, but they are one and the same. He is extremely dangerous. If he contacts you, you need to alert us immediately."

"If he's such a monster, then why was he so sweet to me?" she demanded. "I've known him for almost ten years." Her eyes narrowed. "He walked me home from work when the murders first began because he knew how frightened I was. If he was the murderer, then why didn't he kill me too?"

Kenneth gave her a hard look. "You were lucky."

****

Thaddeus ruffled his grandson's hair. He looked at T.J. and Tyler. "Your mother would be so proud of you boys."

"I wish she could have seen her grandchildren," T.J. quietly said.

Tyler nodded. "Not a day goes by that I don't think about her, Dad." His eyes filled with tears and he quickly brushed them away.

His daughter toddled over to Thaddeus and threw her chubby arms around his legs. Papa," she shyly said, flashing Thaddeus a bright smile.

Thaddeus smiled broadly as he scooped her into his arms. "Christy's got your mother's eyes," he said softly, then breathed deeply. "I'm a lucky man to have known her and been blessed with you boys and my three grandchildren."

T.J. cleared his throat. "Why don't you stay in Seattle for a while longer, Dad?"

He shook his head. "No, I have patients who need me. Besides, I want to be in Pittsburgh when Jeremy Talbot is finally caught and arrested."

"Maybe it would be better for you to stay here until he is," Tyler advised.

"I'll be fine." He smiled at his sons. "You two are the best, and I know you're only trying to protect me, but I need to be there. I need that closure."

T.J. and Tyler exchanged sympathetic looks. "We understand."

His eyes traveled around T.J.'s spacious backyard. "Who would have ever believed that you two boys would have gone into business together?" He grinned. "I'm proud of you two, and don't ever forget it," he said with a wink.

Tyler smiled. "I never dreamed that T.J. and I would end up with our own construction business."

T.J. picked Thaddeus III up and hoisted him onto his shoulders as his other son, Danny, grabbed Tyler's leg. Tyler reached down and lifted the youngster onto his shoulders.

"It is beautiful here, and as much as I wish you would have settled in Pittsburgh, I don't blame you for wanting to settle down here," Thaddeus remarked.

"And it doesn't hurt that our wives are from here," Tyler said with a laugh. "But seriously, I love Seattle. Maybe when you finally decide to retire you'll move here. We'd love it, Dad, and you could see your grandchildren every day."

"You never know what the future holds." Thaddeus smiled broadly.

Chapter Thirty-Three

Nicholas threw his arms around Rebecca. "God, it feels so good to hold you again."

She stroked his handsome face. "Honey, everything will be okay. You didn't have to fly out."

"No," he said hoarsely. "I couldn't stand it, Becky, when every time I looked out the window I saw his house. That bastard was spying on you, watching every move you made. He could've done anything at any time."

"Honey, please calm down. We're safe here. They'll get him."

He looked deep into her eyes. "Becky, why do you insist on being so strong? Sweetheart, you've got to let your feelings out. That psychopath has stalked you for ten years." He placed his hands on her shoulders. "For ten years you've been living in fear because of him." Tears sprang to his eyes. "Honey, come on. You have to quit hiding your fear. Look what he's done in one night. Three more murdered victims."

She drew a shaky breath. "We were all there with him at the picnic, Nick—" her voice broke.

Nicholas enclosed her in his strong arms.

****

Jeremy checked the time. He had to get into the apartment. Once Rebecca saw him, it would be over. The police would let him go after they learned what everyone had done to keep them apart. They'd understand that he'd been given no choice. He had to get to Rebecca before she left for the reunion dinner dance. He licked his lips imagining her delight at seeing him. He would embrace her, and her eyes would shine with all the love she felt for him. He cocked his head. "No," he shouted. "You are not stopping me anymore! I won't listen. It's time for me to go to Rebecca!"

The demons gathered closer. *No! This will be the end of you, Jeremy. Your life isn't worth losing for her! She'll never be yours! Destroy her and let her blood give you power!*

"No," he moaned. "Without her I have nothing!" Tears streamed down his face.

****

Blake Bergan looked up at the building. "Anything going on?"

Gary slowly exhaled. "No. Nicholas Adams got here an hour ago."

Blake looked up and down the street. "Sometimes I feel like he's standing in the shadows, watching our every move and laughing each time he outsmarts us."

"I know." He scratched his head. "Why are you so certain he'll show up here? Wouldn't the most logical place be at the reunion?"

Blake squinted. "Annie and Brian Chambers are the only two of her college friends who still live in Pittsburgh. It stands to reason that she would be their weekend guest."

"Maybe he doesn't know that the Chambers live here."

"He's known everything else, so I'm sure he's kept tabs

on them along with everyone else Rebecca has ever been involved with."

Gary frowned. "Well, at least now we know what he looks like." He grunted. "And we know he hasn't attempted to return to his hotel. Where the hell is he?"

Blake looked at his partner. "He's close. I can feel it."

****

Jeremy made his way to the first set of stairs. The elevator would have been quicker but riskier. Someone was bound to see him getting on or off the elevator, but since hardly anyone took the stairs, he could slip up to the tenth floor unnoticed. After he climbed the stairs to the second floor, he cautiously opened the door and peered into the hallway. The carpeted corridor reminded him of a hotel. A table stood at the far end. He wondered if all the floors were laid out the same way. He crept up another flight of stairs. Annie and Brian lived on the tenth floor, and he calculated how much time he would need to reach their floor. *Jeremy, what are you doing? You have no plan!* the demons shouted repeatedly as he climbed the stairs.

Jeremy panted as he reached the fourth floor. "Leave me alone," he whispered. "You know what my plan is! When Rebecca is mine, you will finally be gone. I'm ridding myself of you. You've done nothing but destroy all of my dreams."

****

"Are the police going to follow us to the college?" Nicholas asked Brian.

He nodded. "Yeah, they've been here all night and day." He patted Nicholas's shoulder. "How's Becky doing?"

His eyes narrowed. "She's hanging in there. She keeps blaming herself for ever befriending Talbot."

278

"I hope you convinced her that nothing is her fault," Brian said.

"I'm trying."

Luke walked over to them and gave Nicholas a bear hug. "It's so good to see you, buddy. Cassi and I are going to take off, but we'll see you tonight."

"Definitely."

Cassi slipped her arm through Luke's. "Are you ready, honey?"

He lifted his eyebrows. "For you, I'm always ready."

She playfully punched him in the arm. "He'll never change. One track mind."

Brian and Nicholas laughed.

Annie walked into the room. "What's so funny?" she asked.

Cassi rolled her eyes. "Just Brian being Brian."

Annie smiled as she turned to Nicholas. "Becky wants you to run to the store if you don't mind. She needs a new pair of panty hose." She handed him a piece of paper. "Make certain you get this exact shade and size."

"Don't you have an extra pair, hon?" Brian asked.

She laughed. "I have loads, but unfortunately none of the shades I have match her dress."

Nicholas slapped his forehead. "Oh, heavens, we can't go to the dance with the wrong shade of panty hose on."

Brian and Luke laughed mimicking him.

"Okay, you guys, you don't know how much trouble we go to making ourselves beautiful for you," Cassi said.

"And we appreciate it all," Luke said, sweeping her into his arms. "But you three are already so beautiful that you don't need to do anything to enhance your looks."

"Always the charmer," Cassi said with a smile.

"I'll go with you, Nick. We can walk Cassi and Luke

out." Brian looked at Annie. "Is there anything else you need, hon?" he asked with a smile. "Watch, the minute we get back she'll have thought of something else." He laughed, turning toward his friends.

"Get going," she said, playfully pushing him toward the door. "I'll see you and Luke tonight," she said to Cassi, giving her a quick peck on the cheek. "Tell your mother I said hello."

****

Jeremy reached the tenth floor and slumped outside of the stairwell door. Sweat poured from him. He was confused. Why was it so difficult for Rebecca and him to be together? His head pounded. He rubbed his temples, but the pounding only seemed to worsen. He opened the door slightly, listening. He heard voices cheerfully chattering. He wished they'd just go about their business. Their incessant babble was making his headache worse.

Forget it, Jeremy! It's too late! She loves Nicholas!

No! his mind screamed. *She's mine! She's always been only mine! As soon as Rebecca and I are together, I told you I am banishing you from my life forever!*

They hissed and laughed. *We'll always be a part of you. You'll never be free of us.*

"Just leave me alone," he mumbled. He peered through the crack of the door. His heartbeat quickened when he saw Nicholas, Brian, Luke, and Cassi moving toward the elevator. He watched as they pushed the button.

Don't do it! The demons warned again. *She's not worth it. She's a whore just like the others. She gave herself to Nicholas, not you.*

"No," he moaned. "She had no choice."

She had a choice, and it wasn't you, they laughed.

"No!" he screamed as he ran out of the door and down

the corridor, just as the elevator door was closing.

****

"What the hell was that?" Luke asked. He pushed the open button on the elevator, but it was too late and had already made its descent to the lobby.

Cassi shuddered. "I've never heard anyone scream like that before. We'd better get back up there."

Luke grabbed her arm. "No, honey, not you. As soon as we get to the first floor, run outside and get the police." He looked at Nicholas and Brian. "We'd better get right back up there."

Nicholas's face was pale. He watched the elevator buttons. They seemed to take forever to reach the lobby.

"What's going on out there?" Annie asked. She frowned as Rebecca moved closer to the door.

Rebecca shuddered. "That was a horrifying cry. I wish the boys hadn't left when they did." She nervously clasped her hands together.

Annie listened carefully. "I don't hear anything now. Maybe I should look." She glanced questioningly at Rebecca.

"I don't know if you should."

"Don't worry. Jeremy can't get anywhere near the building. It could be a neighbor needing help." She took a deep breath. "I'll just crack the door and take a peek." She slowly opened the door, but it was pushed back with such force that it startled her and sent her reeling backward.

Rebecca screamed as Jeremy came barreling into the room. He spotted her and lunged at her.

"I'm here," he gasped, placing an arm tightly around her waist. "Now we can be together just like you always dreamed. You and me forever, Rebecca."

Rebecca was numb with fear. Blackness closed in

around her, and she knew that she had to force herself not to faint. "Jeremy," she whispered. "Please let me go. You're hurting me."

He looked at her with pained eyes. "I would never hurt you, Rebecca. I love you." He touched her smooth skin. "I've waited a long time to touch you. Tonight we'll finally be together. Just like I've been telling you for years."

Rebecca felt a wave of nausea come over her. "Not this way, Jeremy," she pleaded. "Please not this way."

He cocked his head. "But this is what you always wanted." He grinned. "Remember that day you told me what a wonderful writer I was and that I would be famous some day? You were right. You inspired me." He ran his fingers through her hair. "We belong together. Just you and me."

"No," she whispered.

His eyes glazed over.

We warned you! She's never wanted you. She's only been playing you!

"What do you mean? Rebecca, you belong to me."

She tried to pull free from him. "No, Jeremy. I was only trying to be your friend. I never wanted you in any other way." She felt his body tremble, then grow rigid.

He rapidly shook his head back and forth. "No!" he shouted. "You love me! Tell me you love me!"

Tears poured from her eyes. "Please let me go, Jeremy. Please don't hurt me."

"Let her go, Talbot," Blake Bergan called.

"Get your fucking hands off my wife!" Nicholas shouted.

Jeremy moved his arm to her throat. "Get away from us," he ordered. "She doesn't love you, Nicholas. She never did. She belongs to me. Now all of you get out of my way.

Rebecca and I would like to leave now. We have a lot of catching up to do."

"Let her go!" Blake repeated.

Nicholas, Brian, Luke, Cassi, and Gary Benson stood behind Blake as he inched his way into the apartment. "All of you stay here in the hall," he ordered.

"Don't come any closer or I'll break her neck," Jeremy warned.

"Why would you do that? I thought you loved her," Nicholas said.

Rebecca's eyes met Nicholas's.

"Tell them about our plans, Rebecca," Jeremy panted. "Tell them how we've planned this for years." He cocked his head. "Tell them!"

"No," she moaned. "Please let me go, Jeremy."

It's over. You should have listened to us. We were the only ones who ever cared about you.

He tightened his grip on Rebecca's neck. "Tell them now!"

"Jeremy, please," Rebecca pleaded through her choked sobs.

"Don't be afraid of Nicholas. He can't hurt you. Tell him the truth now, Rebecca, for both our sakes. Tell him that it's me you've always loved."

****

Annie cowered behind Rebecca and Jeremy. It dawned on her that Jeremy had forgotten about her in his haste to get to Rebecca and hadn't seen her move to the back of the room. She quickly looked around. She spotted the poker near the fireplace. Quietly she made her way to the fireplace.

Blake briefly shifted his eyes as Annie carefully reached for the poker with trembling fingers. It tinkled slightly against the holder. Holding her breath, she slowly removed it.

Jeremy turned his head and glared at Annie. She sucked in her breath and tightened her grip on the poker.

"Drop it!" Jeremy demanded.

With all the strength Annie could muster, she swung the poker.

The poker made a sickening thud as it connected with Jeremy's skull. He let go of Rebecca and grabbed his head.

Annie looked in horror at the blood gushing from Jeremy's head. The poker slipped from her fingers and she ran to Brian.

"Good job, honey," he said huskily.

Rebecca started toward Nicholas's outstretched arms.

"No!" Jeremy screamed. He grabbed Rebecca's shirt with one hand and with the other stooped and picked up the poker.

Rebecca twisted away from him.

Jeremy raised the poker. A powerful blast caught him in the chest. His eyes widened as he fell back onto the carpeted floor. He placed his hand on his chest. "Why, Rebecca?" he whispered. His breathing became labored. "Tell me you love me. Tell me you'll never leave me," he choked.

We'll never leave you, Jeremy, the demons promised. *We'll always love you.*

Join our Newsletter & Receive Release Day Announcements, News, and Special Sales!

Before You Go...

Share your voice and help guide other readers to these wonderful books. Even if it's only a line or two your reviews help readers discover the author's books so they can continue creating stories that you'll love. Login to your favorite retailer and leave a review. Thank you.

Susan K. Droney
AUTHOR

Writing is Susan's number one passion. When she isn't writing, she enjoys reading, spending time in her garden, and visiting family and friends. She has many novels, short stories, and magazine articles to her credit. Raised in western New York, she now resides in New Jersey. For information about Susan's current and upcoming titles, please visit http://www.susandroney.com or http://susandroney.blogspot.com

www.ingramcontent.com/pod-product-compliance
Lightning Source LLC
Chambersburg PA
CBHW030237200626
46816CB00002BA/400